Only a
MOTHER

Elisabeth Carpenter lives in Preston with her family. She completed a BA in English Literature and Language with the Open University in 2011.

Elisabeth was awarded a Northern Writers' New Fiction Award, and was longlisted for Yeovil Literary Prize (2015 and 2016) and the MsLexia Women's Novel Award (2015). She loves living in the north of England and sets most of her stories in the area. She currently works as a bookkeeper.

Also by Elisabeth Carpenter

11 Missed Calls
99 Red Balloons

Only a
MOTHER

ELISABETH CARPENTER

ORION

An Orion paperback

First published in Great Britain in 2018
by Orion Books
an imprint of The Orion Publishing Group Ltd
Carmelite House, 50 Victoria Embankment
London EC4Y 0DZ

An Hachette UK Company

1 3 5 7 9 10 8 6 4 2

A CIP catalogue record for this book
is available from the British Library.

ISBN 978 1 4091 8147 7

Typeset by Deltatype Ltd, Birkenhead, Merseyside

Printed in Great Britain by Clays Ltd, Elcograf S.p.A.

www.orionbooks.co.uk

To Mum

1

Erica

I step outside and close my front door. Out of habit, I examine it quickly from top to bottom. My shoulders relax. The green paint is covered in tiny cracks, but there's no writing sprayed on it today, no excrement wiped across or pushed into the keyhole. The door's been free of graffiti for nearly eighteen months, but it won't stay that way for long.

It was always the same words: *Murderer; Get out; Scum.* It was like they thought *I* did it. I used to wait till after dark before taking a scrubbing brush to it. There was hardly anyone around at three o'clock in the morning, and I didn't have to be up early for anything. I still don't – well, except for Wednesdays.

I don't know why we settled on Wednesdays. I suppose it's because it was my day off when I worked at the ... No. There's no point thinking about that: my other life.

The clouds are grey and heavy and it's raining. I like it best this way; people have their heads down or under umbrellas. I open mine and catch sight of the bit of tinsel lingering in the inside corner of next door's window; it's been there for over a month. Don't they know it's unlucky? Though I don't believe in luck. My mother used to be superstitious. No new shoes on the table, no passing anyone on the stairs. For years after she died, I imagined what she'd say to me. *You can't become a single mother, Erica! What would the neighbours think of you?* Or *A job in a supermarket, Erica? I pictured you doing so much more.* I expect it's for the best that she passed before my Craig was born. Then me being a single parent would've been the least of her worries.

I wait at the bus stop in the rain as the shelter has long since been destroyed by vandals. A car splashes me, driving through the small lake of a puddle near the kerb. I forgot to step out of the way. I need to concentrate, stop daydreaming. I'm sure drivers take great delight in drenching pedestrians these days. I try not to take it personally – not everyone knows who I am. I'm soaked to the skin, but it'll dry on the bus. They're always too hot when it's raining; all the windows'll be closed.

At last, the bus pulls in. I step on, into the sweaty warmth.

'The bus sta—'

'One eighty,' the driver says.

Why is it always him? I pull the coins out of my purse one at a time, placing them slowly on the money tray. He doesn't even look at me; he's staring out of the window.

I grab the handles as I walk down the aisle, trying to

stay upright as the bus sets off. There's someone in my usual seat – two from the back – so I sit on one of the middle ones next to the steamed-up window. I smile a little as I picture Craig as a child, drawing silly faces in the condensation. My heart drops when I remember where I'm going. I wipe the memory from the window with the palm of my hand. I like to see outside, anyway.

I take my magazine out of my handbag and try to focus on the words. It's one of those real-life magazines. *All problems are relative*. I don't recall where I read that, but it's true. It helps to read about other people's lives. It's good to feel a connection – even if it's a distant one, like on my forum: *PrisonConnect*. Families of prisoners from all over the world can talk in a *safe space*. I've been on it so long, I'm a moderator now. I've never told Craig about it – he wouldn't like being talked about by strangers, though he must be used to it by now.

The bus stops at the traffic lights. I look out at the bakery on the corner. It used to be the pet shop – must be nearly thirty years ago now. We'd look at the kittens and the rabbits in the window on a Saturday morning on our way to Kwik Save. Craig always felt sorry for them. 'Can we take them all home, Mummy?' he said, every week. 'It's not fair they're stuck in there all day.'

It's like he knew where he'd end up. I blink the memory away.

The engine idles as the pedestrians cross the road in front.

It's then that I spot her.

I try not to look out for her; I haven't seen her for

3

years. She's standing there, in the rain outside the newsagents, staring into space. Gillian Sharpe, Lucy's mother. She's the only parent who stayed in this town. So many names imprinted on my soul. There was another girl, Jenna. But my Craig wasn't convicted for that. It doesn't make sense, and I often think this, that surely the two are connected. The two happened just a week apart. If they thought he wasn't responsible for Jenna, then why imprison him for Lucy? There's a killer out there and they've not caught him. Or her; it could be a she. You never know.

What I *do* know is that my son would never harm anyone.

I lower my gaze; my face burns. I can't look at Gillian Sharpe any more. When I do, I see her daughter's face, her photo in the newspapers. I've kept them all, organised in date order and highlighted with the information I need to help me prove Craig's innocence.

How old would Lucy be now?

No, no, no, no.

I pinch the skin on my wrist so hard that my nails almost meet in the middle.

I stand in line with the other relatives: the girlfriends, the wives, the friends, whatever or whoever they are. I recognise some from their clothes, their shape, but not their faces – I never look at their faces.

When I first started coming here all those years ago, a few of them muttered under their breath, called me a stuck-up bitch, but that's stopped. I was no different from the rest of them; they soon realised that. Some even brought children with them, which is understandable – you have to maintain contact, even for the briefest of visits. But prison's no place for kiddies. The world's bad enough without them seeing the worst of it. Well, almost the worst.

The prison officer opens the door dead on two; never early, never late. I suppose it's because it's owned by the Queen. I've read the royal household is quite strict when it comes to time. I hand over my card and they usher me in. I give them my handbag and they place it in a locker. I hold out my arms and they pat the whole of my body. Even though I recognise them, and they know my name, my face, I must show them my passport. It's ridiculous that I have one, really, seeing as I never get the chance to leave the country. I have so many places that I want to visit, things I want to do: see the Northern Lights; travel along Route 66 in a convertible. I read a bucket list of places in a copy of the *Telegraph* at the doctors', but they didn't mention the Lake District, which I thought was a bit short-sighted of them.

Usually, I bring Craig a paperback. I get them from the jumble sale in the church hall in the next village. I've been filling the bookcase on the upstairs landing at home for months. I hope Craig turns to reading when he's home and doesn't fill his head with notions of mixing with the wrong crowd. He can't have made any nice friends while he's been inside.

I won't tell him I saw Gillian Sharpe on my way here.

The first time I visited, Craig was crying, his head in his hands. 'I'm innocent, Mum,' he said. 'You do believe me, don't you?'

'Yes, Son,' I said. 'Of course, I believe you.'

He doesn't speak about it much now. It hurts him when I mention it. We've had to find other things to talk about since.

The guard calls my name. He lets me into the visitors' room and Craig's already sitting at the table waiting. He stands as he sees me – he always looks relieved. As if I'd not come.

We hug for a few seconds. I'd love to hold him for longer, but this is all we're allowed.

'Hello, Mother,' he says, as usual, pulling away from me. His northern accent's stronger in here than it ever was at home.

'Hello, Son.'

I sit on the plastic chair and shuffle it towards the table that divides us. He used to be such a skinny child – he was slim, even as a teenager. He took up weight-training after the first few years in here, said he didn't want to be a victim any more. Looking at him now, it's like he's doubled in size. That grey sweatshirt used to drown him.

'There was a documentary on last Friday,' he says, 'about penguins on the Falkland Islands. Did you see it? I thought of you when I watched it. I said to myself, *Mum'll be watching this, she likes—*'

'No,' I say. 'I didn't, sorry.'

'But it was only on at seven.'

'I don't sit and watch television all day,' I say sharply.

I must've fallen asleep. I don't sleep well. Unless I'm doing the shopping, I'd rather sleep during the day. Then at night I can go out into the backyard and breathe in the fresh air.

Out of the window to my right, there's just the right amount of sky and trees visible to remember there's a world out there.

'What's wrong?'

'Nothing,' I say. I look at him as he stares down at his hands – his nails are bitten so badly; the tops of his fingers are smooth and shiny. I glance at his face; such lovely long eyelashes. 'I'm sorry if I was short with you.'

'Has everyone heard?' he says. 'Are they giving you a hard time again?'

A hard time. He makes it seem like a cross word or a quarrel over parking spaces.

'No,' I say. 'But I'm worried about you ... about what'll happen in a fortnight. We could move away, you know. Start afresh. I've always fancied the Lake District.'

'How the hell would we afford the Lake District? You're dreaming again, Mum.'

It's all I have, I want to say.

'I know I've asked this nearly every time you've visited,' he says, 'but I thought I'd ask one more time. For tradition, I suppose. One last time. Have you found him?'

'No. No, I haven't.'

7

His shoulders drop, and he lowers his head.

He means Pete Lawton. The man Craig has always said he was with the night Lucy was murdered. There's been no sign of him since, and I can't find anyone that'll vouch for him working at the garage when Craig was doing work experience there.

'Anyway. About your bedroom ...' I say, trying to distract him. 'I hope you don't mind, but I put some of your old things in boxes – only your boyish things ... didn't think you'd want to be looking at them. I've not thrown them out – they're in the loft.'

He smiles slightly.

'I can't wait to be home, Mum. It'll be like old times.'

I give a small smile. I don't want to mention that the *old times* meant he was never home, barely giving me the time of day.

'Have you had a visit from probation yet?' he says.

'Yes, but they're coming again tomorrow.'

'I told them I want to be a personal trainer.'

'Oh,' I say. 'What did they make of that?'

He tilts his head and shrugs.

'They said it's not likely ... I'd need one of those background check things. But what do they know?'

'I suppose,' I say. 'If you put your mind to it, you could do anything.'

My words hang in the air like a moth hovering before a bare flame.

'I want to make a life for myself.' His knees bounce up and down underneath the table. 'If it doesn't work out, I promise we'll move. How about that?'

8

I stretch my fingers as close as I can towards his and he does the same back.

'I'll help you all I can, love.'

I know he doesn't mean what he says. He'll not want to be living with me for long – seventeen years is a long time to be trapped inside. He'll want to see some life.

Too soon, it's time to go. He quickly lists the items he wants me to buy. I'm not sure if it's allowed, him having two phones, but I tell him I'll get them anyway.

'I love you, Son,' I say.

'Right back atcha, Mum,' he says, as usual.

I stand. I'm leaving this prison for the last time. Inside this place, he's safe, he's warm, he's fed. He doesn't know what he's coming home to, does he? Everyone thinks he's guilty; they'll probably think he's got a nerve returning to the town where it happened. They'll be angry, I know they will.

And I don't have the power to protect him from it.

2

Luke

Luke Simmons sits too heavily on his chair and it wheels visibly backwards. The work experience lad next to him purses his lips, suppressing a snigger probably, which is rare for one of these millennials; they usually feel the need to share bloody everything. They'll be comparing shits on Snapchat soon, given a few months.

God. How has Luke's belly got so big that he can't even sit on a chair without sounding as though he's been winded? It's not as if there's much fat on the rest of him. It's his wife Helen's fault. She's been on a diet of only five points a day or whatever, and the mere idea of zero-point crap soup makes Luke crave his mum's proper chip-pan chips from when he was a lad.

He sniffs the air. The Greggs cheese and onion pasty that's been keeping his left nipple warm in his jacket pocket smells like BO. Great. Overweight, and now everyone within five feet of him reckons he's a soap dodger.

Ah sod it, he thinks, taking it out and pushing the pasty up from its paper bag. He can taste every glorious calorie and it warms his soul. *Oh, how I've missed you*, he says in his mind. It's been a long week – thank God it's Friday tomorrow.

Afterwards, he immediately feels that he shouldn't have eaten it. He can feel the cholesterol coat his arteries and the fat adding another layer to his abdomen. 'It's for the kids,' Helen said on Sunday as she was chopping celery and carrots into batons. 'We're older parents – we're not far off forty. We need to think about *them*.' Yes. Luke should've thought about them. He'd read enough crap editorial copy to know that eating pastry wasn't the key to eternal youth.

It's just too hard to resist. It's a well-known fact that life's shit these days. Baby boomers and happy-clappy hippies are what his parents were. What do we have now? Brexit and Donald Trump. And it's pissing it down outside. Luke rests his chin in his hand.

'Luke!'

It's Sarah, the news editor – who's also his line manager, head of PR and something else. When had it all got so corporate? It used to be more about the story. But that was when this place was bigger, had more staff and more actual paper copies were sold. Luke sits up, grabbing a pen from the pile on his desk.

'Sarah!' he says. 'Light of my professional life.'

She frowns.

'Are you trying to be funny?' She leans towards him. 'You know there's a fine line.'

'I ... No. I was only trying to lift the mood.'

'What mood?'

'Sorry, Sarah. I don't know.'

Luke lowers his head a little. He doesn't know what to say any more. Back in the day, everyone joked with each other. Now there's HR, PR, HSE, and God knows what else.

'Craig Wright is out in less than a week,' Sarah says.

'I know – I'm putting a piece together. I'm going to contact his mother, see if she'll talk to me again ... find out if she still believes he's innocent after all this time.'

'Good idea. Plus, he's planning on moving back to the area. Thought we should warn the community in a roundabout kind of way.'

Luke glances at Sarah. What age might she be? Twenty-nine? Thirty? She's not from around here – she won't remember when it all happened. The year 2000: a year that promised a fresh new millennium but warned that planes might fall from the sky if computers failed. Craig Wright had been a 'normal' lad – well, he'd appeared to be. He'd never told anyone what had motivated him to kill. Whatever it was, Luke doesn't believe that seventeen years in prison will have changed him for the better. He's going to reoffend, there's no doubt about it.

'I was thinking of interviewing the witnesses,' says Luke. 'See if they remember anything new – perhaps dig a little deeper into his childhood and what made him do it. I'm going to look into the second victim, too – try to come up with some more details about her. Craig's mother, though ... she might be a tough one. She's been through a lot.'

'It's not our fault she chose to stay here. If a murderer lived on my street, I'd want to know about it. Wouldn't you?'

'Yes.'

Luke has thought about Erica often over the years. He's the same age as her son. How different their lives had turned out – did Erica ever wonder how different Craig's life could've been? He managed to get a brief interview with her after Craig's sentencing. It hadn't felt right at the time. He'd not long started at the *Chronicle*; the most serious crime he'd covered was illegals working at the takeaway on the high street.

Erica hadn't known that Luke worked for the newspaper when he spoke to her – perhaps she assumed he was a concerned bystander. He'd known that he wouldn't be able to use what she told him, but perhaps it would get him a new angle, help him get his lucky break – maybe he'd make the nationals.

He found her down one of the side streets, taking a drag from a cigarette. Luke remembers she wore black and was shivering. He'd wanted to put his arms around her, like he would've done had it been his mother at a funeral. He wasn't sure if Erica dressed like that for her son, or the girl Craig murdered.

Luke doesn't need to read his article again to recall her every word; there weren't many. 'Do you think he did it?' Luke had asked, pretending not to know who she was.

'Of course not,' she said, looking at the floor, then to the crowd in the near distance.

Her voice was barely a whisper. She appeared so small, like she wanted to disappear, blend into the concrete.

The detective leading the case had read out a statement saying how justice had been done – that a dangerous, calculating and manipulative young man had rightfully been put away. The victim's relatives huddled behind him, clinging to each other to stay upright, while cameras captured their grief, pain and tears.

Erica Wright had sat alone during the trial. There were no friends or relatives there to support her. Luke recalls glancing at her as the photographs of Lucy were shown to the court. Unlike others in the courtroom, there were no gasps from Erica's mouth. Her eyes glistened with unshed tears, her mouth remained pressed into a straight line. Why had she done that to herself? But then, Luke thought, why had the victim's parents sat there, too? Who would want to see their child's lifeless body, or listen to what happened in their last moments?

Craig had looked at the photographs, too. Of course, he'd already seen the body in person, hadn't he. He showed no emotion as he gazed at them. Perhaps he got some sick gratification, as though reliving the memory. Craig remained detached when Lucy's mother ran out of the courtroom in tears. Only a person so cold, sociopathic, could ignore suffering like that.

Down that side street, Erica threw her spent cigarette on to the ground. She fumbled with a crumpled packet for a new one. Luke always carried a lighter, alongside a pen, notepad, and a packet of fags, even though he didn't smoke. As he held the flame up to her and cupped his other hand to shield the wind, he said, 'Will you visit him in prison?'

She narrowed her eyes at him.

'Of course. He's my son. I love him.'

Tears rolled down each side of her face. Then she turned her back on Luke and walked away.

He wondered if she had visited him. What had they talked about for all these years? Did they talk about the most serious of subjects, his guilt? Luke would've loved to have been a fly on the wall during their visits.

There was another girl: Jenna Threlfall. She went missing a week after Lucy did. Everyone feared the worst for her after Lucy's body was found in woodland outside Preston. Their fears were realised when Jenna Threlfall was found in the playing field. She was right in the centre, star-shaped as though she were in the middle of making snow angels. Dog walkers found her. It's always dog walkers, isn't it? They're out so early, in random places and the dogs can smell it: death, bodies.

The police interviewed Craig about the second girl, but he had an alibi – the MO was different. There was no evidence to connect the two. Only circumstantial, and that wasn't enough. But people thought it was him. Otherwise, why hadn't the police pursued anyone else?

'I'll get on it,' Luke says to Sarah.

He retrieves Erica's number from the database, lifts the receiver and dials.

She picks up after ten rings.

'Hello?' Her voice is quiet.

'Erica? It's Luke from the *Chronicle*. Do you have time for a chat?'

'I ... No. I've people here.'

She hangs up.

People? So it must be true. After seventeen years in prison, Craig Wright is coming back home. He's bound to slip up – he can't be that bright to have been caught in the first place. He's going to make a mistake and Luke is going to make sure he's there when it happens.

3

Erica

I haven't slept for more than two hours at a time these past two weeks. I drank three strong coffees this morning in preparation for their visit and now I could do with a fourth.

They waltzed into my house like they owned the place and now they're sitting in my living room with gadgets instead of notebooks. I carry the tea tray through, grasping it tightly. I spaced the china far enough apart so it wouldn't clatter if my hands tremble. I place it on the table in the middle of the room.

Patrick Nelson from probation was here four weeks ago with a young man, but he's brought a young lady, Hannah McIntyre, with him today. Perhaps he prefers being with females. I know his type.

Hannah's looking at my photographs on top of the telly. Craig was a normal little boy, I want to tell her – a mummy's boy. He probably still is. She gazes at the landscape prints on the walls, the bare bars of the electric fire. At least my house is clean, tidy.

I wonder what she thinks of me. Does she pity me?

Or does she hate me? Perhaps she thinks I created a monster.

If I talk normally to them this time – I've practised since the last – then it could be the final time I have to deal with the authorities. I know as I think this that it won't be the case, but it's a step closer. It might all be over soon – we could have a chance at a normal life. Once Craig realises what it's like living back here, he'll want to move away – like I've always wanted to.

'Thanks so much for seeing us again, Erica,' says Patrick. 'I hope you don't mind but I thought we'd go through things again. I want to get Hannah familiar with everything as she'll be organising Craig's voluntary work. As I mentioned last time, Craig will already know his supervising officer.' He glances at the paper on his lap. 'Adam Bardsley.'

It's a fake smile he gives me. I don't return it.

'So,' says Hannah, running her finger up her electronic tablet, 'you've no children who visit the premises?'

'No,' I say. 'No one visits here.'

She shifts her bottom on my chair; people always feel uncomfortable around me. It's like they think it's catching or I'll not be able to help myself.

'How do you think Craig'll cope with being in the outside world?'

'You're in a better position to answer that question, aren't you?'

They exchange a glance.

'Sorry,' I say. 'I don't mean to sound obtuse. It's just that I only see him once a week. You lot – I mean, you

18

being his advisors, have worked with him on a closer level, I imagine.'

Hannah tilts her head in a quizzical manner.

'But you're his—'

'I suppose what Hannah is trying to gauge,' interrupts Patrick, 'is how you think Craig'll cope with the animosity he might face on his return?'

'I suppose,' I repeat, 'we won't know until it happens.'

He frowns. 'We don't really want that kind of unpredictability.' He shuffles in his chair too. 'Saying that ... we are pleased with Craig's rehabilitation. He speaks openly about how sorry he is. Has he said much to you about that?'

'I ... He knows I'm here to listen if he ever wants to talk.'

I want them out of my house. They don't belong here, with their smart suits and big job titles. It's like they want to trick me.

After fifteen minutes, they run out of things on their list to say and take themselves for a tour around my house. I stay seated in the living room, listening to their footsteps upstairs. Why do they need to go into my bedroom? What are they expecting to find? They go from my room to Craig's. I've spent weeks getting it ready. For years, I left it the way it was. I tidied it after the police ransacked it, of course, but the door remained closed until last year, when the matter of parole was first mentioned.

I've cleared the clothes from his wardrobe – they're

19

too small for him now, anyway. I've taken the television out. I don't want him spending all his time in there – not like it was before.

The phone rings in the hallway.

I stand and pace the living room. If I talk to anyone in the hall, those two'll be able to hear upstairs. I don't like people listening to me on the telephone. This house has thin walls.

I walk out of the room; it'll only be PPI – no one else rings me.

'Hello?'

I expect a robot to speak, but it doesn't.

'Erica? It's Luke from the *Chronicle*. Do you have time for a chat?'

'I . . . No. I've people here.'

I don't say goodbye. I place the receiver in its cradle, my hands shaking. I want to sink to the floor and curl up into a ball. I would if I were alone.

I didn't think I'd hear from that reporter again – what's he doing, still working there? He must be stuck here like the rest of us.

So, the people at the newspaper know. Soon everyone else will, too. And it's all going to start again.

4

If I close my eyes and think of Lucy, I can smell the scent of her skin. It's the most powerful of the senses; memories can be instantly evoked with just a whiff. White Musk, she said it was. I found it in one of those hippy-dippy shops afterwards ... bought a few bottles of it.

Lovely Lucy.

I remember our first date. We went to the pictures to see Meet the Parents ... I sneaked vodka into the cinema, funnelled it into SodaStream bottles. I didn't concentrate on the film much. Ironic, given the film, that Lucy wouldn't let me meet her parents.

Ironic. I know words like that now. Been doing a bit of reading.

She was quiet, that night. I'd wanted to take her out for a date for ages. She'd noticed him first, of course. Everyone always does, but not for the right reasons. He liked to think he had the pick of all the girls, but he was deluded. Thick shit.

Women. I have to call them women now. I'm not a boy any more, Mum.

I bet he *was introduced to her mum and dad. The slimy fucker. Gets everywhere, like sand in my crack.*

Lucy and I ended up in my car. I only had an old banger, then. We sat on the back seat. I said I had a tape that I'd made for her.

'You shouldn't be doing things like that for me,' she said.

'Why not?' I said. 'I love you.'

It was as simple as that. I did.

'You don't love me,' she said.

'Your skin's so soft,' I said, stroking her cheek with my index finger.

She tilted her head towards it like she'd never been touched before but craved it, like a kitten getting its ears tickled.

'Thanks,' she said.

Well, I thought that's what she said.

She had a glint in her eye – she knew what she wanted.

I traced my finger down her mouth, her neck; lingered on her breasts, put my palm on her nipple. She sighed, leaned back slightly.

Oh, my lovely Lucy.

I thought she was shy, but she wasn't. I kissed her neck and all the way down her.

After twenty minutes, she changed her mind.

'Don't you like me after all?' I said.

'What do you mean?'

'You can't start me off like that, Lucy.'

'I didn't mean to . . . but I can't do this. It's not right.'

Oh, Lucy.

Lucy, Lucy, Lucy.

My most precious memory of you is when your breath had left your body; your skin was growing cooler with every minute. You wouldn't have wanted to grow old anyway, not with a face like that. Beautiful, smooth. I did you a favour.

You left this world unspoiled. Well, almost.

It won't be too long. Soon I can find another one like you.

Girls like Lucy are ten a penny.

5

Luke

Luke taps gently on the front door, a queasy churning in his stomach. Is it hunger or nerves? Why is he even in this job? He can't remember the last time he left the house in the morning without a feeling of dread. Mondays are the worst. Then again, even on Fridays he presses the snooze button at least four times before getting out of bed.

He knocks again, a bit louder.

The last time he talked to her was seventeen years ago, a few days after Craig Wright was imprisoned. Luke had admired her strength, the way she held it together for the forty-five minutes he interviewed her, while he felt like an intruder. Her words, 'He's torn our lives apart,' made the paper's headline.

So many quotes in Luke's head – most of which he'll never use again. He wishes he could format his brain; clear the unnecessary, unpleasant words – and images – out of his memory.

Gillian Sharpe: mother of Lucy, the first girl, opens the door.

'Hello, Luke,' she says. 'I'd say it's nice to see you again, but we've never met in the most pleasant of circumstances, have we? No offence.'

'None taken,' he says, stepping inside the house.

People say that to him all the time: 'No offence'. Most of them don't mean it. At least he's not as salacious as other reporters. He'd never sensationalise anything. Well, he hadn't with Gillian's story. Back then, he'd just learned how to interview the newly bereaved. *Avoid doorstepping; offer breaks where necessary; prepare to be distressed yourself.* He's sure many of his fellow students hadn't adhered to those rules, especially that bastard Damian who currently works for *Look North*. Given the chance again, though, Luke's not sure he'd observe the guidelines either; he could've been working for one of the nationals by now if he hadn't.

Back then, Luke could tell Gillian cared about her appearance. Her smooth shoulder-length bob was almost black, and she always wore make-up; her mascara never streaked with her tears. Perhaps that was a distraction for her – a mask she wore in public. But now her hair is lighter, pulled into a scruffy bun at the base of her neck, and her face is free of make-up. She's thinner now – almost too thin.

He follows Gillian into the kitchen. The floor is white, the cabinet doors are white, and the massive island in the middle is topped with white marble. Everything is spotless, gleaming.

'Can I get you anything to drink?'

Luke's tempted to ask for a shot of that vodka he spots in the drinks cabinet.

'Black coffee, no sugar, please,' he says.

She raises her eyebrows.

'I had you down as a builder's tea, three sugars kind of man.'

'I was last week.'

She flicks on the kettle and gestures for Luke to sit at one of the bar stools. He tries to mount it as gracefully as he can, but his hands are full with his leather satchel and mobile phone. Gillian has the courtesy to turn away as he places everything on to the marble top before sitting.

His questions are listed on a notepad and a recording app is ready to go on his phone. Gillian places the steaming coffee in front of him. He'll have to wait at least five minutes before he can attempt a sip – she hasn't topped it up with cold water. But he's not in a café; that's another of Helen's phrases.

Gillian sits at a ninety-degree angle from Luke, a herbal tea in a glass cup in front of her. There are bags under her eyes that seem to threaten tears at any moment.

He's about to ask the first question when his stomach growls. The room is so quiet that she must've heard it.

'Did you miss breakfast?' she says. 'You reporters must be so busy. Would you like a biscuit?'

She's talking as though she's his mum. It must be terrible for her, being a mother when her only child is dead. Luke banishes the notion from his head.

26

'I had breakfast, thanks. It was a smoothie.'

Shit, why is he being so unprofessional today? Luke's usually so together, but he feels edgy around her. He can't imagine losing one of his daughters, especially in that way. It's like he's too close to the tragedy and that just being part of it will harm his own family.

God. Stop it. He can't think like that. How bloody disrespectful.

Luke picks up a pen and taps the pin code into his phone.

'Are you OK to start?'

She nods, slowly, wiping a strand of hair from her face. Her shoulders are straight; she's so composed, given the circumstances.

'How do you feel about the imminent release of Craig Wright and his intention to come back to the area?'

'Straight to the point as usual, Luke.' She picks up her glass cup and sips the tea, a slight shake to her hands. 'As you know, my husband has never done interviews ... didn't want to read Lucy's name alongside that man's. He says he'd kill Craig if he ever saw him in the street. Brian agrees with me ... that Craig coming back shouldn't be allowed. Life should mean life – that's what people say all the time, isn't it?

'Why drag everything back up again?' She rests her elbows on the counter and leans towards Luke. 'What he did in the first place was evil enough.' She reaches a hand out and places it near Luke's mug. 'Please don't refer to my husband in the article.'

'I won't.'

'Good,' she says, sitting up straight again. 'Most of them don't care about our feelings when they've written about Lucy. You're the only one who's kept to your word. It's why I agreed to this interview. I'm not going to speak to any other newspaper.'

'I appreciate that.'

'I bet you do.' A brief smile crosses her face before she frowns. 'Anyone who's committed crimes like that shouldn't be allowed back into any community. What he did to my daughter and Jenna Threlfall was … inhuman – not that he was ever convicted for Jenna. What must her family be going through?'

'We can't write about Jenna in connection with Craig, unfortunately.'

She doesn't register Luke's words.

'And he confessed near the end … The trial had nearly finished! What sort of person does that? He was thinking about himself, to get a reduced sentence. Did he want the world to hear about what he'd done? Have my child's image shown to a room full of strangers?'

Luke sees them in his mind as clear as the first time – he wishes he couldn't. Lucy's burgundy T-shirt pushed up around her neck, her face white, lips blue, eyes wide open. A single straight open wound on her abdomen – her intestines tumbling out after small animals had begun to eat her, inside out.

Gillian gets up from the stool and plucks several tissues from a box on the counter. She turns away from Luke as she dabs at her face and blows her nose.

'I'm sorry about that,' she says, sitting back at the

island. 'I never know when it'll hit me. I could be sat in traffic, see one of her friends pushing a pram, or on their way to work, and it'll overwhelm me. Lucy never had any of that. She'd barely turned eighteen. She will always be eighteen. If it'd been a month before, she'd have been classed as a child ... Craig would never be released.'

Lucy seems such a young person's name, he thinks. Would she still've suited it if she'd had the chance to grow older?

'Would you like to take a break?' Luke says.

'A break?' She gives a bitter laugh. 'I never get a break from this. It makes some people uncomfortable when I cry ... even my own father. He thinks I should be over it by now.' She covers her face with her hands for several moments, her shoulders rising as she takes a deep breath. 'He's always been so cold, especially when *I* was a girl. How can anyone get over losing a child?'

'I don't know.'

Luke feels pathetic, helpless. He hates his job sometimes. What's the point of it all if you can't change anything? All he does is tell readers about events after they've happened. Helen says it's important, that people have the right to know what's going on in the world. She wouldn't feel the same way if it were her own life being read about by thousands.

'Did Lucy know Jenna Threlfall?' says Luke. He's probably asked the question before, but there's nothing about it in his old notes.

'Vaguely,' says Gillian. 'They went to the same

29

school, same college, but they didn't spend much time with each other. I'd never met her – didn't know she existed until . . .'

'But they could've spent time together at college and you might not have known about it?'

'I suppose so.'

'It's just too much of a coincidence that they went to the same place and were both—'

He stops himself, knowing he's pondering aloud to one of the victims' mothers.

'I know,' says Gillian. 'The police would've looked into it at the time, though, wouldn't they?'

After a few minutes' silence, Luke says, 'Have you ever thought of moving away, like Jenna's parents did?'

Her mouth falls open; she leans back, and Luke worries she might topple from the stool.

'Why should I leave?' she says, raising her voice for the first time. 'Lucy's room's upstairs. How could I get rid of that? She's still my daughter. I'm still a mother. She's with me every single day, I can feel her. Where would she go if I weren't here? Don't look at me like that, Luke. I haven't lost my mind. But when you lose a child, you have to believe there's something else after this. Otherwise, I couldn't carry on living. I want to do her proud . . . live my life for her because she can't. She was passionate about so many things. I volunteer in several of the places she did . . . I'm not going to list them now because I think it should be private. Can you believe an eighteen-year-old volunteered in her spare time? It was like she—'

30

Loud footsteps sound from the staircase above.

'That'll be Brian.' Gillian slips gracefully from the stool. 'Do you have everything you need?'

Luke stops the recording app on his phone, places it in his pocket, and swipes his notepad off the counter. On it, he's drawn thirty or forty triangles of different sizes, the imprint of the pen gouged into the paper.

'Thanks for your time, Gillian.'

She stands at the kitchen door, almost beckoning him out. The heavy treads stop, and Gillian's husband appears in the hallway. He's a tall man: around six foot two.

Luke's forehead feels cool with newly formed sweat.

'Luke was just leaving,' says Gillian.

Brian nods and stands aside to let Luke by. His right shoulder tingles as he passes Lucy's father. Luke's always had a vivid imagination – he pictures Brian grabbing him by his collar and flinging him out of the front door. He's surprised when he steps out of the house unscathed. He wants to run to the safety of his car but turns to face Gillian.

'Bye then.'

She closes the front door gently.

Luke wishes he could speak to people without sounding like a bumbling schoolboy. Perhaps he should get on with writing that novel instead of reporting real life and mixing with the public.

He gets into the car and pulls away from the Sharpes' house, turning left at the end of the road.

There must be a connection between Lucy and Jenna.

Gillian didn't mention where her daughter volunteered, but Luke knew it was at an animal sanctuary. Perhaps Jenna visited there, too. He makes a note of it on his pad.

He passes the shops on the parade three miles from the Sharpes'. The houses are smaller here: rows of red-brick terraces with different coloured front doors. There are people on the street: some alone with shopping bags; others chatting on their doorstep or next to the postbox.

Another left, then a right and he's driving on Erica's road. He slows before he passes the house. The front door is still painted green, though he can tell from here that it's seen better days.

Erica's curtains are closed, but that's not unusual. Every time he's passed before, it's been the same. He checks his watch: five to ten. *Homes Under the Hammer*'s on soon. Luke watched it every day when Megan was off school with chicken pox.

Erica must have her own routine; he doubts she goes out very much. Why the hell does she stay here? For her son? It's a question Luke asks himself whenever he thinks about her, which has been a lot these past few days.

He sees movement in the upstairs bedroom window and looks away quickly. Is that Erica's room? He re-members how he and a colleague, Rebecca, spent all day out here, waiting for any activity inside the house or from the police officer guarding the front door.

Luke presses his foot on the accelerator. Within the week, Craig will be back here. As a young man he did such horrific things. God help the people living on this street. Someone like that can't be rehabilitated, thinks Luke. He's seen it before – there are plenty of cases like it. Sometimes within hours of release a person will reoffend. How has Craig convinced the authorities he's changed? Luke can't help but shudder. This man murdered two young women one week apart. There must be evidence linking them, and Luke feels a new determination to find the connection.

6

Erica

He always loved potato waffles. He used to make them into sandwiches; he made everything into sandwiches, even mushy peas. I add them to the shopping list of his favourite foods – things I never eat. I always have the same meals so I don't have to think about it. Today is Tuesday, so I'll have beans on toast for dinner and a cottage pie ready meal for tea. Sometimes, I get the notion of trying something different, perhaps an avocado or an artichoke – I've seen things like that on *Come Dine with Me* and *MasterChef* – but there's no point making all that effort for only one.

I can't believe Craig's coming home tomorrow. I thought something might come up that would stop everything; it hasn't. I've imagined over the years what it would be like to have him home, but I'd pictured him as he was before he went inside. He's a different person now. I'm afraid he'll either withdraw into himself or enjoy his freedom a bit too much.

I've had so many messages from my forum friends.

AnneMarie2348: He'll be a bit shell-shocked at first. He might be quiet for a few days while he gets used to being free.

Anne Marie's from Bristol, so we're relatively close – she's the one I talk to the most.

TexanDude: Why not throw him a party? We had a little get-together for our Shane and it went down a real treat.

Trevor's from Texas, obviously. I just said I'd think about that. I don't think a convicted murderer partying the night away on release would go down very well in this town.

I cross out the cans of lager I wrote on my shopping list.

Some of our members can be a bit strange, but I try not to judge. I have to lead by example, being a moderator. It can get out of hand sometimes. The worst fallout was when a victim's relative found his way on to there. I don't know how he found the site, or how he knew that Martha was on it. He said that he was going to hunt her down and kill her family after what Martha's brother had done to his daughter. She left because of that, which is a shame because she was a really sweet person.

But that's in the past. There are more stringent verifications for admission to our group now.

*

I look at the first-ever picture of Craig on the TV cabinet. My friend, Denise, took the photo and gave me the print. He was premature. So tiny, wrapped in a blue hospital blanket.

I was sitting in this very chair when I felt pains at thirty-three weeks. I thought it was those practice ones, Braxton Hicks, but then my waters went. I ran out into the street, my skirt sopping wet, still wearing my slippers. Denise lived on the next street. I'd known her since we were at primary school. She was the only blonde in a classroom of mousy heads. Bit gobby, too, which was OK if you were on the right side of her.

I waddled all the way to hers, my hands between my legs in case the baby fell out. I must've looked a sight, but you don't think about that when it's a case of life or death.

'Whatever's the matter?' Denise said, opening the door to my banging and screaming. She was carrying her baby boy; his chubby legs gripped her waist, but her blond hair was perfectly styled, make-up always intact.

'My waters have gone,' I said.

'OK, OK. Calm down, love. It's going to be all right. How far apart are your contractions?'

'I don't know. I've only had a few, I think. I had a couple of twinges in the frozen section at the VG, but I thought it was only growing pains.'

She ushered me in.

'Right,' she said. 'I'll give the hospital a ring – ask them what to do.'

She was always helpful. I was twenty-three, but I knew nothing about life, even though I thought I was experienced in the ways of the world. When my mother died, I had no one. My brother didn't visit much, but he didn't even when Mum was alive.

Denise only asked about the baby's father once. I was silent on the subject and she never asked again. She must've known I'd made a mistake. I'd known her since secondary school and we used to tell each other everything. It was shame holding me back.

An ambulance took me to the hospital and I was in agony for nearly twenty-four hours on gas and air before Craig made his appearance. He was silent; everyone said babies should scream when they come out. I saw the panic on the midwife's face, though she pretended everything was fine. She whisked him out of the room and I was left on my own for an hour before anyone came to talk to me. It was one of the longest hours of my life. I imagined the worst – that he'd died, and they couldn't bring themselves to tell me. I was in pain with my stitches, so I couldn't even go and find him.

Eventually, they told me his lungs weren't as good as they should be because he was early.

I didn't see him for three days. I lay there on the ward while all the other mothers tended to their little ones. I pulled the curtain around my bed because I cried all day, thinking they'd soon tell me he was dead. The nurses dragged it back open every time. 'It's best if you're not alone.' I didn't know why some of them were in the job; they obviously didn't like people very much.

They kept me in for a week before I was discharged. 'How can I go home without my baby?' I asked, but they said they needed the beds. I travelled every day on the bus to come and see him before they let me take him home three weeks later. I finally had him to myself and I didn't want him to leave my arms.

Kit Kats. Craig loves Kit Kats.

I write it on my list.

I see Denise in the street, sometimes. My heart yearns for that closeness, for the times we knew what the other was thinking without saying. Our children grew up together – they were inseparable during the school holidays.

But I don't talk to Denise any more. Not after what she did.

It wasn't that far to the Co-op. It's in the next town and I could've taken the bus, but I have to watch the spends this week if I'm buying all this extra food – my money only stretches so far. I've been putting away something each month for my travels – money I used to spend on ciggies. I gave them up years ago. There've been times when I think *Sod it, I'll buy some. Who needs dinner?* But when I tried going without food for a whole day, my stomach won. It's difficult to concentrate on anything else except food when the body's starving. I didn't go further down that dark route, though. Instead, I opened a tin of tomato soup and tried to forget about the *nicotine monster* (a phrase I read in a self-help book from the library).

If they know I'm Craig's mother in this shop, they never let on – not like the one at the top of my road. They treat me as though *I'm* the criminal.

I've found everything on my list and watch as the young lad scans and packs everything into my bag-for-life. They're good like that at the Co-op.

'Hello there, Erica.'

A man's voice, loud and self-assured behind me.

I turn around, relieved to see it's only Jason Bamber. It's not often I see a friendly face out and about.

'Hello, Jason love,' I say.

I turn back to the cashier. The bill comes to £27.50! That would do me a fortnight, but I shouldn't complain.

I can sense Jason standing behind me. He's always been kind since Craig's been inside, and I've known him since he was born.

'Great news about Craig,' he says.

He strides towards me and takes me in his arms. I've only one hand to return the gesture. He's wearing a suit today, but I don't know for sure what he does for a living – I've not had a proper chat with him for ages. He must be doing well for himself. I feel an actual pain in my chest when I compare him to Craig – how my son's life could've been so different.

'I ... How did you know?' I say, but I know the answer.

I've avoided looking at the newspapers since that reporter Luke Simmons telephoned the other day. I glance at the row of papers near the door and I see it: *Murderer to Return to Preston.*

My fingers start to tingle; I tighten my grip on the carrier bag.

I knew they'd run with something, but I didn't think I'd be in a shop full of people when I read it. What did I expect? A warning from that reporter? No. He owes me nothing because I gave him nothing.

'You OK?' says Jason. He follows my gaze. 'They don't half print some crap these days. Must've been a slow news day.'

I smile at him, knowing he's trying to console me. A convicted murderer returning home *is* big news, though.

'Yes, yes. I'm fine.'

How will I get home now? It's a mile away and my legs are like jelly. I walk out of the automatic doors. Cars whizz past; the road's so busy. Oh God. I knew everyone would find out, but I wasn't prepared for it, mentally – not today.

I wish I could buy every single copy of that newspaper and burn the lot.

I could start packing up our stuff when I get home. Craig won't want to stay around here, I know it. I hear a car pull up next to me.

'I'll give you a lift.'

It's Jason. How did he get his car here so quickly? I didn't see him leave the shop.

'It's OK. I'll be all right. Don't worry about me, love. I'm sure you've got things to do.'

His car crawls alongside the kerb as I walk.

'Erica!' he shouts. 'Come on. I wouldn't want my mother walking so far on a day like this.'

I look up to the sky and he's right. The clouds are grey and heavy; it feels like it should be six o'clock at night. I stop walking. The hairdresser's on my right has a sign in the window: *Highlights, cut and blow dry, only £50*. Imagine spending that much money on hair! Mine was about fifty per cent grey the last time I looked.

Jason gets out of his car, the engine idling. He takes the carrier bag from my hands.

'I know Craig's innocent,' he says, looking solemnly into my eyes, his lips pursed as though he might burst into tears. 'He'd never do anything like that.'

'I know,' I say. 'Craig really appreciates you believing in him. Not many people did.'

He puts my shopping into his boot then opens the passenger door.

He'd never do anything like that.

'I saw Lucy's mum the other day,' he says, as we set off.

The blood in my arms and legs runs cold. Jason's never mentioned the past before – though we haven't said more than a quick hello in passing recently.

'Did you speak to her?' I say.

'God, no. What would I say? I doubt she'd recognise me now, though. We've all changed so much since back then.'

He glances at me. There's sweat on his top lip and down the side of his face. He smells strange ... sickly sweet.

'Do you still live with your mum, Jason?' I say.

He gives a short bark of a laugh.

41

'Shit, no. Can you imagine that? She'd bloody nag me all day. No. I'm a free man, me.' He looks at me again. 'Sorry. No offence, like. And pardon my French.' He laughs again.

'It's all right,' I say.

I can't imagine Jason's mother ever using language like that, but at least he's not talking about Gillian Sharpe any more.

We pull up outside my house. I daren't look.

I don't need to.

'Oh God,' says Jason, after undoing his seat belt and opening the car door. 'I'll find the little shits, Mrs Wright. I'll tear their fucking hair out.'

I put a hand on his arm.

'No, no, love. I'll be OK. I knew it'd start again. And they might not be so little these days.'

He gets out of the car and opens the boot, lifting out my carrier. We walk to the front door and stand two feet from it. The smell is awful; I want to gag, be sick, run away.

'At least the keyhole's clear,' I say.

'I'll get Stu the window cleaner round. He's used to clearing up dog crap.'

'I'll be fine, Jason. Thanks for the lift.' I grab the bag from his hand. 'You take care, now.'

His mobile phone bleeps and he takes it out of his pocket.

'Give me a ring if you need me,' he says before leaping back into his car and screeching off.

I stand a little closer to the door. I'd almost forgotten the smell.

The letters, this time, are vertical: *WHORE*. I'm surprised they managed to collect enough shit to write it in such big letters.

It shouldn't hurt, but it does. It's the worst thing anyone could ever call me; I've tried hard to learn from my mistake.

I don't look around because I don't care who's looking at me. I open the door and carefully step inside; there's nothing on the doormat this time.

In the kitchen, I put the frozen food into the ice compartment and leave the rest on the counter in the bag. Still in my coat, I kneel on the kitchen floor, leaning against the back door. I should be heating my cottage pie; *Tipping Point*'ll be on in a minute. My knees are shot; I might never get up. I allow myself a few minutes to wallow before I try to stand. There's so much to do. They didn't break me last time, and they won't now. I'm stronger than I was then.

7

Tick tock, tick tock.

Soon it'll be time. Can you imagine what I've been thinking about for all these years? I've not been able to do anything about it – I need the timing to be perfect, like before. And it's nearly time.

I need to be a bit more careful now, though. They know more these days. People are filmed almost everywhere; phones are tapped, computers are monitored. You might think – if you're an ordinary person – that no one is watching you, but they are. Especially online, because that's easy. Those big internet companies get away with so much. Have you ever wondered why? They know everything about us. So you need to be clever about it. If you want to do something ... under the radar, so to speak ... you can never have a phone with you (those gadgets are always listening), and you must always know where CCTV is. People – normal people – have cameras pointing at their driveways ... they like to protect their property. I suppose that's reasonable, but why don't they protect their loved ones in the same way?

It would only take one sighting and I'd be inside. Again. Though it might be worth it.

So I have to work quickly; get as much done as I can.

Lucy was so good, you know. So pure. With her white-blonde hair, she was almost an angel ... so trusting. Perhaps she's looking down on me now: my very own guardian angel. We will always be linked. Sometimes, I talk to her and she always replies in some way.

I don't think about the words she said near the end. She didn't mean them. She loved me, I know she did. She brought out the good in me.

It was different in those days. Not as many mobile phones – there were those shit Nokia ones – if you had one at all. But Lucy didn't have one. Her parents didn't trust them.

They trusted me, though.

Her dad was ever so protective. He never wanted her to grow up ... didn't want men to spoil her.

He doesn't have to worry about that any more.

8

Erica

I was two hours early, just in case. I've walked around the housing estate opposite three times. They could do with a coffee shop or something around here.

I'm so tired. I set my alarm for three a.m. this morning, but I needn't have. There were taps and bangs on the front door and living room window all night. I was too scared to sleep until they stopped. It sounded like children, but surely their parents wouldn't have let them stay out so late. What's the point of things going wrong if people don't learn from our mistakes?

When it finally got to three, the alarm rang out and scared me half to death. It was quiet outside, so I went downstairs and put the kettle on, getting the Dettol out of the cupboard. I had several pairs of marigolds, scrubbing brushes, and there are four big bottles of bleach that I can't remember buying. I'm sure I didn't have that many.

It hadn't rained since four the previous afternoon, so I expected some of it would've dried into the cracks of the paint.

I cried the first time I scrubbed dog dirt off the door, but last night I just got on with it and imagined what I'd cook Craig for tea, where we'd sit, and what we'd talk about. I couldn't think of many subjects. He's had a television in there, and that's all we've had in common so far.

I know I shouldn't be nervous now, waiting outside the prison for him, but I am. I haven't told him many details about my life as it is. He wouldn't be interested in my online group or my knitting. To be honest, I'm not bothered about knitting any more. Mother tried to teach me, but I only got the hang of the basic knit stitch. *Concentrate, Erica! You look like you're going to stab yourself!* I've knitted enough squares to blanket the whole of Lancashire, I expect.

I could talk to him about the books I've read (though they're silly, romantic novels); the documentaries we watched at the same time in different places. And I've got my folder of places I want to visit, even though that's not something I've actually *done* yet. I'll tell him what favourite foods I've bought him, and that I recorded that film he used to love.

After buying those treats yesterday, I can't stretch to a taxi home for us. I hope he doesn't mind getting the bus.

No, it'll be fine. He'll just be glad to be out.

I stand next to the towering doors. It's strange, waiting here alone. People passing don't even glance at me; they must be used to it. I want to tell each of them that my son is coming home, that he's going to be free! My hands are shaking but I don't bother to hide them. I don't care. This is the day I've been waiting for after seventeen long years.

At eleven o'clock, on the dot, the door opens.

Adrenaline surges through me. It creates a strange combination of feelings: excited, happy, nervous.

Craig steps out. He towers over me, but there are tears in his eyes. He holds out his arms.

'Mum!'

I rush into him. I promised myself I'd be strong, but I can't stop the tears. The slam of the door makes me jump, so Craig hugs me tighter. It feels so good to hold him tightly and not have to be mindful of the time.

'I can't believe it,' he says into my hair.

His tears are warm on my scalp.

'Oh, my boy. I've missed you so much.' I stand back, holding his arms. 'Look at you! Haven't you grown?'

He laughs a little as he dabs his eyes with his jumper.

'You've seen me every week, Mum.'

'I know, but it's not the same. You're in daylight, now ... in the real world. I can see the colour of your hair properly – it's gone darker. Did you notice that? Oh, you must be freezing – don't you have a coat?'

He shakes his head.

'I got your favourites in ...' I say. 'Mushy peas, crispy pancakes ... You still like all of those things, don't you? I suppose you will, after the terrible food they've been giving you in there. And you'll like a nice hot bath, won't you? I got you some bubbles ... they're only Co-op's own, but they'll be as good as—'

'Mum?'

'Yes, love?'

'Can we go straight home?'

'Course we can, Son. I hope you don't mind the bus, it's just that I—'

'The bus is fine.' He puts his arm through mine as we walk slowly. 'I've never heard you talk as much.'

'It's hard to talk freely in there. I thought of so many things to say to you on my way here, but they've gone right out of my head.'

'I'm sure you'll think of them. And the food inside wasn't so bad, you know.'

I squeeze his arm towards mine. I never want to let him go.

I can't stop staring at him. It's like when he first came home as a baby and I didn't think he was real. I'd gaze at him for hours as he slept, afraid he'd stop breathing at any moment.

His crispy pancakes and potato waffles are heating in the oven and he's sitting in his old chair next to the telly. I'm not sure about his choice of programmes, though: *Banged Up* or something, I think it is. If *I'd* just come out of that place, it'd be the last thing I'd want to watch.

'One of the guys inside said that when his missus was pregnant,' he explains, as I stand in the doorway, 'she'd watch *One Born Every Minute* all the time. He didn't get why she'd want to put herself through watching it ... She carried on recording it for weeks after the birth until she got fed up of being knackered all day ... Never watched the programme after that ... well, until she got pregnant again.' He scratches his head. 'We talked about loads of rubbish, you know. It wasn't all bad stuff.'

He's wearing the jeans and jumper I ordered for him from the catalogue. They seem to fit him well, and he hasn't complained about them. He's so much bigger now. The last time I bought him clothes was when he was thirteen years old.

'I can't go out in this!' he'd said, holding up the black T-shirt.

I'd spent ages in town searching for it; they weren't as easy to find as you'd think.

'There's nothing wrong with it,' I said. 'It's as plain as I could find.'

'Exactly. People'll know we got it on the cheap – it hasn't got a label.'

'Course it's got a label. I didn't steal it!'

He rolled his eyes – always so dramatic.

'Not that kind of label, Mum.'

I'd thought myself lucky that he still spoke to me. Anne Marie from the forum said that before her daughter, Ashley, went to prison, she barely spoke to her. She knew she was hiding something because she'd rush straight upstairs after coming home. Drugs were to blame for what she did, Anne Marie says. *Makes them secretive, erratic.* I'll have to ask her what drugs they were because secretive *and* erratic isn't a combination I've ever heard of.

'Something's burning, Mum,' says Craig.

His voice is so different now: deeper, confident. Perhaps that's how he needed to be in there. Especially after what happened to him for the first five years.

'Oh, good grief,' I say.

I open the oven and luckily find that only the edges of the crispy pancakes have caught. I plate them and pick off the burnt bits. They're probably better than the food he's been used to.

I put it on a tray and carry it through.

'Good old crispy pancakes!' he says. 'I'm surprised you can still buy them. They're so seventies.'

'Some things never change, Son.'

'You not having any?'

'I'm too excited to eat.'

I watch as he layers up his fork.

'Oh, man, that's hot,' he says with a mouth full. He chews it quickly and swallows. 'I'd forgotten what really hot food was like.'

I pat his shoulder; I'm hovering near the doorway, unsure what to do. He's going to get fed up of me if I carry on like this.

'I'll get you a drink.'

I fill a tumbler with water. It's so strange having someone else in the house. It's like the place has come back to life – that the wallpaper and the carpets aren't as drab as they were yesterday.

'Here you are, love.'

He raises his eyebrows briefly.

'Don't suppose you have any beers in? Haven't had one of those in a while.'

'No, Son. And it's only four o'clock.'

We sit together in companionable silence. His prison programme has finished and *Tipping Point*'s just started. His eyes glaze over as the theme tune ends. This is the life I'm used to, but I don't think it's going to be enough for him. It might be like going from one prison to another. I'm itching to get on to my computer and tell my friends that he's home, but I can't just go and sit in the corner – not on his first day back. I get the notifications on my phone. There are twenty-three so far, but it would be inappropriate to talk about him while he's still in the room. I can catch up with them all later.

The letterbox sounds. There's a burning smell.

I rush to the hall, where a scrunched-up piece of newspaper smoulders on the wooden floor. I pour the jug of water I keep on the window sill over it. I hadn't put the litter tray down ... I hadn't wanted Craig to see the reality so soon. He's only been home three hours.

Everyone on the street will know now – it's like that around here. I walk calmly back into the living room and draw the curtains.

'What was that?' says Craig.

'Just takeaway flyers,' I say. 'I wish they'd stop wasting the paper.'

'I can smell burning.'

'Don't worry, it's only the oven – I forgot to turn it off.'

His plate is clean, and the knife and fork are at six o'clock. At least he's retained his manners.

'Why've you closed the curtains?'

'Didn't want the light to get in your eyes while we watch telly.'

We both know it's a lie; the sun isn't showing itself today.

I take the tray from his lap and place it next to the sink. I'll wash it up later; there's no point wasting hot water on a few dishes.

I thought we might've had at least one evening with a bit of peace. My son spent all that time in prison when they should have been targeting the real killer. It might be seventeen years too late, but I'll prove them all wrong. I've been searching for the man named Pete Lawton for so many years now. He worked at the Anderton & Campbell garage on Poulton Street. Craig had given the police the details of where he was when Lucy disappeared, but the police couldn't find a man by that name who worked there. I've written to every Peter Lawton I can find the address of. I've only had one reply. It was from a Mrs B. Lawton, telling me that her husband had passed away, he'd never set foot in Preston, and had certainly never been a mechanic.

At first, I was excited by my search, but after all these years, I'm beginning to lose hope. I've messaged twenty-three Peter Lawtons on Facebook – most have ignored me, but there are three who have yet to open the message. They thought Craig was making him up, but I knew my son wouldn't invent something like that. And the truth will always find a way of finding us, won't it?

Car headlights dance across my bedroom curtains. It's quiet and I feel safe with Craig in the house. It's like our roles are reversed. I was meant to keep *him* safe – it should've been an easy job, but I couldn't even get that right. It can't be because I brought Craig up on my own – my mother did a good job with us – my brother and I have never been in trouble, unless you count my getting pregnant while unmarried, but that's not even unusual these days.

I wonder if *my* father's even alive. Mum said he was around for the first few weeks of my life *then scarpered*. She'd say it was history repeating itself, but she'd be wrong. I never told Craig's father he had a son. Not straight away, at least.

Perhaps my brother managed to trace our dad, but never told us. 'He's got ambition, that one,' Mum said about Philip. 'But you've got the brains. You could really do something with your life, Erica. Not like I did with mine.'

She said it as though bringing us up on her own was a cross she had to bear, but it wasn't as bad as that. She never made it feel that way.

I turn on to my side, punching the pillow until it's plump. I feel a little better knowing I put the litter tray under the letterbox after Craig turned in. When I went upstairs, I listened at his door for a few moments before knocking.

'Come in, Mum,' he shouted.

I opened his door and he was tucked up in bed, his covers across his chest and his arms out either side. He was holding a book from the bookcase on the landing.

'Which one have you chosen?' I said, excited as I'd read them all before I put them there.

'*The Da Vinci Code*.'

'Do you like it?'

'I'm not sure yet. I'm not much of a reader.'

'But ...' I stopped myself.

I must've given him at least three hundred books over the years. I wish he'd told me it'd been a waste of time. But, to be honest, *The Da Vinci Code* wasn't the best book I've read either. Mother would've hated it; she was a staunch Catholic when it suited her.

'Do we still have that portable TV?' he said.

'I don't know. I'll have to check,' I said, a bit too quickly. 'Night, Son.'

I walked out and closed the door. I didn't want him to see my face. It was silly of me, getting upset over a few books.

I close my eyes, shutting out my old-fashioned bedroom curtains that always let in too much light.

I picture in my head a detached house with a crescent-shaped drive that has two gates: one for in, one for out. Inside, three children are sleeping (two girls and a boy) in their own bedrooms, with nightlights that create constellations on each of their ceilings. Downstairs, I'm sitting at a large pine table with three chairs on one side and a long wooden bench on the other. A man – I can't see his face – passes me a cold white wine in a glass decorated with silver stars. He puts a bowl of pasta (creamy tagliatelle topped with pieces of roasted artichoke and parmesan) in front of me.

A car door slams outside and my dream disappears.

I wipe the tear that's dribbled down my right temple. I've never liked white wine anyway.

9
Luke

For the first time since he doesn't know when, Luke almost jumps out of bed – despite being a little hungover.

Two nights ago, the *Chronicle* published links of Luke's article on to the Facebook page, as they always do. Since then, it's gotten over three hundred sad and angry faces, which was pretty good for a local paper. Luke can't help but picture people making those expressions as they clicked the button. People are acknowledging his work, seemingly for the first time in months – perhaps even years.

Craig's mugshot was the image they used as clickbait. But that picture was nearly twenty years old. Luke doubted Craig looked the same now. When researching Craig's case at the start of the millennium, he'd seen pictures on the internet of a child who killed several other children decades ago. He felt sure he'd recognise her in the street. But now, he remembers his daughters; Megan had blonde hair for the first two years of her life and then it turned into a mousey brown, now it's darker. And his own wife has seen pictures of Luke as a nine-year-old and didn't recognise him.

Last night, he'd been watching Megan do her homework. She had to write a story about the scariest monster she could imagine. She'd drawn a picture of her creation; it had a mouth that filled two-thirds the size of its purple face and contained at least fifty pointed teeth. 'I wish all monsters were so obvious,' Luke had said to Helen before he took the girls for their bath.

He read to them, as always, on his and Helen's bed. Megan on his right and Alice near the wall as she feared she'd fall off the high bed, still used to sleeping in the toddler bed she won't let her parents get rid of. They were half asleep when he finished reading *Room on the Broom*. He gazed at their little faces, their eyes trying to battle against sleep, and he vowed to always keep them safe. Then another thought washed over him: what if one of his daughters harmed someone? He conjured the scenario: Megan at twenty-one years old, a dark-haired taller version of Helen; she's kneeling on top of someone – her hands around their neck. A shiver ran through Luke's body. Why does he have to imagine every situation he thinks of so intensely? His imagination is so vivid, these tableaux almost become memories.

He ushered them into bed, handing Ted to Alice.

'Thank you, Daddy,' she said.

He thought then that he would do anything to protect his daughters.

Later, Helen, sitting crossed-legged on the dining chair in her pyjamas, had the laptop open on the kitchen table (it was always cluttered, like the rest of the house) reading the Facebook comments from readers. He had never had so many and couldn't believe people were still reading it over twenty-four hours later. The paper must've sponsored the post.

Helen poured them both a glass of prosecco, not even mentioning the points value (though she'd heard it was less calorific than normal wine). He gazed at her as she leaned towards the laptop. He always loved the way strands of her blonde curly hair dropped on to her face and she seemed not to notice.

'Can you believe,' she said, 'that a lot of slim people don't even count the calories from alcohol?'

'Have you been reading those celebrity diet magazines again?' said Luke. 'They lie, you know. Most of them don't bloody eat anything. It's probably the booze keeping them alive.'

'You're so cynical.'

'Well ... yeah, I am. It's called being a realist.'

She tutted and rolled her eyes. He loved it when she did that – it meant they were getting along. Helen had been working the previous night, so they hadn't had the chance to sit down and talk about his article. She was a charge nurse at Royal Preston Hospital and he'd always felt slightly jealous of her career choice: she actually helped people.

'Oh, look,' she said. 'Someone's just commented that they live on the same street as Craig's mother. *She's a bloody loner. Weird. Nothing's right with that family. I've been there for over ten years and I can tell with people like that*. He didn't put any apostrophes in. That must drive you mad. He got ten likes though.'

Luke gulped his minuscule glass of fizz down in one.

'You know me too well,' he said. 'Shit, Helen. What if people target Erica again?'

She turned to look at him, her head wobbling slightly. Dieting made the drink go to both of their heads. This healthy-eating lark could have its benefits, he thought. They'd save a fortune and he'd be slim again, if a little bad-tempered during the day. He didn't know why Helen wanted to lose weight, though – she was perfect as she was.

'Did you kill anyone, Luke?' she said, refilling his glass.

'Eh?'

'Well, it's not your fault then, is it?' She tilted her head to the side, looking at Craig's picture again. 'He doesn't look like a murderer, does he?'

'I don't suppose many people do, until it's too late.'

'But look at him. He's so slight. And those eyes are so sad.'

'They're sad because he got caught. Don't fall for it, Helen.'

She nudged his elbow, almost spilling a drop of precious prosecco – though he didn't usually drink it, he was grateful for it tonight.

'I'm *not* falling for it,' she said. 'But I can see why his mother still loves him.'

'What? You're basing that on looks?'

She took another gulp from her glass.

'Sorry. You forget sometimes ... when you look at someone's photo ... what they're capable of. They're all human to me. I guess it's because I have to care for people whoever they are, whatever they've done.'

'You wouldn't think that if you were in court during the trial. Didn't you read my article? I mentioned that in the past, convicted killers have gone on to kill again ... sometimes only weeks after their release.'

'Sorry ... sorry. No, I haven't read it. I will, though. Tomorrow.'

Luke paused to look at her. When had she stopped reading his words? She used to read everything he wrote; she'd been so proud of him. But then, Luke doesn't blame her. Until now, all he'd written about was petty criminals, village fetes, and takeaways.

'Wasn't there another teenager who was killed around that time?' she said.

'Jenna Threlfall. Found in the middle of a playing field. The police couldn't link her to Craig. No evidence. With Lucy, he was seen with her just before she went missing and he had no alibi for the time of her death. But there was nothing that concrete with Jenna.'

'Aren't the police still looking for her killer?'

Luke shrugged. 'I suppose they thought they'd found him.'

'What must her mum and dad be going through? At least Lucy's parents had some sort of justice.'

She stared out of the kitchen window, even though it was dark outside and all she could see were reflections. Luke wondered what was going through her mind. Did she picture imaginary events like he did? Perhaps she was visualising what—

She slammed the laptop shut, making Luke jump.

'I think the kids are asleep,' she said.

'I should hope so,' said Luke. 'It's ten past eleven.' He looked at his wife as her eyebrows went up and down. How much had they drunk? 'Oh. Right. Yes.'

She stood and cleared the glasses.

'A few years ago,' she said, 'you would've jumped on me if I said that.'

'Sorry. It's just that ...'

'Whatever.' She lingered at the doorway, staring at him. 'You've not been yourself for a while now, Luke. It's like you're only half present most of the time.'

'But we've been talking tonight,' he said.

'Yeah, I suppose.'

She went upstairs and was asleep in the ten minutes it took Luke to make sure the house was secure. He was relieved. What was wrong with him? Was it because he was so unfit (he got breathless just walking up the stairs) and thought that having him panting over her would put his wife off him?

But that was last night. He didn't want to think about anything negative this morning. He'd actually got out of bed as soon as the alarm had sounded. It was progress. OK, a person's life may have been affected by his words a few days ago, but someone else would've written it if he hadn't.

Luke had finally started to make his mark. He had several leads to go on: he could interview friends of

Lucy and Jenna — perhaps find a link between Jenna and Craig that no one had found. Today was going to be a good day.

10

Erica

I've been up since six and keep hovering at the gap in the living room curtains. I've had four coffees so far. I'm not used to all this caffeine; my hands are shaking.

At 2.15 a.m. this morning, a sound woke me. I sat up in bed and stilled my breath.

It came from *inside* the house this time.

My heart pounded. What if someone had broken into the house? Would they try to harm Craig? We weren't prepared for that.

I stood, listening at my door before opening it. Moaning, whimpering, coming from across the way.

'Craig,' I whispered in the hallway. 'Are you OK in there?'

No reply.

I pushed the handle down and slowly opened his door. The light from the landing was enough to see that Craig was in his bed. He was fast asleep, but tears lined his cheeks.

I crept out again. It would've been cruel to wake him – he might be ashamed of crying, though he needn't be.

During the first five years in the first prison, I watched, week by week, as he gradually became a shadow of the person he was. Sometimes, he would sit opposite me with tears pouring down his face, yet he didn't sob or put his hands up to cover them. It was like he was dead inside. I wanted to put my arms around him, to comfort him and tell him everything was going to be all right. But I couldn't; I was helpless. It was one of the most heartbreaking moments, when I could do nothing to help my child. He'd never tell me what was wrong or if other prisoners were hurting him. I wish he had, because what I imagined instead was horrific.

'They treat me like a kid in here,' he said. 'And not in a good way.'

'What do you mean?' I said.

'You don't want to know. Please, Mum,' he said. 'Tell me about home. Do you still go to your pottery class on Thursdays?'

I lied and said that I did because I wanted him to think life was carrying on as normal, just waiting for him to slot back in. But I hadn't been to pottery since Craig's arrest. Not one of the members of the group spoke to me in the street after that, so it was pointless. I'd thought they were quite an open-minded bunch, but you can never tell with people, can you? I didn't tell him that I didn't work at the shop any more either, but he probably knew that already as I'd taken so much time off during his trial.

I cried for the rest of the day after that visit, even on the bus home. No one asked if I was all right, assuming they even noticed. They probably thought I'd snap at them, like I was unable to control my emotions in public.

I wish I'd asked Craig more about his troubles, raised a grievance or whatever they do in prisons. I had a feeling it would be worse for him if I did, though. But I should've pushed him for an answer, complained to whoever would listen. It's an internal argument I have with myself all the time. About Craig and what I could've done to make things different. I think it might have hardened him – after that, there was no hope, no light behind his eyes.

Hearing him cry last night brought all those memories back. I went back to bed, but I didn't sleep much after that.

I've switched off *This Morning* because *Granada Reports* will be on again soon. I caught it in between *Good Morning Britain* earlier. They used the photo of Lucy wearing her school uniform – even though she was eighteen. They tried to make Craig out as some child killer, when he isn't. I wished they'd mention the other girl – that he was arrested for her, but the police didn't have enough evidence. If they didn't think it was him, then surely it casts doubt on his conviction. But they're biased, these television reports. In the past, there have been loads of people who've been wrongly sent to prison and it's ruined their lives. I read a government website where a prisoner can make a claim for compensation if a sentence is overturned. It probably wouldn't be much, but it would give Craig a good start; the start in life that he deserved.

The news articles on the local station usually only last a day, so hopefully it'll be done and gone by six o'clock. I'm surprised they didn't run with it the day *before* Craig was released.

I should know better than to have it on in the first place. When it first happened, the news was so raw, so horrific. But sometimes, it's like it's happened to someone I don't know. I've had to distance myself from it, you see. I'm not as hard as you think I am. I can't imagine my son doing ... See, I can't even think about the details.

Would Mum have made it better or worse for Craig and me if she were alive? I can't envisage what she'd say about it – I've never been able to. She was so loyal to her loved ones in public.

No one around here cared about me after she died. All they talked about was how her husband left her and how she had to look after her spinster daughter – as though there was something wrong with me. Mother knew everyone around here. She was always talking about everyone's business, and everyone else was the same. What they gossiped about was only true half the time; the rest they made up to fill in the blanks – I'd heard them when I was forced as a child to sit at the back of the church after the service with a lukewarm orange cordial.

Mother didn't know the lengths I went to to keep my other life secret from her. I didn't want to disappoint her because I knew what I was doing was wrong. She had such high expectations of me. She had no idea I had a boyfriend, let alone that I was pregnant *out of wedlock* (as they used to say). I had no other choice but to live with her – I had no money to start up on my own, even though I was working. Single people didn't have as many points as families to get a council house, and this area was made up mainly of married couples with children. Mother inherited this house when she was only twenty-three. Her parents – I was only two when they died – were killed in a road accident, but I never asked my mother to elaborate. I wanted to ask how they managed to die like that. Wasn't it rare in a place that didn't have many cars? Had they been drinking? I didn't have the courage to ask any of those questions.

There was one picture she kept in a display cabinet. In it, my grandfather's wearing a light shirt with a knitted vest over the top, and my grandmother's in a proper 1950s dress, belted in the middle. I like to imagine it was yellow and her belt was patent black. They were both smoking cigarettes and looking off camera, standing in front of a house with grass under their feet, so it can't have been this house. It was as though they were so used to having their picture taken. They looked kind. I must still have that photograph somewhere.

My mother always used to tell me how wealthy her parents were, that they were involved in the cotton industry, but she never said how or what she did with the money– never showed an interest when the last mill closed. Instead, she said, 'I could've been rich, too, after they died, had I made different life choices.'

I took that personally, of course, but she didn't mean it in that way.

And now I'm in the same position as she was then. My mother and I might not have been that different after all, but we never found that out, did we?

Well, not until the end.

Now I'm six years older than she was when she died, yet I picture her in my head as an old woman, even though she was only fifty-four. She never let herself relax, and I wished she had. I suppose I'm like that now – I never drink alcohol, I worry about things that will never happen, and I can't sit still for more than ten minutes. Is it inevitable that we turn into our mothers?

She didn't leave a will, so I've been paying my brother rent for his share of the house since she died. I constantly wonder if he'll announce he wants to sell. I'd get half, but what could I buy for that? A one-bedroomed flat probably – and I'd be grateful of that – but what would happen to Craig?

I shouldn't worry about something that's not happened yet.

There've been no goings-on outside so far today. People have been walking to work and not giving us a second glance. It helps that only one person on this street has lived here from that time; most have moved on. Those who stayed live up near the shops. Many of these houses are rented out now – it's where the profit is; I hear that all the time on *Homes Under the Hammer*.

It's only at twenty past eleven that I hear Craig moving upstairs. He hasn't said what time he was usually woken, but I doubt they gave him a lie-in. I've been dressed since I got up in preparation for him coming down. I don't usually bother getting up until just before ten as that's when the postman might knock. Sometimes a new one'll be at the door with a package for a neighbour five, or even ten, doors down, which is ridiculous. It's worse around Christmas – why don't people have it delivered to their workplace? They must be so busy that they can't be bothered going into town to buy presents. If I had the money and people to buy for, then I'd love to.

Oh well.

The regular postie knows I don't take anything in. What neighbour would want to knock at *my* door to rescue their parcel?

Craig thuds down the stairs and leans into the living room.

'I'm going to make some toast. Do you want any?'

He doesn't wait for a reply, just carries on into the kitchen. I get up and stand at the doorway.

'I've eaten, love,' I say. 'Do you know what to do?'

'I didn't die and come back to life,' he says.

I frown at that, but he doesn't see. I don't think he realised what he said. He begins humming as he takes the loaf from the wooden bread bin that I've had for so long the pine-coloured varnish has worn off. He puts two slices in the toaster. It's like he's in his own little world and everything's fine.

'I worked in the kitchen for three years,' he says. 'I chopped onions, made sandwiches. It was fresh food,

70

you know. Everyone has to work … and my mate Rob got a degree with the OU.'

I don't say he already told me most of that during our visits over the years. Though when he'd said he worked in the kitchen, I thought he meant washing up, serving food – I hadn't imagined they'd given them sharp objects. Why hadn't I asked at the time? But it's good news; it means they trusted him.

'What time's your supervising officer getting here?'

He turns his back to me, his shoulders tense as he leans on the counter. The toast pops up and he scrapes butter on it. He takes a bite; almost half of it in his mouth at once.

'Half twelve,' he says, his mouth full. 'Surprised they arranged a meeting at lunchtime. I could've done with a longer sleep.'

I follow him into the living room. He's so tall, but he can't have grown since he was last in this house. The markings on the doorway only go a bit higher than I am because he wasn't interested in measuring his height once he was an inch taller than me.

Looking at him now, bulked out with his weight-training, it seems like he could be capable of anything. And he must've learned some new things in prison, too.

Craig doesn't want me there while Adam, his supervising officer, talks to him. I was allowed to answer the door, though. '… Just so he can see you're around. I wouldn't want them thinking I was lying about moving

71

in with you. You don't want to be bothered by all that official stuff though.'

Adam seems nice enough. Young – though of course everyone is these days. I feel so much older than sixty. My mother used to say she knew she was *past it* when police officers started looking younger than her. Mum always seemed old, even though she wasn't – such old-fashioned hair. All mothers looked the same when I was a child: permed hair (I imagine they thought they were Marilyn Monroe), skirts to the knee, and powdered faces. They never swore in public, but then got to a certain age when they thought they could get away with saying whatever they pleased, even if those words hurt people.

I'm trying not to eavesdrop on them downstairs, but I'm itching to know what they're talking about. This is my house, after all. I tiptoe to my bedroom door and open it slightly. They have the living room door open, so whatever they're saying can't be that bad.

'So, to go over this again: travelling abroad is a no-no at the moment. You have to declare your record when applying for employment, although we have approved organisations that'll offer you certain positions – some-times on a volunteer basis to begin with, but it all helps ... ease you back into life on the outside.'

'Yes, yes. I know all this.'

'Well, here's a list of volunteer positions available to get you into the swing of things. Have you any ques-tions?'

There's silence for a moment.

'No. I think we've covered everything.'

'We have courses you could enrol on, so you could—'

'I've been on enough courses.' Craig almost shouts these words, but then clears his throat. 'But thank you.'

'Here's that leaflet again,' says Adam. 'It covers everything, and it's laid out clearly.'

'I'd say. It looks as though it's written for a five-year-old. *Number one: Be good*. Isn't that a bit obvious?'

'You'd think so, wouldn't you? Have you got a mobile yet?'

'No. Should be getting one soon.'

'Let me have the details about that when you do. And only one phone – text only for the moment. No photographs.'

'OK.'

Craig's sounding impatient – I hope Adam doesn't pick up on it. I've read the leaflet they're talking about. It is a little basic, but he has to behave in these meetings. His freedom is so precarious and I'm not sure Craig fully realises that.

'Lucy's mum still lives around here,' says Craig. 'They only told me the other day. I hadn't expected anyone from then to be here now – except Mum of course and ... .'

'And?'

'I can't remember the name.'

'Gillian and Brian Sharpe live far enough for it not to be a problem – we did check that out. But you know not to contact them.'

'Right.'

'And you're not to mix with any known criminals.'

'I know.'

'Good. Here's a card with details of your counselling session next week. Be on time – early, if you can.'

'Are they really necessary?'

'You know they are. It's one of the conditions of your release.'

Craig didn't mention anything about counselling.

They're still talking downstairs when there's a screech outside – a car breaking suddenly. I creep to my window, not wanting Craig to realise I've been listening at my door. I push the nets aside.

Standing in the middle of the road is a teenage girl. Her hair is blonde; her skin is pale. She's staring right at the house.

The driver in the blue car that stopped for her puts a foot on the accelerator; the engine revs, but the girl doesn't move.

She meets my eyes and raises her hand to wave, but her palm stops mid-air.

It can't be her, can it? Ghosts don't exist. It would be impossible.

I can't take my eyes from hers.

The car horn sounds and my gaze is drawn away; there are another two cars behind the blue one. By the time I look back into the road, the girl is gone.

I stagger backwards till I land on my bed.

She looked just like Lucy.

*

I wait a good two minutes after Adam leaves the house before going back downstairs.

In the living room, Craig is in his chair, unmoving, looking out of the window. There is no one standing outside.

'Craig, love?' I ask tentatively. 'Did it go well?'

He purses his lips; his eyes narrow. No reply.

'Can I get you a brew?' I say, trying to sound cheerful.

'A special one.' Still he looks out of the window, his voice monotone.

'Eh?'

'Never mind.' He stands, towering over me and stretching his arms backwards, making his chest look inflated. 'I'll make us both one.'

I want to follow him into the kitchen, but resist. Instead, I look to the window, half daydreaming.

My heart jolts when I make out a face that's pressed against it. Young, female, blonde.

A knock at the door.

I stand motionless – hoping that will make me invisible.

Lucy might be haunting us now that Craig's been released. I shake my head. No. That's ridiculous.

'Shall I get that, Mum?' shouts Craig from the kitchen.

I dart out of the living room and join him in the kitchen, shutting the door.

'No, no,' I whisper. 'We can't open the front door. We don't know who it is.'

'Of course we don't,' says Craig, too loud. 'But that's usually the way.'

Another knock; the letterbox flaps open and shut.

'Oh no,' I say. 'I forgot to put the litter tray down.'

'Litter tray? What are you talking about?'

I look up at my son – his face in a frown.

'It's for ...'

He rubs his forehead, then pulls open the kitchen door, almost running to open the front one. He stands on the pavement, looking left and right for several minutes before coming back inside. He bends down and picks up a leaflet. It was only a silly leaflet.

'You haven't been getting threats ... things through the door, have you, Mum?'

I blink quickly. 'I ... no ... I ...'

I thought it might have been the girl standing outside.

'Shit. You have, haven't you? Why didn't you tell me? You should've told me ... I could've had someone protect you.'

'Protect me? Like who? And how?' I shake my head. 'No, no. That's not been necessary, has it? Look at me: I'm fine.'

He stares at me, hard, frowning again. If he weren't my son, I could imagine myself being afraid of him.

'Yes, you're fine,' he says. 'But, Mum ... you look different, you act differently. Being here isn't what it was like when ...' He puts his hands on my shoulders – they're so big and his grip is so tight that it hurts me a little. 'You'll never have to worry about things like this again. OK?'

I nod. 'Yes.'

Even though I know that will never be true. Craig used to be such a gentle soul. But I've noticed that something in him has changed. Perhaps he was never gentle – that might have been a picture I painted of him while he was away.

It's now three in the afternoon and there have been no further dramas – unless you count Craig getting up and down from his seat to peer through the curtains, mumbling, 'Where the hell is he?'

He said it so quietly, I didn't want to ask what he meant by it.

I can't concentrate on the telly. The girl outside looked so much like Lucy it was uncanny. Her hair was the same colour, the same style. I remember Craig brought Lucy to our house one afternoon. She was ever so quiet, but very polite. She declined my offer of tea and biscuits, while Craig was mortified at the mere suggestion of refreshments.

'We're not staying,' he said. 'I only came to get something from upstairs.'

When he came down, whatever it was must've been in his pockets because he wasn't carrying anything. I was happy at the time that he'd found someone. I thought it might calm him down if he had a sensible influence. Before that, he was always off gallivanting with Jason, getting home at silly o'clock in the middle of the night.

He never did answer me when I asked if she was his girlfriend. Perhaps he wanted to keep some things private from me. I had to accept that.

I can't have imagined someone being outside earlier – the car had stopped for her. They say everyone has a doppelganger, but they're never in the same area. What was she doing, staring at the house – and was it her who peered through the window?

There's a bleep on my phone telling me I have a notification from my forum. Craig didn't seem to hear it, so I open the application.

It's from Anne Marie. She's online now.

AnneMarie2348: How is Craig settling in?

NorthernLass: I'm not sure. He seems different to how he was inside.

AnneMarie2348: How?

NorthernLass: He was quiet, vulnerable in there. It's like he's a different person. Seems taller but his temper's shorter. He seems frustrated or angry with me for some reason. Does that sound strange? I'm almost afraid of him sometimes, but I suppose I can't read his behaviour in the same way I could before all this.

AnneMarie2348: No, not at all. Although Ashley was the opposite. She seemed smaller when she got home. It was almost like she didn't want to be here. It took a few months for her to stop missing her friends inside. Said they were the only ones who understood her. Can you imagine how hurtful that was to hear? But I suppose I shouldn't be selfish.

NorthernLass: You're not selfish. It's as though Craig doesn't want to be here either. It's not how I thought it would be.

78

AnneMarie2348: It'll take time.

Craig gets up and walks to the window again.

NorthernLass: Better go. He keeps getting up as though he's waiting for someone.

AnneMarie2348: Take care, Erica.

'Where is he?' says Craig, louder than he did before.

'Where's who, love?'

He puts his hands on his hips, still facing the gap in the curtains.

'Jason. He said he'd be round as soon as ... he's a day late.'

'But how would you arrange that? He's not psychic.'

'Psychic's not a word I'd associate with Jase. We planned it ... when I was away.'

'Over the phone?'

'No,' he says. 'You weren't the only visitor I had inside.'

11

Luke

When he got into work, Luke had expected a round of applause – like Jerry Maguire or something – but his piece was days old and no one gave a shit about Facebook likes until they were well in the thousands.

At times like these, he remembers the words of his arsehole of a PE teacher: *must try harder*. He needs something more, to dig deeper. Luke's tried telephoning Erica, but admittedly gave up after four rings. He can't believe he's afraid Craig will answer the telephone. Erica isn't the person he should be chasing for an interview anyway. The person he should be talking to is Craig Wright, but will the man talk to him?

Sarah's not asked him for a story featuring the killer himself so perhaps he'll surprise her with it. He's already written the articles needed for tonight's edition, and he has several others he needs to complete by midday tomorrow (a man with over three thousand indecent images of children sentenced to eighteen months; a woman arrested for benefit fraud totalling £52,000; a piece on a local artist's exhibition), but his mind keeps drifting back to Craig. There must be something that everyone has missed.

Luke goes into his old files, clicking on the notes for the article he'd written about Jenna Threlfall. There were certain bits of information that he'd gleaned from a police officer at the time, though he'd had to change the details when the CPS terminated proceedings against Craig. Luke thought they'd find new evidence; he imagined the frustration of the police when they found nothing. The police officer who helped him had retired now. Luke makes a note to track him down – he must be frustrated that the Jenna Threlfall case remains open.

Luke's article is sparse; there was so much more he wanted to say:

A 20-year-old man from Preston has been arrested on suspicion of murdering a woman who went missing on New Year's Day. Jenna Threlfall, 18, was found after a lengthy search by police and locals in the early hours of Wednesday morning. She had been raped and strangled.

A post-mortem suggests that death occurred three days before the body was found.

Police are appealing for witnesses. It is believed that several items of clothing were missing from the body.

He goes back into his notes. There were facts about the crime that were under embargo: the body was cleaned with bleach after death; her remaining clothes were dowsed in White Musk perfume. Jenna's T-shirt and necklace were missing and have never been found.

Lucy's body wasn't cleaned. She was strangled, too, but there were traces of DNA on her body that put Craig Wright in the frame. Her body was hidden, but Jenna's wasn't — it was almost on display, like the killer was proud of what he'd done and wanted everyone to see it.

Luke leans back in his chair.

'Get us a coffee, would you, Mikey?' he says to the work experience lad next to him.

Mikey looks at him, his young face scrunched in a scowl.

'I haven't been taught how to do that yet,' he says with a smirk.

'What the—'

'I'll get us a drink,' says his colleague, Amanda, sitting opposite him. 'I've been staring at that screen for hours. I could do with a break. Come on, Mikey. I'll show you how it's done.'

The lad tuts before standing.

Luke doesn't know why Mikey bothers turning up. It's clear he's not interested in serious journalism. He's been engrossed in gaming forums since he started last week.

Shaking his head, Luke brings up his article from a few days ago.

MURDERER TO RETURN TO PRESTON
Life should mean life, says victim's mother

Craig Wright, who was found guilty of murdering local teenager Lucy Sharpe in 2000, is to be released after seventeen years behind bars.

Wright was 20 years old when he committed the crime that made a huge impact on the community. Lucy Sharpe was 18 years old at the time of her killing. Wright strangled then raped the teenager before dumping her body in woodland.

The mother of Lucy, Gillian Sharpe, spoke exclusively to the *Chronicle*.

'Lucy was passionate about so many things,' said Gillian. The teenager volunteered at several charities.

Lucy's parents were both present at Craig Wright's murder trial. They listened to details of their daughter's final moments, before the trial was sensationally halted after Wright changed his plea.

'Did he want the world to hear what he'd done?' said Gillian Sharpe.

Wright's assumed return to the town will no doubt cause unease in the community. But Gillian Sharpe refuses to move. 'Why should I leave?' she said. 'My daughter will always be eighteen, but I'm still her mother.'

Luke remembers that Craig hung around with a local lad – they'd been inseparable, from what people had said. He clicks back on to his files on the case and finds him. Jason Bamber.

He types the name and *Preston* into Google and clicks on the News tab. Several articles appear on the screen.

29 June 2001

LOCAL MAN SPARED JAIL

Jason Bamber, 22, of Wignall Street, Preston, was sentenced to six months in prison after he was found guilty of collecting three weeks of his grandfather's pension after his death, amounting to £217.50. The judge said, 'I've taken into consideration that you have no previous convictions and appear to be remorseful.' Bamber's grandfather, Fred, who was a popular figure in the area, died 22 February 2001 after a short battle with cancer. Fred Bamber's close friend Derek said, 'I can't believe Jason would do this. He's always been a bit of a handful, but he's gone too far this time.'

The next article was written by Jeff Stanley, who retired two years ago. Luke remembers him for his bad temper and bad taste in ties, but he taught Luke a lot. His style was more 'tabloid' than the more neutral tone of the *Chronicle* – he was wasted here.

31 December 2005

NOTORIOUS PRESTON CRIMINAL CAGED FOR ASSAULT

Serial criminal, Jason Bamber, 27, has been jailed after being found guilty of assault. Bamber, of Holden Road, Preston, punched Robert Gregory, 24, in the face, and held him by the throat, causing him to lose consciousness.

Bamber pleaded guilty in Preston Magistrates' Court and was sentenced to six months in prison.

21 January 2010

DRUG DEALER JAILED

Local man, Jason Bamber, 31, pleaded guilty of possession with intent to supply after being found with 2 kg of cannabis on his person. Bamber, of Water Lane, Preston, was sentenced to two years in prison.

Most of Jason's articles were only a few lines. None of them printed his photo. Luke wonders if Craig's probation team are aware of his delightful friend. It must be in his terms not to keep the company of criminals. He can't be so stupid as to hang around with him now, can he?

Jason must know things about Craig that were never brought up – the pair were close growing up. Luke types Jason's name into 192.com and writes down the address.

Luke stands and grabs his jacket, just as Mikey places a pale cold-looking coffee on his desk. The lad looks rather pleased with himself.

'Sorry, Mikey,' says Luke. 'I've got serious journalism to be getting on with.'

'But it took me ages to make that.'

'Why don't you have it?' Luke checks for his keys and heads to the door. 'And a little less milk next time.'

Luke pulls up outside a convenience store a few streets down from Jason Bamber's house. The inside is pretty full, considering it's ten thirty on a weekday. Don't these people have jobs to go to? There's an older gentleman talking to a woman with a voice that hurts Luke's ears. She's wearing a waterproof jacket that's printed with pictures of cartoon dogs. An acquired taste.

Luke lingers next to them, pretending to ponder the microwave rice.

'... Brian Sharpe was in here the other day, Reg. Fuming, he was.'

Luke's interest is piqued at the mention of the name.

'Was it about that Craig lad?' asks Reg.

The woman tuts. Luke imagines her rolling her eyes and sees her shaking her grey-haired bob out the corner of his eye.

'Have you seen him, then,' says Reg, 'since he's come back?'

'Not yet. But you know me ... I'm a busy person ...

86

I haven't the time to spend getting involved in other people's business.'

'Right you are, Pam,' says Reg. 'Anyway, I'd best get off. Eileen'll be wondering where I've got to with the paper.'

'Oh, all right, then. See you later.'

Pam sounds disappointed. It seems she could have talked about it all day. Luke can't resist – he knows the type; they love a bit of attention.

'You know Craig Wright, then?' he says.

'*Know* is a bit strong,' she says, turning towards him and talking to Luke as though he were an old friend. 'But I've lived here all my life. It was such a shock – I can't get over it.'

He's grateful she didn't castigate him for eavesdropping; she's probably used to it. She leans closer to Luke.

'He'd better not start hanging round with young girls again. I'll be straight on to 101 if I see any of that.'

'How will you know who he's hanging around with?'

'I like to think I'm more observant than others around here. I've seen his friend, Jason, driving around – he's got tinted windows on that flash car of his. God knows what he gets up to in the back of that.'

'Does he still live on Croston Street?'

'Yes,' she says, narrowing her eyes at Luke. 'You're not from around here, are you? Are you a reporter?'

Luke holds up his hands.

'You're a canny one. Miss Marple's got nothing on you.'

She looks pleased with his assessment and she smiles, revealing perfectly straight, white teeth. They must be false – the woman must be in her eighties.

'I like to look out for my community, that's all.'

'Is Craig's dad not around?'

'No ... though there's been plenty of talk about who the father is. Was a bit of a scandal at the time, although I like to think of myself as open-minded ...'

'Sure you do.'

'They never expected anything like that from Erica. I mean, she never had boyfriends or anything ... she always kept her head down. She must be good at keeping secrets – I didn't have a clue that she was even seeing anyone. I suppose living with that mother of hers would've driven anyone a bit potty. She was always in Erica's business, that Maria. She wanted Erica to go to university – make something of herself.'

'Maria?'

'Erica's mum. Yes – it's a youthful name, isn't it? Anyway, she hardly let Erica go out on her own ... would only allow her to hang around with Denise Nuttall – that's her maiden name. Those two were always together until, well, you know ... Anyway, when Erica got her job down the road, she had a bit more freedom.' Pam leans conspiratorially towards Luke. 'Although that freedom must've gone to her head, if you know what I mean. And of course, she went back to work a few years after Craig started school ... well, she had to after that terrible business with her mother ... fifty-four's no age at all. Did you hear about that? Found dead at the bottom of the stairs. You know, sometimes I wonder … it's not surprising Craig turned out as he did. And his friend, Jason. Well, those two were close … some even reckoned … you know … that those two had a thing.' She cocks her head to one side and raises her eyebrows. 'Like I said, I'm open-minded, but it wouldn't have been right, not in those circumstances.'

'I see.'

Luke has no idea what she's going on about. Pam narrows her eyes at Luke, tilting her head.

Luke fishes a card from his inside pocket.

'I'm looking into their family history,' he says, thinking on the spot. 'But don't let anyone know, will you? Here's my contact details – if you think of anything else, give us a bell. I'll even give you a mention if you want – or if there are any events you've got going on, I can give you a plug.'

She takes the card.

'I'll have a think,' she says, grinning and placing the card against her chest. 'Oh, you've made my day.'

She pulls out a piece of paper from her pocket and writes on it.

'I'll give you my number too, in case you think of any other questions. My name's Pamela, by the way. Pamela Valentine.'

'Nice to meet you, Pamela.'

That's one Valentine he'd be disappointed receiving on the fourteenth of February.

Luke leaves the shop and jumps into his car, feeling nauseous at the thought of knocking on Jason's door.

He reaches the house in minutes. Outside is a black BMW 5 Series. It must've cost ten grand at least.

Luke gets out of his car.

The front door is red, spotless. He bangs on it using the lion-head door knocker.

The door opens, but not so much that Luke can get a look inside the house. It's a woman of about thirty-five; she's wearing far too much make-up to be lounging around in a dressing gown.

'Is Jason in?' says Luke.

She narrows her eyes and pulls the collar of her dressing gown together, resting her hands on her chest.

'Who's asking?'

'I'm Luke from the *Chronicle*. Just wanted a quick word.'

'Who is it?' shouts a man's voice from inside.

'Some journo,' the woman hollers back.

Another hand grabs the door and opens it fully. Jason. He has dark hair with flecks of grey, and his face is clean-shaven. His shirt is expensive-looking, and he's teamed it with jeans and loafers.

'I'll deal with this, Becks,' he says. His voice is quiet, well-spoken, even though Luke knows he grew up in this town and is as northern as the rest of them. 'Liv wants some more toast.'

'Is Liv your daughter?'

'Yes. Why are you here?'

'I'm doing a piece on Jenna Threlfall. You knew her, didn't you?'

'Yeah, we went to the same school,' he says, frowning,

'but we weren't close. Listen, you're wasting your time talking to me, I don't know anything.'

'Did Craig ever go out with her?'

'No.' The man takes a deep breath. 'You're chasing the wrong story here. What happened to Jenna had nothing to do with Craig. Don't you think he's been through enough? And his poor mother. Do you know what people round here have done to her? They covered her front door with dog shit, they spat at her in the street, she was ostracised. But she stayed here for Craig.'

He goes to close the door. Luke's tempted to place a foot inside but imagines it might not come out in one piece. His rant about Craig and Erica has left Jason red in the face. The door opens again.

'You're not allowed to name Craig in connection with Jenna, you know,' he says. 'We had all this years ago. It wasn't taken to court – so leave him alone.'

'I just want to know what Jenna was like as a person – who she hung round with.'

'You're the reporter – do your fucking job. I'm not doing it for you.'

He slams the door shut.

Luke takes a few steps back, glancing up at the bedroom window. Rebecca is now dressed, her arms folded as she stares at Luke. She gives him the briefest of smiles but he's unsure whether it's mocking or genuine. She tilts her head to the side.

He gets back into his car and switches on the engine. Jason seemed clued up about the legalities of naming suspects in connection with crimes. Luke's sure he knows more about Craig and Jenna than he's letting on, but he's covering for his friend. Why would he flip like that – calm one minute and raving the next? He's definitely hiding something. Luke looks back up to the window, but Rebecca has gone. Jason might not talk to Luke again, but *she* might.

12

Erica

There's a knock at the door. It's 10.35 a.m. and I'm still in bed. As usual, I didn't sleep well. I close my eyes and hope that whoever it is goes away.

Why, now that Craig is back home, does it feel as though these walls are closing in on me? Maybe he brought some of the prison back with him – the feeling of hopelessness, perhaps. I don't even want to get up.

Jason didn't come round yesterday. I thought Craig would explode by eight in the evening. It had gotten dark outside, so he'd stopped going to the window. He was upstairs and silent in his bedroom by half past. I hadn't wanted to bother him; I couldn't tell if he was asleep or not. I know he couldn't have been reading. I'm trying to forgive him for that, for not telling me about those books. It's never good to dwell on such slights. It's likely he meant nothing by it – he probably hadn't wanted to upset me when he was in there after I told him I'd chosen each book so carefully. It doesn't matter in the bigger scheme of things. He's out and I should be happy enough about that.

I wish I'd appreciated him more when he was younger – treasured him, loved the little moments instead of counting the minutes until bedtime when I could finally get some peace. It's both a blessing and a curse that I have such a good memory.

Someone's whistling outside. Knocking again. Louder this time. It sounds like they're using their foot instead of their hand.

Craig pounds down the stairs and opens the front door.

'Are you coming out to play?' says a man's voice.

'Jason!' says Craig. 'About fucking time!'

I doubt he realises I'm listening.

'What kind of a welcome do you call that? After everything I've done for you.'

'Come in before anyone sees you,' says Craig, laughing.

'You ashamed of me?'

'Yeah, very funny.'

They go into the living room.

I sit up in bed and swivel my feet to the floor. I quickly dress and walk quietly across the landing.

'Will you look after this for me?' says Jason in the living room.

'What is it?' says Craig.

'Just some stuff ... Becks has it in her head I'm seeing someone else. If she finds this, she'll probably kick me out.'

'*Are* you seeing someone else?'

Jason laughs. 'Maybe,' he says. 'Anyway, I had a

visit from some reporter yesterday ... he was asking questions about Jenna.'

'What did you tell him?'

Craig sounds worried.

'Don't worry,' says Jason, 'I didn't say a word. They won't be able to find anything, will they?'

'I had nothing to do with Jenna.'

'But you were seeing her.'

'I was going out with Lucy.'

'Don't worry, mate,' says Jason. 'We've all got our little secrets.'

I tread loudly down the stairs. Their voices quieten, and Jason comes to the living room door.

'Morning, Erica,' he says.

'You're up and about early, Jason,' I say, even though it's nearly quarter to eleven.

'You could say that.'

He winks at me. Does he think I'm someone else?

'I'll put the kettle on.'

'None for us thanks, Mum,' says Craig.

I go into the living room where Craig's sitting on the settee, a cardboard box on his lap.

'What've you got there?'

'A few bits Jason got for me.'

'Is that a computer? A phone?'

'A laptop, and yeah. No offence, Mum, but neither of the phones you got me sends pictures. I'll give you the money back for them.'

'What do you want to be sending pictures for? I

thought you weren't supposed to have anything like that. Your supervising officer said—'

'Everyone has them these days. It's not like I'm some criminal mastermind organising human trafficking on the internet.'

'What a strange thing to say.'

'I was joking.'

He pockets the mobile telephone and brushes past me as he takes the box upstairs. Jason and I look at each other. He's dressed smartly again – his suit looks expensive.

'No more trouble then?' he asks. 'Since the dog muck.'

'Just a firebomb through the door.'

His eyes widen. 'Really.'

'Oh, I'm used to them, Jason. I've got myself a fire extinguisher.'

'But what if you were in bed? And they poured petrol in first?'

His face is expressionless. Is he joking with me? It's not very funny. And it's a terrible thing to suggest if he's being serious. I fold my arms.

'Well then, I'll be done for, won't I?'

'We'll take care of you,' he says, lightly touching my shoulder – he's a good seven inches taller than I am. 'Though I think we're off to the pub now.'

'Aren't you working today?' I say. 'You're dressed for the office.'

'No boring office for me. Don't want to be tied down by anything like that. I work for myself ... choose my own hours.'

Craig comes down the stairs and jumps from the third-to-last step.

'You're going to the pub?' I say to him. 'It's not even eleven.'

'It will be when we get there, Ma,' he says. 'I've got a lot of drinking to catch up on.'

'But what if someone sees you? I really don't think this is a good idea. I could go and buy you some drink, if that's what you want.'

He walks slowly towards me, his eyes dark. I have to look up as he gets closer.

'I do wish you'd stop trying to control me.'

When he bends down, I almost flinch. He plants a kiss on my cheek.

'Bye, Mother,' he whispers into my ear.

'Bye, Erica,' says Jason.

'Don't forget,' I shout after them, 'you can't stay out late.'

By the time I finish speaking, they're gone. The mirror on the wall wobbles from the draught.

This isn't how I imagined it would be. I thought Craig would be shell-shocked. I thought he'd spend days recovering from his ordeal.

But I suppose he might not think of it in that way – perhaps he made friends, misses the routine, like Anne Marie's daughter. He doesn't miss whoever it is that gave him nightmares, though. He always was a sensitive soul. Was. His and Jason's conversation earlier has unnerved me. Why would he be anxious about Jenna

Threlfall if he's got nothing to hide? He always told me he barely knew her.

I'm still standing in the hall. I'll give it a few minutes to make sure they've really gone. I sit down on the bottom step. Hardly anyone goes past the front door, but it's mid-morning now – most people'll be at work.

Last night, Craig asked me what I'd been doing since I stopped working at the supermarket.

'Charity work,' I told him.

But that was a lie, wasn't it? What have I been doing all these years? The days seem to have merged into each other. Obsessing about finding Pete Lawton, reading, watching television, going to the library once a week, chatting to my friends online, and trying *not* to think about those who wronged me.

I go into the living room and switch on my computer. Today might be the day that one of the Lawtons I contacted has got back to me. I bring up my Facebook page and click on one of three remaining unopened messages. One of them has been read. It says he was only online several minutes ago – he mustn't have set his privacy settings that tight.

I wait, staring at the screen, willing him to reply. I click on to his profile, but there aren't any pictures of him. Just cars, motorbikes, photos of what appear to be his grandchildren. This could be him.

After five minutes pass, I realise looking at the screen won't make him message any faster. I switch my notifications on and increase the volume.

I walk back into the hallway.

Craig and Jason would've been back by now if they'd forgotten something. I stand and go up two stairs at a time, happy that I can manage that with my temperamental knees and my health the way it is.

Craig's bed is made, perfectly so. It's the tidiest I've seen this room, but he doesn't have many things.

I know I shouldn't be snooping. Especially after how much I regretted it the first time.

It was five days after Jenna Threlfall had gone missing: 6 January 2000. Craig hadn't been himself since New Year; he wanted me to stay at home with him more, flinching when there was a knock at the door. I thought he was having a crisis of confidence – people sometimes feel low at that time of the year when their life isn't how they imagined it would be. Craig always wanted to be a chef, but every kitchen job he had only lasted a few months. I suspected he was unhappy living at home with me, watching as his friends got their own places.

He was obsessed with the news after Lucy went missing; he could barely sleep from worrying. I tried to comfort him, but he withdrew into himself, barely eating. I had to stand over him to make sure he'd get something down him.

As a photograph of Jenna appeared on the television, I asked him if he knew her. He said he didn't, but they went to the same school, in different years. He'd never talked about her.

'I need to pop to the shop,' I said. 'I've run out of cigarettes.'

He sat up straight in the chair.

'Really? Do you have to go out?'

'Unless you want me clawing at the wallpaper in ten minutes, yes.'

He stood, hands deep in his pockets rooting for money.

'I'll go for you, Mum. Actually, I feel like a jog – I'll not be long.'

He was only out of the door a few seconds before I dashed to his bedroom. I didn't know what I thought I'd find. I looked under his bed, pillows, inside his wardrobe. Nothing.

I went to his chest of drawers. Among the old coins and dead batteries was a necklace – a choker with a large daisy pendant. It could've been there for years, could've come from anyone. So I left it. Closed the drawer. Nothing of importance. How could I have suspected my own son? I felt awful. *I'll do his washing to make up for it*, I thought to myself. From the age of seventeen he'd been doing his own laundry; he was usually pretty good at it, but that week he'd done nothing except sleep, eat, and watch telly with me.

A mistake. I wish I'd never emptied the damn basket.

At the bottom of it, under piles of socks and pants, was his light blue T-shirt. Blood covered the collar, there were blobs of it down the front. I dropped it on the floor in a panic.

'Got your cigs, Mum!' he shouted from downstairs.

I piled everything back into the laundry basket, everything except for that T-shirt. I darted into my bedroom and stuffed it under my bed.

'Thanks, love,' I shouted back, hoping he didn't hear the quiver in my voice. 'I've got one of my hot flushes. I'm just having a lie-down.'

He never asked questions if I mentioned anything to do with *women's problems*.

Then, his bedroom was cluttered, covered in old Lego creations he hadn't wanted to part with, rows of VHS films, an *X-Files* poster above his bed. Now, it's a shell of a room, like one in a hotel. Anyone could be sleeping here.

The box Jason brought round is on the desk. Inside is a silver-coloured laptop, a few magazines (which I hope were a joke) and a bottle of vodka. A little inappropriate, but nothing out of the ordinary. He always said Craig was like a brother to him, always protective of him. They haven't seen each other properly for so long – only the short visits in prison. I suppose they have a lot of catching up to do.

Most of Craig's clothes are piled next to the box. It's like he's not stopping, that he doesn't want to stay with me.

No, I shouldn't think like that – he's adjusting to being here, that's all. He's not had a chance to buy new things yet.

His black holdall is on the floor near the radiator under the window. I pick it up and place it on his bed. Unzipping it releases a strange smell: chemicals and stale sweat, mixed with other odours I can't put my finger on. There are socks paired in balls; underpants piled together and rolled. So neat. Underneath these is the last book I gave him: *Pharaoh* by Wilbur Smith. It makes me smile a little that he brought it home.

I feel along the bottom of the bag; there's a lump in the middle. I prise the plastic base up and lift it out. There, gathered in a tan-coloured elastic band, is a bundle of letters.

I flick through them. Teenage scrawl, words punctuated with hearts.

There are no envelopes and they are all from the same person, signed:

L xxx

The blood rushes from my head; I feel dizzy. I perch on the end of his bed. These letters can't be from Lucy, can they? Written years ago, that he kept? She's never going to go away, is she? Haunting me as though it's my fault. I've read about strange goings-on in *Take a Break's Fate and Fortune*. I always thought people made it up, but what if there's something in it? Finding these letters and seeing the girl yesterday could be a sign. Maybe she's angry that the real killer hasn't been found. Yes, that must be it.

I'd been restless since I found the letters in Craig's bag – only sitting down for five minutes at a time – looking out of the window to see if I could see him, or the young girl I saw the other day, but there was nothing out of the ordinary. They finally rolled in at half past eight, drunk. Over ten hours of drinking after Craig

102

not touching a drop of alcohol for years (although he has said in the past, 'Nothing is impossible in here' – I pretended not to hear that).

They brought back some tinnies. Now, Jason's sprawled along my settee and Craig's sitting cross-legged on the floor. They're watching a film on BBC One about swimming, but it has Kevin Costner in it, so it's not all that bad.

'Mind if I smoke?' asks Jason.

I might be an ex-smoker, but I'm not pious with it.

'I'll get an ashtray,' I say, wearily, but Craig jumps to his feet, swaying slightly as he gets his bearings.

'*I'll* get it, Mother,' he says.

'What've you been up to today?' Jason asks me.

'Learning Cantonese on YouTube.'

'Oh.' He nods slowly. 'Right. Fair play.'

I roll my eyes. He takes me ever so seriously, it's too hard *not* to wind him up – plus he's as drunk as a newt. I've only ever watched music videos on YouTube – it's amazing how far back they go. They even have the ABBA collection on there.

I've wanted to go to bed since they came back, but I didn't want to feel pushed out of my own living room. Once I start that, it'll become a habit. Just like when I let Craig have everything he wanted in his bedroom as a teenager: a television, a video player, his meals. I hardly saw him. That might have been where the trouble started.

Craig leans over to Jason and whispers something. He laughs in return.

It must be a remnant of my childhood that I always think someone's talking about me if they whisper in my company.

'What about that one with the fringe?' says Jason. 'She was well after you.'

'Nah she wasn't. She was probably curious.'

'Oh, *curious*. When did you start talking all posh?'

I've had enough. I stand, clearing my throat.

'Night, boys,' I say.

I linger at the doorway.

'I was thinking, Craig. I could sort the dining room out ... it could be an extra living room.'

I know it's as bad as him being cooped up in his bedroom, but I don't think I can face the anxiety of today ... wondering when they'll be back – worried about how long Jason'll stay.

'Really?' says Craig.

He's frowning and swaying as he sits.

We've never used the dining room. It's only tiny and it has my mother's furniture in there. I still can't look at her things. All those pieces she inherited from her own parents that meant so much to her. But they're a heavy presence – taking over a whole room of the house that I never use. When she died, I gave all her clothes to the church. I didn't even look at them individually; I couldn't, without picturing her wearing them. It was too upsetting. Especially as I could have saved her.

*

Four-thirty in the morning and I can hear the television blaring from downstairs. I must have drifted off for an hour or so, but I keep thinking about those letters in Craig's bag. I had only read snippets from one of the letters: *I think about you all the time* and *I feel like we know each other inside and out*. I didn't want to think about the last sentence too much – not after what happened to Lucy. He must have written back for her to keep sending so many letters. Will his replies still be in *her* bedroom? Or perhaps her parents have put away her things – the pain of seeing them a constant reminder that she's not coming home.

I jump as the front door slams shut. Jason must've left.

I go downstairs, but there's no one in the living room. I grab the remote, flick off the television and my ears ring with the silence. Once in the hall, I notice that the light in the dining room is on, the door ajar. I push it fully open; it stops against a mahogany dresser, and I find Craig sitting near the back window in my mother's old chair. It's a tall wing-backed one; the fabric patchy, threadbare in places. He looks incongruous in it. His feet are on top of her occasional table. I'm surprised it takes the weight – it's such a flimsy piece of furniture.

I shimmy my way past the white wicker laundry basket, two chests of drawers, and some cardboard boxes. It smells musty in here, like a garage: damp. Even though I leave the radiator running during the day so mould doesn't breed.

Craig's eyes are focused on the five pictures – ordinary

nondescript landscapes, framed in various woods – that are leaning in a bundle against a small chaise longue. It's surprising how much furniture can fit in such a tiny room.

'Are you all right, love?' I say. 'Craig?'

Silence. Does he realise I'm standing in front of him? He's wiggling a bottle of beer that he's holding by its neck. They must've gone out for more drink after I went to bed.

'I might as well be inside.' His eyes quickly meet mine. 'What's the point of me being out, if I have to be home at a certain time like a bloody teenager?'

'But it won't be forever.'

'I thought it would be different being free. That people – even if they thought I was guilty – could see that I've been punished. My life has been destroyed. I can't be the person I want to be – there are too many rules I have to follow. How am I supposed to live a normal life when I've all that hanging over me? I was so naive to think I could be a personal trainer. God, what an idiot.'

He speaks so eloquently for someone who's been drinking for almost twenty-four hours. He must've drunk himself sober, if there's such a thing.

'We could move, if you want.' I say it quietly, slowly. I don't want to let on that I've been dreaming of moving for so long.

He raises his eyebrows.

'I'm nearly thirty-eight. I should be thinking about branching out, shouldn't I? But the only job they'll give me will pay a pittance. Is it really worth it? And I've got that ridiculous counselling session I have to go to. I must've had my blinkers on inside. They said it'd be hard, but I didn't listen. My best mates are still in there ... they're the ones who know the real me. Not even Jason ...' He sits up straighter. 'Did I tell you that one of them'll be out in a couple of days?'

'No. What's he inside for?'

He shrugs. 'The usual.'

'What's the usual?'

'We didn't really talk about the past. We talked about the future.'

'OK.' I fold my arms. It's so cold in here. 'What's the counselling for, love?'

'To help me settle,' he says, almost shouting. He doesn't even look at me.

'Are you sure?'

I can't tell him I was listening in, but why would his supervising officer say he needed to go if there was nothing wrong?

'I wouldn't lie to you, would I?' he barks. 'What would be the point in that?' He leans back, takes a deep breath, and closes his eyes. I give him a moment to calm down. I wanted to ask him about the letters I found, but he's in no mood for that. And he wouldn't take too kindly to me snooping among his things.

'They'll put you in touch with organisations, won't they? Somewhere you can feel useful.'

He opens his eyes, but he's looking at the ceiling.

'Useful?' He gives a short laugh then sighs. 'Yeah. I've always wanted to feel useful.'

Is he making fun of me?

The grandmother clock behind him suddenly begins to tick – for the first time in over thirty years. My mother loved that clock, but the sound of it used to make me so anxious. The house was rarely quiet, except for when Mother was in one of her moods. She could go from being cheerful to affronted in a second. Granted, I was a little clumsy as a child – always knocking cups of tea over. She recovered as quickly, though. Always apologetic, but during her silence all I could hear was the ticking of that stupid thing.

'Did you wind that clock up?' I say.

He shrugs. 'No one ever believed me when I said I could never have done those things to Lucy,' he says quietly, 'but you did, didn't you, Mum?'

His eyes are glazed and won't meet mine. He must've taken something; this can't be just from the drink. I can't predict his mood from one second to the next.

Tick, tick, tick. I want to smash that thing with a hammer.

'I never thought you were capable of doing something like that.'

The clock is taunting me.

He brings his head level again and his eyes meet mine.

'Why won't you tell me who my father is?'

I unfold my arms and rest my hands on my hips.

'What?' I say. 'Where did that come from?'

He finally lowers his head and meets my gaze.

'I've had a lot of time to think about things,' he says, tilting his head to the side. He's almost *too* calm now.

'I didn't want to bring it up during our visits – wanted to keep them nice and light for you ... well, most of the time. I was ignorant at the start – unseasoned, you might say. But I've always wondered about my father. How could I not? Did you think I'd just forget about him?'

I can hear my pulse pounding in my ears.

'I ... I've nothing else to tell you. I don't know his name.'

'You've said that before, but you're not like that ... you were never one of those women.'

'What sort of women? There aren't *those* women.'

He shrugs again.

'He gave me the wrong name,' I say. 'I tried looking him up in the phone book when I was expecting you. He wasn't listed.'

'And he wasn't local?'

I shake my head. 'No.'

'Does Denise know who it is? Did she meet him?'

'How could you bring her name up in this house – after what she did?'

'For fuck's sake, Mum!' he shouts. He leans towards me and I startle, taking a step back. 'Stop changing the subject all the fucking time!'

My whole body is shaking.

'I wasn't trying to change the subject, I was only—'

'A lot of people have wronged me,' he says, leaning back again. 'I used to believe in karma, but now I know it's a load of bollocks. Bad people get away with murder, and good people ... they're the ones who suffer.'

He's staring at the wall behind me, with a look on his face that's chilling – like he's wearing the mask of someone I don't know.

Slowly, his eyes meet mine again.

'Yes, Denise. Good old Denise, eh?' he says. 'I wonder what happened there. Did you say anything to her? About what you did for me?'

'No, of course I didn't. And I wouldn't have done that if I thought you were guilty. She betrayed me, too, Craig. We were friends for over thirty years before she did that – she was like a sister to me. What she did hurt me – and you – so much. She'd known you since you were a baby. I'll never forgive her.'

'Jason said she was asking about you.'

'I don't want anyone talking about me.'

He takes a deep breath that lasts for nearly ten seconds.

'Mum, Mum, Mum.' He's shaking his head. 'I asked you about my dad and you've turned it around.' He brings up the bottle and toasts it in the air before taking a sip. 'You're clever. I'll give you that. But I'm not a kid any more!' He barks the last sentence through gritted teeth.

'I don't know his name, Craig!' I shout. 'What would it solve now?'

The tears are building behind my eyes, but I don't want to cry in front of him.

'Just because it happened to you – that *you* never knew your father – doesn't mean everyone is like that. I want a name, that's all.'

'It's something I can't give you! How many times do

I have to repeat myself? What do you want me to do, make up a name? That would be pointless!'

I wipe my face. The tears stream from my eyes despite my efforts.

He sits forward suddenly, making me jump, but he's only reaching for my hand.

'I'm sorry. I didn't mean to make you cry. I know you've been the one who's been there for me. We'll save this conversation for another day.' He drops my hand and looks around at his grandmother's belongings. 'Why do you keep all this crap? You don't have people round much, do you?'

'It's not crap. And I don't mind not having visitors,' I say. 'It's better for me that way.'

'Why?' he says. 'Why is that? What have you got to hide?'

I wipe my face.

'Nothing. But if you don't get close to someone, then they can't hurt you.'

The sentence hangs in the air. I'm always saying stupid things.

He tilts his head to the side.

'What if I already know who he is?'

'What?' I say, feeling a panic that almost strangles me. 'How can you know that?'

He wavers from my gaze and shrugs.

'It doesn't matter. I don't know his name. You get yourself to bed. I'm all right here. I need to think about what I'm going to do next. I don't think this is the life that I wanted.'

'What do you mean? You have to give yourself a chance – make something of yourself.'

'But what if I'm broken? I've been treated like shit. Where's the justice in that?' He leans forward and rests his elbows on his knees. 'Nothing's fair in this world.'

'You need to get some sleep,' I say. 'You're not thinking straight.'

'I'm thinking just fine. Goodnight.'

I start to back out of the room. The conversation has finished because he's shut down; the barrier has built up between us. As I reach the door, in the quiet I notice that the ticking of the clock has stopped. I close the door tightly and walk to the foot of the stairs. I grab the banister post for support.

Why is Craig suddenly asking about his father again? How easily the lies came out of my mouth. I should be ashamed of myself.

But he can never know who his father is. The truth would break him even more.

13

I knew it wouldn't be hard to find another. It was almost too easy. I had to do the groundwork first, of course. Lay down the trap, so to speak. And I've learned a few more things since then. There's a whole internet's worth of chemicals, instruments, weapons, if you look hard enough, though I've been researching them for a few years anyway. And preferably, you should have a different address to send things to.

I should write a book on it. Wouldn't that be a first? A person like me getting a book out there to help others. It'd have to be a work of fiction, though. And who's to say life isn't just one long storyline? A mate of mine inside – let's call him Mark – said to me one night, years ago when neither of us could sleep:

'What if this is all a simulation and we're not really here? I read an article that said our whole life experience might be computer-generated and there are glitches visible to the naked eye. We might not even be lying down here at all. This might all be a test. We could be different people, playing this as a game.'

'Where the fuck did you read that shit?' I said.

'Hey, it's not shit,' said Mark. 'It could be real. How the fuck would you know? And I read it in the Guardian, probably.'

'Keep your nose out of papers like that,' I said. 'It doesn't suit you. You don't want to be believing any of those conspiracy ideas.'

We had to put on an act, you see, in front of everyone else inside. If we were as soft in public, talking about newspaper articles and life's glitches, then we'd get the shit kicked out of us.

I've spotted a couple of old cars for sale at Barry's Motors. I know someone there who'll write false registration details for me.

The police won't find me until it's too late.

Fucking genius, me.

14

Erica

It's pouring down, so there's hardly anyone on the streets. Craig wasn't there when I woke up. Downstairs was a handful of flowers he must've picked from someone's garden in a pint glass of water. He didn't used to be one for flowers. He must've been drunk or hungover when he woke up. He'd also left a folded piece of paper with the word *Sorry* written on the front, alongside a five-pound note.

Craig and Jason had eaten almost everything in the fridge, and most of the decent stuff from the cupboards – as well as the asparagus soup and tinned peaches. I hadn't noticed the mess when I came downstairs at four in the morning. He's left all the dirty plates and bowls in the sink. I know I shouldn't be angry – it'll take him a while to adjust – but I didn't want to leave the house today. I've got a pain in my right side and it's niggling me – I don't think I can walk far today.

I walk past the end of Denise's road. I put my head down but glance along her street. Jason's car is parked a few doors down. If we were still speaking, I'd ask her if she'd seen my son. Why did Craig even mention her? He was acting so strangely last night; it must've been the drink. I should've messaged Anne Marie about it all, but I didn't want to put it in words. There was never any doubt in my mind about his innocence – and I can't go back on that now, but something's cast a shadow over it. The letters in Craig's bag, and his behaviour towards me only a few hours earlier. No, last night was just a one-off. Letting off steam.

Craig said Denise asked about me. How dare she? She told lies to that newspaper – made up things about my son – and she should've known what the fallout would be after it was printed. I bet they paid her for her lies. I wonder how much she got. Was it worth a few hundred, maybe a thousand pounds, for all those years of friendship? She always said that Craig was like a son to her. She used to watch him when I had a later shift at Morrisons. Once, I came back to find him under a blanket on her sofa, sleepy, watching *Coronation Street*. Her husband Jim came through the back door.

'Didn't you see Erica waiting at the bus stop?' she hollered to him from the living room.

'Don't worry about it,' I hissed to her. 'I like the bus. I don't want people thinking I'm after lifts all the time, because I'm not.'

'Well, it wouldn't harm him to offer occasionally.' She leant towards me. 'Was he on his own in the car?'

I shrugged. 'I didn't notice.'

She didn't used to be suspicious of him. I can't remember when that started. Gradual, I suppose, like these things tend to be. I don't even know if they're still together. I'm not privy to any gossip these days. People used to tell me everything when I worked at the supermarket. Some of them just wanted someone to talk to, have a bit of a chat. Some would say I'd be the only person they'd talk to all day – which is ironic really, now I don't speak to many people. Others thought me invisible, part of the backdrop of the shop, so they used to discuss their problems with their friends as they walked around the aisles. And the older people got, the more honest they were about their problems. I've heard them all: *Mrs Waterhouse has the depression, you know,* or *Gayle's husband ran off with the man at the tyre workshop,* that sort of thing. But now I know nothing.

God, I hate this town. Rows and rows of terraced houses; the back alleys with heaps of rubbish the council have given up clearing away, the bloody clouds and the bloody rain. I've lived here for most of my life. In the same house I'm in now.

I spot Brian Sharpe in the distance. My knees weaken; I rest my hands on a garden wall for support.

Deep breath. Deep breath.

What's he doing around here? He must know Craig's home now. He might be looking for him.

I stand up straight and turn into the alley on my right. If I walk slowly he'll be gone by the time I get there.

The cobbles are uneven beneath my feet. Either side are wooden gates leading to the backyards of the terraces that block out the sun. There's not as much rubbish down this one. No doubt Denise had something to do with that – she was always vocal about the goings-on in her precious street.

I'm almost at her gate and look up at the house. I can see from the movement behind the frosted glass of the window that there's someone in the bathroom. I don't want to be caught being a peeping Tom, but I steal a glance inside her bedroom.

There's a man leaning against the window. It doesn't look like Jim – this man's taller, has all his hair. I walk slowly; I'm parallel to Denise's bedroom window. It's Jason; I'm sure of it.

He stands, and a head pops up from next to him. It's a young girl; she only looks about seventeen from here; fair hair and she's wearing a bright red top. She looks like the girl from earlier – Lucy ... No, it can't be. It'll be my imagination, seeing her everywhere.

Oh God, she's seen me.

She waves at me.

My face flushes with heat.

I put my head down as Jason is turning around. I hear a tapping on the window, but I don't look back as I rush forward. I almost run to the other end of the alley. It brings me out on to the street and now the shop's on my left.

I knew going out around here would be trouble. What did I come in for?

I fumble in my anorak pocket for the five pounds and the list and head to the fridges.

Oh God, it's Pamela – every time I've ever been in

this place, she's always bloody here. She's with two others I don't recognise. The reason it's quiet on the streets is because everyone's in this damn shop.

Milk, bread, beans, sausages. That's all I need and then I'll be done.

I wish I'd got a basket; now it looks as though I'm thieving it all.

I reach the vultures and they're standing in front of the tins. I'll have to leave it; I've got tomato sauce at home anyway.

'Are you wanting something behind me?'

Pamela folds her arms and grimaces like she's on an episode of *Prisoner Cell Block H* or something. She'll think I'm scared of her, but I'm not. I just don't want the bother.

'Beans,' I say.

'Hmm,' she says standing aside.

'Thank you.'

'Most I've heard her speak for nearly two decades,' she says to the other two, who burst out laughing.

Oh Lord, I really want to ignore them, but there's this feeling in my stomach and it's coming up to my chest.

Walk away, walk away, I tell myself.

'But she looks as though she's aged forty years,' says another. 'I reckon she'll move on soon, now that monster is back. What the hell were they thinking, letting him out? Life should mean—'

'Excuse me,' I say, walking slowly towards her. 'If you've got something to say, then say it to my face.'

'Well, that wouldn't be as much fun, would it?'

119

'What's wrong with you people?' I say. 'Haven't you got your own lives to get on with? He's done his time.'

The clichés coming out of my mouth are straight from *EastEnders*, but I can't help myself.

'You can't expect people to ignore it – he's only just come out! And if I remember rightly, you loved a bit of gossip when you worked at the supermarket.'

'I ... there's no point arguing with you. It's my life you're talking about.'

My heart is pounding. I'm as bad as them – spouting stupid rubbish that means nothing.

'You're lucky it's only me,' says Pamela. 'If my Gordon were here, he'd have given you a few stronger words. He saw your Craig in the pub yesterday – off his face, he said. He would've given him a good kicking if he wasn't with that smarmy friend of his.'

'If your Gordon didn't weigh thirty stone and could lift his leg higher than the kerb,' I say.

Her mouth falls open. Finally, I've managed to silence Pamela Valentine.

I walk away. Why did I engage with them? It happened when Craig was first arrested – it's like the conversations are on repeat. I'm living the same life over and over again.

'People like him never change,' shouts one of the other old cronies to the other. 'I give it six months and he'll be back inside.'

We'll show them, I think to myself. My hands are shaking.

The cashier won't look at me as she scans my items.

She doesn't bag them for me, and when I ask her three times for a carrier bag, she flings it at me.

'I'm a paying customer, the same as everyone else,' I snap.

She's standing there, holding out her hand for the money while I'm flapping with the bag. Why are they so hard to open? I throw in my things and hand her the five-pound note. She pinches it off me – holding it as though it were covered in dog shit. She holds it up to the light, even though she doesn't need to with these new plastic ones.

'Hmm,' she mutters, placing it in the till.

I hold out my hand; she drops the money into it, and shouts, 'Next!'

This is why I go to the Co-op in the next town.

I turn to leave, but find there's a man standing there. It's Brian Sharpe. I really shouldn't have left the house today.

'I can't believe I'm seeing you in my shop,' he says to me.

'It's not your shop, it's—'

'You know what I mean.'

I go to open the door, but he stands in front of me.

'I only came in for a few bits,' I say.

He brings his head a little closer to mine. 'You and that bastard son of yours don't deserve to be living around here.' He barely opens his mouth, speaking quietly so no one else can hear. 'I can't believe you've got the gall to show your face. Do you not get fed up, eh? Of everyone hating you? Can't you feel it in that shell of a house you rattle around in?'

The shop door opens.

I've never been so glad to see Jason in my life. Brian stands slightly aside to let him past.

'What's going on?' says Jason, frowning.

'Was just telling Erica she's not welcome in here.'

Jason turns; his face two feet from Brian's.

'Is that right?'

Brian pulls his head back, but his feet remain.

'It's upsetting, seeing her,' he says to Jason. 'What that evil cunt did to my daughter ... my only child. You'd feel the same ... I know you would.'

'But Erica wouldn't hurt anyone. You know that.'

Jason opens the door and ushers me outside.

'No, I *don't* know that,' Brian hisses to him. 'She never leaves that house ... she obviously has something to hide. He must've inherited the badness from somewhere.'

I don't hear what Jason says in reply.

He links his arm in mine and guides me down the road as if I were eighty years old.

'Any time you want to go out again, Erica, I'll come with you.'

'Really, there's no need. I won't be coming here again. It's only because ...'

I was going to explain the pain in my side, but I think I've lost him. His eyes are glazed, focused on the road ahead. I expected Brian or the gaggle of women to be calling after me, but they don't. It's not like all those years ago when emotions were so raw that it was like everyone had been hurt. They were quite restrained today.

There's someone waiting outside my front door.

It's the girl who's been watching the house.

She turns as we approach, rubbing her hands from the cold.

'All right, Jason,' she says, giving Jason a shy smile. She looks at me. 'Is Craig in?'

So, she is real.

I look quizzically at Jason. He glances at me, slightly rolling his eyes.

'What are you doing here?' he says to her.

'Who is this, Jason?' I ask him.

'This is Leanne,' he says. 'We met her in the pub the other night. She seems to have taken a shine to our Craig.'

The girl's cheeks flush.

What is Craig doing, having a teenage girl calling for him? It's not right. Hasn't he learned anything from the past?

I open the front door, hoping I can close it on today and leave the horrible world behind.

'Thanks ever so much, Jason,' I say, 'for the help at the shop.'

'No worries. Any time. You know I'm always here for you.'

'I'll see you soon.'

I go to shut the door, but the young girl pushes it open, goes past me (she's such a slender thing) and

123

stands in my hallway. I wouldn't have dreamt of doing that when I was her age.

'Is it OK if I wait for Craig?' she says. 'It's really important I see him.'

'I'm not sure when he'll be back, er ... What's so important that it can't wait? You're not in any trouble, are you?'

She shakes her head. 'No, it's nothing like that. It's so nice to finally meet you.'

Finally meet me? What the devil is she on about? She holds out a hand and I shake it. Have I stepped into a parallel world? I've seen too many people today; I need to be on my own.

'Five minutes should be all right, I suppose,' I say wearily, 'but he might not be back for hours.'

'That's fine,' she says, taking off her coat and hanging it on the end of the banister.

Jason's waiting outside.

I peer out of the door.

'Who is she?' I hiss at him. 'Didn't I see you with her earlier?'

He shrugs.

'Nope. One of Craig's new fans – I don't think I'm dangerous enough for her.' He taps the side of his head with his index finger. 'Probably a bit cuckoo, but she seems harmless enough.' He looks at his watch. 'I'll see if Craig's down the pub. If not, I'll give you a knock and I'll take the kid— I mean, Leanne, home.'

'But how do you know where she lives? Is she a relative of yours?' I say.

'Something like that,' he says, walking away from me.

I look either side of the street before closing the door, but there's no one about. I don't want anyone thinking I'm up to any funny business, letting teenagers come into my house. I'll have to tell Craig that he can't do this. I'm on edge as it is. I turn to go into the living room, but she's in the kitchen, filling up the kettle.

'What are you doing?' I say.

It comes out a little too forceful, but she has the gall to be so brazen in *my* house. I should throw her out, but she seems so young.

'Thought you could do with a cup of tea,' she says.

'Did you?'

She shrugs. All this shrugging. Mother used to hate it. *There are enough words in the English language to not rely on your shoulders to say it for you.*

'Were you over at Denise's before?' I say, suddenly.

'What?'

'I thought I saw you with Jason earlier.'

'I don't know anyone called Denise.'

'Really? I must've been seeing things, then.'

I narrow my eyes, trying to read her expression, but there is nothing. Why can't they just tell me the truth – it's all so odd.

She pours the boiling water in a mug from the tree, then opens the fridge.

I put the carrier bag on to the counter.

'The milk's in here,' I say.

She takes the bag. Why am I standing here observing

125

while a stranger makes a cup of tea in my own kitchen? It must be the shock from at the shop, and her presence here is so unnerving.

I watch as she looks out of the window, waiting for the kettle to boil. There's nothing much out there to look at, just the side of the yard fence, which needed repainting years ago. She tilts her head from side to side as though dancing to music in her head. I get a waft of her perfume or hairspray; it smells like White Musk. I remember it from years ago. Where do I recall that from?

She smiles at me as she catches me staring at her, but I don't smile back. She opens the biscuit tin and peers in.

'Oh, there's only one left,' she says.

'I'm not hungry,' I say.

'You don't have to be hungry for biscuits!'

She's talking to me like we've known each other for years; it's like we're in a bizarre dream.

She tears off a bit of kitchen roll and places the malted milk on it.

This must be what it's like to have a daughter. Pre-empting what you need before you know it yourself. Though I wasn't that kind of daughter myself – I wasn't allowed to be. Mother wouldn't let me near the cooker, which I didn't mind, really.

Craig and I have a different relationship to what my brother and I had with our mother. I never felt as though I was missing out not having a father around – she could play both roles perfectly. Stern when she needed to be, but mostly nurturing, kind, funny, although she did have her darker moments. It hurts to think about her sometimes.

Leanne carries the tea through and places it on a coaster on the coffee table.

'You've a lovely house,' she says, perching on the end of the settee, looking around.

'Really?'

She jumps up to look at the books on my bookcase and I flush slightly. There are too many Mills & Boon, and only a few of the thrillers people like to read these days. She takes a thick book out.

'Oh, *The Thorn Birds*! My mum loved this book. Can I borrow it?'

'Wouldn't you like something a bit more recent? I ... well ... I've no intention of reading it again, so you're more than welcome, but I don't think it's appropriate really. How old are you, Leanne?'

'I'm nineteen,' she says, but the little red patches on her cheeks betray her. 'She watched the series as well.'

'What? Who?'

'My mum. She had a bit of a thing for the priest guy ... said she liked him when she was a kid, which was weird because she wasn't religious.' She laughs self-consciously, brushing a strand of her blonde hair away from her face. 'She hated organised anything – politics, the police, social workers. From what I remember anyway. She's dead now.'

My hand automatically goes to my mouth.

'I'm so sorry, love.'

'It's all right. It was years ago ... that's why I'm in Sunningdales now,' she says quietly. She clasps her hands together; a formal gesture that doesn't suit her. She's so young, vulnerable. 'Dad tries, but, you know. He hates real life and that. My mum loved life, but then you would if you were off your face all the time, wouldn't you?'

What a life she's had. There's something about her that makes me want to put my arms around her and tell her everything's going to be all right.

She only looks about fourteen, but I'm out of touch with youngsters nowadays. The ones I've seen in the Co-op all have a face full of make-up and what looks like mascara lathered all over their eyebrows.

'Where did you meet Jason, Leanne?' I say.

'Always known Jason, really. About a year ago, he started sitting in a beer garden near Sunningdales.'

'What's that?'

She laughs.

'Yeah, it sounds like an old people's home, doesn't it?' she says. 'It's great to meet you, by the way.' She says it in a faux-posh voice and I'm not sure if she's pulling my leg or not. 'Craig talks about you all the time.'

'Really?' And then the penny, or rather the pocketful of rusty, dirty coins, drops. 'Have you been visiting Craig?'

'Oh no,' she says, her voice wobbling for the first time. 'We were talking yesterday.'

'I see. From what you said, it was like you'd known each other for years.'

'It feels like we have.'

It's not far to the pub – where the heck is Jason? He needs to take this child home.

'I don't mean to be rude,' I say, 'but ...'

Her eyes widen; she hugs the book, anxious suddenly.

'That's OK. Craig promised he'd meet me ... an hour ago ... but it was Jason instead of him. They all want something, don't they?'

'What do you mean?'

Her eyes dart around the room.

'Guess it's different these days ...' she says. 'What with the internet and everything.'

'I ... I don't know why that's—'

A knock at the door.

It's Jason here to collect her. If it were Craig, he would've used his key. I swallow.

'Listen, love,' I say to her. 'If you're in some kind of trouble, you can trust me, you know. You don't have to go anywhere with Jason. I can ring Sunningdales ... tell them to come and get you. You're welcome to stay here. I can say to Jason that you're going to help me with something. How does that sound?'

Five minutes ago, I wanted her out of my house and now I feel as though I need to protect her, make her sit down and tell me everything she knows about my son.

Because I don't think I know him at all any more.

'I'm fine,' she says, standing. 'Honestly. Don't worry about me. I've had to learn to take care of myself.'

'If you're sure, love.' I reach over and touch her

slender arm. 'If you ever need someone to talk to, I'm here. Don't ever feel alone.'

She places a hand over mine. Briefly, her eyes glisten with tears before she blinks them away.

'You're kind,' she says.

Another loud knock on the door makes us both jump. Leanne follows me into the hallway.

I open the door to Jason.

'I found Craig at the pub,' he says. 'But he's a bit merry.' He glances at Leanne standing next to me in the doorway. 'I can drop you off home instead, if you want? He can get a bit ... maudlin after a few.'

'That's OK. I want to see him.' Leanne almost leaps from the doorway. She turns to me. 'Thanks, Erica. For the tea and everything.'

'Any time,' I say.

She looks up at Jason, smiling. She trusts him. Does she trust my son as much? Do I?

I watch as they walk together down the street – a sense of foreboding grips me.

Nothing good is going to come of this, I can feel it.

15

Luke

Luke takes a detour past Erica Wright's on the way to work – for the third time in six days. He's already late with the monthly review of the newly released 'bestsellers'. He doesn't know what he's hoping to find down Erica's street. Perhaps he'll see Craig appear at the door – or he'll follow him and witness the crime he knows Craig's going to commit. He'd be the hero. Or he could see an angry mob of locals confronting him with placards; a fight on the street. He knows these scenarios are ridiculous. As if he'd see it at precisely the right moment, his phone ready to film it. It would be such a scoop. Some of the nationals picked up his most recent piece – even used his quotes from Gillian Sharpe – but they never mentioned him. They just lifted the words from the *Chronicle*'s website, with a pitiful link on the word 'reported' that no one ever clicked on after they'd been told it third hand.

He slows as he passes Erica's, but as usual the curtains are closed. Nothing to see there.

Luke continues towards Jason Bamber's house but

stops seconds later when he sees a familiar face. But the face is the only recognisable thing about him. Craig Wright. Shaved head – a number two by the looks of it. Broad shoulders, thick neck, but still the same face.

He's waiting at the corner on the end of the street, looking around. What is he doing? Craig gets out a mobile phone but puts it away when a car turns on to the street. An older car – an Astra – stops. Craig leans into the passenger window. Luke can't see if there are any passengers.

He hears Craig swear at the driver, even with his car window up. Luke lowers it down as Craig says, '... fucking piece of shit'. He kicks the car door.

Luke gets out his phone to capture it, but the car speeds off.

As though he can sense Luke watching, Craig slowly turns to face him. His gaze is unwavering.

'Shit,' says Luke.

He knew he should carry a baseball cap and sunglasses in his glove compartment. Now Craig has seen his face. Luke presses on the accelerator. Craig glares at him as he passes – Luke can feel it even as he tries to keep his eyes on the road.

Luke's going to have to be more careful about this. God knows what Craig would do if he knew Luke was trying to get a story on him. Unlike all those years ago, Luke has a family now. He can't put them at risk.

He turns into Jason Bamber's street, relieved that the black BMW isn't there. Luke waits a few minutes, his eyes on the rear-view mirror in case Craig is on his way here.

Nothing.

This time, Becks opens the door straight away. She's wearing a silk blouse with tight blue jeans, but her feet are bare.

Full name: Rebecca Savage, an unfortunate surname. Date of birth: 7 March 1981, almost two years younger than Jason Bamber. They're married, but she kept her maiden name for some reason.

'Thanks for coming round again,' she says. 'You can't be long, though. I never know when he's going to come home.'

She opens the door wide and Luke steps inside.

'Go through to the lounge,' she says, heading towards the kitchen. 'Do you want a drink?'

'No, I'm fine thanks,' says Luke.

If Jason were to come back, he doesn't want to seem too at home with a cuppa.

The living room is small; two leather settees and a chair take up most of the space. On the wall is a fifty-inch TV that's almost as wide as the mantelpiece below it.

Luke flinches as a piercing scream comes from the corner.

He turns to see a baby in a crib. Luke needs to calm down.

'Don't mind her,' says Rebecca, coming back in, placing her drink on the side table next to her before sitting in the leather chair next to the baby Jumperoo.

She tucks her legs underneath her as she gets comfortable. 'She likes new faces.'

Luke gets his notepad from his inside pocket.

'You're not going to mention my name, are you?' she says, frowning.

'No, of course not. I'm only after a bit of background about Craig.'

'That bloody man,' she says, shaking her head. 'Jason's always going on about him. They were best friends even though they were in different years at school.'

'Did you all go to the same school?'

'Yeah. Me and Jenna were two years below Jason.'

She brings her legs to the floor and sits straighter.

'You knew Jenna?'

She nods slowly and wraps her arms around herself.

'Well?' says Luke.

'Well what?'

'Did you know her well?'

'Oh, right. Yeah, I guess. We went to the same primary school, too. Hung around with each other until we were about fifteen, but then we drifted apart. These things happen. She was very ... you know ... into doing homework and stuff. But they say it's always the quiet ones, don't they?'

'The quiet ones who what?'

'Get into trouble.'

'But it wasn't her fault she was murdered!'

'I'm not saying that.' She raises a hand in protest. 'But she was sneaking around with him, behind Lucy's back.'

'With Craig?'

'Yeah. I saw him with Jenna the night she disappeared. Not that she knew Lucy, but you know – everyone knew Craig had a girlfriend.'

'Did you report this to the police at the time?'

'Of course. But there was no evidence to connect him with it – and he had an alibi for the time of her death. He was with his mother – even had another witness, which is bullshit.' She turns to look at the baby. 'Sorry, Liv.'

She takes a sip of her tea.

'They were both as bad as each other, you know?'

'Craig and Jenna?'

'No, Craig and Lucy. Apparently, she was seeing someone else as well. It was all a bit of a mess. But we were all so young – it was so long ago, another lifetime almost.'

'Do you know who she was seeing?'

She glances at the baby. 'No.'

'Then how do you know it's true?'

'People talk,' she says, shrugging as though it were nothing.

'OK.' Luke sighs.

'I think I've said enough,' says Rebecca. She suddenly stands, looking at the clock. 'You'd better go.'

'Well, thanks for talking to me. Any chance I could ring if I have any further questions?'

She laughs. 'Don't push your luck. He'd bloody kill me if he found out I spoke to you today.'

Rebecca leads him into the hallway, to the front door. She opens it and Luke steps outside.

135

'Can I ask a quick question?' he says. 'Why did you talk to me today?'

'We've had this hanging over our head for years,' she says, wearily. 'I want it to go away.' She closes the door and Luke walks back to his car.

Luke is perplexed by her closing words. Why would it bother Rebecca about Craig's involvement in Jenna's murder? Most of what he's just heard is speculation and gossip – apart from the sighting of Craig and Jenna that Rebecca reported to the police at the time. The police chose to believe Erica Wright and the other witness over Jason's girlfriend.

So which one of them is lying?

16

Erica

It's so peaceful in church when there's nobody else here. I used to come here a lot when I was expecting Craig; it was the only place I felt closer to my mother after losing her so suddenly. Being here took away some of the hopelessness, the loneliness – it gave me a feeling that there was something bigger than the situation I was in, although I wasn't religious. It was also the only place I could open my coat in that summer heat without showing all and sundry my expanding belly. Oh, the shame of it. That's what my mother would've said.

There's the smell from the incense I remember, and the fragrance of the church flowers. There must've been a funeral today. It's freezing, though; I feel cold to the bone and I've still got the pain in my side. I've been drinking plenty of water as I'm sure it's a water infection – I've had so many in the past, I've lost count. Antibiotics play havoc with the rest of my body so I'm not in any hurry to visit the doctor again soon. I can usually take care of it myself.

I had to walk here, had to get out of the house. I

hoped that I might see Craig on my way here, as I passed the pub he used to go to.

I don't really know why I came here, though. The prayers for Craig never worked last time, but they might work today.

Craig hadn't got back by the time I went to bed last night, nor was he in when I woke. He's going to get into trouble if he doesn't take more care. I said he was asleep when his supervising officer, Adam, phoned for him at ten o'clock last night. Maybe Craig *was* asleep somewhere. All right, maybe not that early, but I would've heard if he'd gotten himself into bother.

I have Craig's number in my mobile, but I didn't want to call him too early this morning in case he'd had a sleepover at a friend's.

Oh Jesus, what do I sound like? He's not a youngster any more. He needs to get his act together. I should have sent him a message. A text would be far better than a mother ringing her thirty-seven-year-old son asking him if he'll be back for tea, wouldn't it? I hate not knowing where he is, though. I don't know why I'm in church; he'd never come here. He never did like churches. Too quiet, I expect. Too many thoughts race through the mind when you're faced with God.

I remember, when he was eleven, Craig was very late getting back from school. He'd been quiet all week, but he clammed up when I tried to talk to him about it. Denise helped me look for him when it got to six o'clock and I was worried sick. It was summer, so the nights were lighter, but it was nearly dark when we found him in the derelict house on Inkerman Street. Denise managed to get Jason to admit their hiding place after she threatened to call the police. Jason said that Craig was being bullied at school, said he was picked on because of his half-mast trousers, and that Craig was a *bastard* and I was a *whore*. It was like we were stuck in the seventies. Denise clipped him round the ear when he said those words.

Jason walked me down the path at the side of the house and round to the back. The grass was overgrown, and the greenhouse's glass panes had collapsed and smashed. Inside were empty plant pots and old seedling trays covered in moss.

'A man killed his wife in this house,' said Jason. 'That's why hardly anyone goes in ... no one'll buy it.'

We stepped inside and there was a pentangle on the wall, painted in red; the drips of it made it look like blood. It made my arms and legs turn cold, but Jason just strolled in. 'He'll be upstairs,' he said. I wanted to run out of there. I'm not a believer in ghosts or anything like that, but the place was ominous, made me feel physically sick.

Upstairs, Craig was sitting on a dirty old settee, reading a comic.

'You want to be careful,' Jason said to him. 'We could've been anyone. Keep your guard up, mate. And your ears open.'

He was talking as though they were on the run from the police or something and he was only twelve.

Craig stood when he saw I was there, too.

'Mum!' He looked out of the window. 'I didn't know it was so late.'

I looked at the floor, where the wrappers of his packed lunch were scattered.

'Have you not been to school?' I said.

Craig glanced at his friend, narrowing his eyes.

'Sorry, mate,' said Jason. 'They were going to call the police.'

They? I held out my hand for him to take it, but then realised he wouldn't do that in front of Jason.

'Come on, love,' I said. 'It's Friday. No school tomorrow. I'll have a word with your Year Head on Monday ... see if we can get this sorted.'

'No, Mum! That'll make it worse.'

'We'll talk more about this at home,' I said.

'Jason'll keep an eye out for him, won't you?' said Denise, nudging her son in the ribs.

'Yeah, sure,' said Jason. 'I didn't realise it got to you this bad, mate.'

Craig shrugged, kept his eyes on the floor.

'Come on, lads,' I said. 'I'll stop at the chippy on the way home and get us all a bag of chips.'

Jason rubbed his hands.

'Nice one. Come on, lad.'

My son got up and followed Jason and Denise, leaving me in the bedroom alone. Its wallpaper peeled from the walls; the old fireplace with its tiny grate held ashes that must've been years old. There was a photograph on the windowsill and I couldn't help but walk over. It was of a man and a woman. She was sitting on his

140

knee, his arms wrapped around her waist and he was grinning. She wasn't smiling. Her eyes were cheerless; a stare at the camera like she was telepathically begging for help. I knew it must be the woman who died here. I put the photograph in my pocket – couldn't bear to leave her there, where it all happened.

I think I have that photograph stashed away somewhere. Perhaps that's what's brought me such bad luck. I should take it back to that old house; it still stands empty, unloved.

The confessional door slams shut. I flush slightly, which is silly, because Father Peter can't hear my odd little thoughts. How long has he been in that box? No one must be confessing today because nobody else left from the other door. He brushes some dust from the top of one of the pews, looks down the aisle at the rest of them and shrugs.

He glances at me, and nods – unsurprised by my presence.

'Cleaner mustn't have been in this morning,' he says. 'Come to think of it – it's been a few days since I've seen Mrs McNally.' He tilts his head and looks to Jesus on the cross to my left. 'Hmm. Must see how she is.'

I smile at him and he turns on his heels, his gown swishing at his ankles.

It must be nice for someone to care about where you are. I might come back at the same time tomorrow. If Mrs McNally doesn't show up, Father Peter might be in need of a new cleaner. It'd be quite pleasant to have somewhere to go every morning, and no one would bother me in here.

He must be in his seventies now. I wonder if he recognises me from when I had to tag along with Mother. This was her church – the one nearest our house looked *too much like a community centre*. She always said she wished she'd married my father here, instead of the registry office in town. Not that it would've made a difference.

It's strange, thinking about her having dreams and wishes. She always seemed content with her life, her friends.

Unlike her, the thought of marriage petrified me. I saw all these women rushing home from wherever they were so their husbands had a meal on the table when they got home from work (or the pub). Denise was one of them, too, in the end.

The night before her wedding, I'd stayed over at her parents' house with her. It was 1975 and we were only nineteen. It was the best night of my life. We laughed so much we were in tears.

Her bedroom was big as she was an only child, and it had a single bed with a yellow and brown flowered quilt. The carpet was orangey brown as well. She still had the poster of David Cassidy above her headboard. It felt surreal that she put that up when we were in fourth year, yet here she was about to get married.

Her wedding dress hung on the front of her wardrobe. It was to the ankle, high-necked and had long flowing sleeves that cuffed at the wrists. It cost £30, but her parents had been saving for a wedding long before she'd even met Jim. They must've been itching to get the house to themselves.

She'd sneaked up a bottle of Cinzano, but didn't have any mixer, so we just took little sips. We drank out of the china cups me and Mum bought for their wedding present, so Denise's parents couldn't see we were drinking alcohol. 'You'll want a clear head on the biggest day of your life,' her mum said. Denise put her fingers in her mouth and pretended to be sick when her mum turned her back. 'I'll leave you girls to it,' she said. 'I'll be up later with a few sandwiches.'

'She's so nice, your mum,' I said to Denise. 'My mother hovers over us ... listens in on our conversations. She's always so protective of me.'

Denise shrugged. 'I guess none of us are pleased with what we've got. But she's not bad, your mum. She's funny. At least she let you come here tonight.'

'Yeah, but I'll bet you a quid she rings me at half eight before she goes to bed.'

Denise took a sip from her mug and giggled.

She'd just learned about face masks from an American magazine and made me apply one with her, so we both looked a fright in our frilly nighties and muddy faces.

'I'm getting married in the morning,' she sang, a little too loud after refilling her Cinzano. 'Ding Dong, his willy will be mine!'

'That's disgusting, Denise,' I said, giggling.

She scrunched up a piece of tissue and threw it at me.

'Stop being such a prude. Don't tell me you haven't daydreamed about it?'

143

'The chance of me meeting anyone is naught.'

'But you've got such a pretty face. You should grow your hair out – that's Twiggy's hairstyle from about ten years ago.'

'I don't like to faff about with it in the mornings,' I said. 'Anyway, my mother would scare anyone who came to our house. She'd question them about everything.'

Denise pulled a face, but it was hard to tell what it was, it being covered in mud.

'What about that lad from school ... what was his name?'

'Billy. He's at university now ... I heard he got into Cambridge.'

'He never did! Well, imagine that ... someone from this town and our school, getting into Cambridge.' She sighed and leant back heavily on the legs of her white stool; it was feeble, and she nearly fell on her back, but it stopped against her matching vanity unit and she didn't notice her close shave. Always the way: Denise never suffered from a crash landing. 'What a different life that would be, eh?' she said. 'Not too far from London. Maybe you could write to him?'

'I doubt he'll want to hear from me – not after meeting all those glamorous posh southern girls.'

I felt my face flush, though Denise couldn't tell. The mud was beginning to crack; there was so much satisfaction in stretching my mouth to feel it break.

'What on earth are you doing?' said Denise.

'It feels so nice when it splits.'

'You definitely need a man,' she said. 'Someone like my Jim.'

I blushed again. 'He's very handsome.'

'One of those silent, brooding types,' she said with a wink. 'Though he's got a bit of a temper on him. I'll have to keep that in check.'

'Yes.' I put on an accent, mimicking how I thought the Queen might speak. 'And make sure you're never late with his sausage and chips.'

'Ooh, Matron!'

I dipped a tissue in the bowl of warm water and started to rub the mask off my forehead.

'I'll hardly see you once you're married,' I said.

'Course you will. I'm not going to be chained to the house ... though ours won't be ready for another fortnight. Can you imagine Jim and me, crammed in my single bed?'

'I'd rather not.'

It was one of the best nights of my life, that Friday night.

And she was true to her word – she did make time to see me, even though it was only once a week when Jim went to the pub. It was better than nothing.

And Denise was right in a way: I *did* meet someone.

It wasn't exactly a lie when I told Craig that his father didn't tell me his real name. I saw him at Christmas in 1978 when it was the supermarket's do. We had a three-course meal down at the Berni Inn (fruit juice to start, turkey with the trimmings, and cheese and biscuits – I'm not a dessert person). The drinks were included in the four pounds fifty we had to contribute. I didn't go out all that often – certainly never to a restaurant – and I didn't have many outgoings then, so I didn't mind spending that much on a night out. I even bought a red V-neck dress with a black belt from Denise's catalogue.

They went straight to my head, the drinks. Needless to say, Mother wasn't a drinker, so we never partook at home (not many people did, then). It was my first taste of sherry, champagne (probably sparkling wine), and port. I was walking to the ladies' and he was standing at the bar on his own. He held my gaze as I walked past, and my face burned. He was the classically tall, dark and handsome man that I'd read about, but he had blue eyes. His hair was longer at the front, so it half covered one of his eyes. He stopped me on my way back to the table, touching my shoulder.

'I've not seen you around here before,' he said. 'What's your name? I'm John.'

I thought he was joking at first, about his name, because I certainly knew *him*. I was almost going to give a fake one myself, but I couldn't think of anything but Agnetha Fältskog, and that would've been silly, especially as I didn't know how to pronounce it.

'Erica,' I said.

'I've never met an Erica before,' he said.

'Well, you have now,' I said, emboldened by all the drink.

He extended his hand, so I held mine out, too. His large hand covered mine, and its dry warmth felt reassuring.

'I bet you've never had a Harvey Wallbanger,' he said.

'What makes you say that?' I said, not knowing what he was talking about.

He shrugged. 'You look innocent. You're probably the only one in here not caked in make-up.'

'You hide it well,' I said.

It took a while for him to get my awful joke. He didn't laugh (the barmaid didn't laugh either). He ordered me a Harvey Wallbanger and I was about to tell him that we hadn't pulled our crackers yet so I should be getting back, but when I looked over at my supermarket table they were getting up to go to the bar, all wearing the paper hats. I tried to hide my disappointment, feeling silly.

'Are you with that lot?' he said, frowning as he peered over my head.

I nodded. He swiped the two drinks from the bar and said, 'Let's take these somewhere a bit more private.' And I followed him.

Denise helped me get ready for my first date with him.

'So it's John what?' she said, her face inches from mine as she applied blue eyeliner under my bottom lashes. 'I can't believe you don't know his surname – why didn't you ask?'

It felt wrong, really, not telling her who I was going to meet, as though I was betraying her.

'I didn't tell him mine,' I said. 'Wouldn't want him to think I was being nosy. Men hate women who pry too much, don't they? They like to be all mysterious.'

I think she rolled her eyes, but it was hard to tell from that close.

'Maybe in your books, Erica. Not in real life. Men love talking about themselves. Jim only stops to let me speak so I can ask a question about *him* and his day.'

She leant back, her eyebrows furrowed as she examined her work. She went over to her wardrobe, opening it while rubbing her back. Her belly was huge now; it was like she'd stuck a pillow up her dress.

'I've been bored, stuck inside most of the week,' she said, 'so I've been going through a few of my outfits for you.'

She pulled out two hangers, both with complete outfits on them, and hung them on the handles.

'This,' she said, stroking the black top and matching narrow trousers, 'is a bit Olivia Newton-John, but I think you'd look great in it.'

My mouth dropped open a little.

'I can't wear that, Denise. He'll think I'm a ... you know ... a bit of a goer.'

'Hmm. Do you reckon? Maybe you're right. Don't want you looking like you're going to a fancy-dress party. The other one it is then. I'll just visit the lav ... for the hundredth time this evening.'

I took the dress off the hanger. I'd always loved it, and she knew that, and I felt teary that she let me borrow it. It looked exactly how I'd imagined it would on me. It was dark blue denim, with pale pink spaghetti straps that tied on each shoulder. It had a matching drawstring waist in a bow around the middle.

'Oh, Erica,' she said, as she waddled back into the room. 'That looks lovely on you.' She walked up to me and played around with my hair (not that there was much to play with). It was all blonde, then, and cut short, barely covering the top of my ears. It was so thick, it just went back in its place, even after Denise had covered it in hairspray. She shrugged. 'Oh well, I tried. So when's he picking you up?'

'At eight. I'm meeting him outside the library.'

'What on earth ... ? Why isn't he picking you up from home? Your mother must want to meet him.'

'I told her I was round here tonight. You don't mind, do you? Only ... I think she'll worry too much about me and—'

'It's fine, it's fine. I wondered how she'd let you out so easily.' She kissed me on the cheek. 'Now go and have a good time.' She flopped onto the bed and lay on her back. All I could see was belly. 'Tell me all about it tomorrow because I can't remember what it's like to have fun. I'm going to be miserable for years, I can tell,' she said dramatically.

'You're going to be such a good mum, Denise.'

'Yeah, I suppose.'

I did have a good time. He drove me to Blackpool and bought me a cone of chips. He didn't even try to kiss me, which was good because I'd never kissed a lad before, even though I'd practised on my hand.

It was the first of many dates. He told me not to tell anyone we were courting. He said his mother wanted him to concentrate on the family business and didn't want him *out gallivanting*. I knew that was rubbish, but I didn't pry.

'He's probably married,' Denise said when I wouldn't answer her questions a few months later. *Where does he work? Does my Jim know him? Does he have any brothers or sisters?*

'Do you really think I can get away with this pink lipstick?' I said instead. Because I didn't want to answer. I knew what I was doing was wrong, but it was exciting – a chance to escape my life – even if only for a few hours a week.

I told Mother that when I went out at night, I was working a late shift at the supermarket. She never thought to check, never thought I would lie to her face. She had no reason to doubt me – I'd always been a good girl in that sense.

The church door opens now, making me jump slightly on the hard seat. There's a draught on the back of my neck. A woman in her eighties shuffles in.

I'd better be going anyway. Sitting in silence is bad for the soul sometimes – I don't want to be dredging up the past. *The devil finds work*, and all that. I shift to the end of the pew and genuflect; some habits never leave.

'Oh, Mrs McNally,' says the priest, appearing from nowhere.

'Sorry I've not been in for a few weeks, Father,' she says. 'My hip's been playing up ... and what with my cataracts ... it's been difficult to get around.'

'Oh, we did miss you,' says Father Peter. 'I hope you're feeling better now?'

What a jolly old liar he is – he thought she'd been absent for a couple of days. If God's own servant can tell a porkie and not be struck down, then there's hope for the rest of us.

It's three o'clock by the time I turn on to my street. Mrs Eckersall from next door is outside cleaning her windows. So she's not dead after all. I haven't seen her in months. I've not seen anyone do their own in years. I can smell the vinegar she's using on the newspaper and I'm a good thirty feet away.

I always think that avoiding someone's eye will make me invisible, but it doesn't today.

'Good morning, Erica,' she says, neither cheerfully nor unkindly.

I hold the key up to my front door, scanning it quickly. The sun has been on the door all morning, and I can smell the dog muck that must've worked deep into the cracks.

'Morning,' I say.

'Nice to have a bit of sunshine.'

She's stopped buffing her windows. I turn my head to face her.

'Everything all right with you?' she says.

'Yes. Why? What have you heard?'

I drop my hand from the lock.

'Nothing, dear,' she says. 'Nothing at all. I just worry about you sometimes. All the comings and goings from your house in the past few days. That girl I saw, the blonde one ... I'm not used to hearing commotion from your side. It'll be making you anxious, I expect. And I saw your Craig at the end of the street before.'

'You don't have to worry about me. Everything's fine. We're all fine.'

I rush into the house, leaning against the closed front door. I wish people would just mind their own business.

That conversation will replay in my head and I will think of a thousand sentences to improve the outcome. The trouble is, everyone around here knows my business and I don't know theirs.

The house is silent.

'Hello? Craig? Are you in?'

I look in the living room, in the dining room. Nothing.

Upstairs, the bathroom door is open, as is Craig's bedroom door.

His bed hasn't been slept in – the towel I put on there two days ago is lying at the same angle, untouched. The black bag remains under the radiator. The letters might still be in there.

Yes, they're in the same place. I sit on his bed and take one from the middle.

1 January 2017

Hi Craig,
HNY!

Sorry about my late reply. You sent me that letter ages ago, but it's been manic here and I haven't been round to my dad's in a while (you can guess why).

152

Can't wait till we can talk proper. Instead, I'll just write about what's happening round here.

Robyn in the bedroom next to mine sneaked a guy into her room last night. She put her chest of drawers against the door, but the guy must've been smoking pot or something because Franny McPhee said she could smell it from outside and almost broke the door down getting in. I don't think they got up to much because Robyn was still in her high-waist jeans and corset top (must've been too much of a job for her bloke to get off. Esp. after the weed). Fran said she knew what Netflix and Chill means (whatever, that's so 2015) and she should rethink her choice of outfits (and blokes) and said she's not allowed to leave the premises for at least a week, but I can't see that happening ('premises' lol). Banned her from Snapchat for a week, though. Harsh.

Jaden downstairs had his bedroom turned over by two dickheads (had Halloween masks on so the CCTV is useless). They took his hamster, which is well shitty because the kid's only eight and he's missing his fam. I think it might've got into the walls because I heard scuffling next to me last night. Freaked me out TBH. Thought it was Robyn's pothead boyfriend trying to get back into the 'premises' (who in their right mind would try to get in here?!).

Got that chain you told me to buy myself for Christmas and I've been wearing it every day, even when I'm in the shower.

I'm gonna put a photo in with this letter. It's only

a few months old. It looks like we're abroad, but it was only Blackpool. Robyn let me have one of her bikinis (she didn't want it back after I borrowed it ha!). Her mum sends her clothes all the time (Robyn calls it spending guilt money). As you can see, I don't tan very easy. 'English rose,' Mr Townsend the gardener calls me, but everyone knows he's a paedo, the old perv (he's about eighty, but ...). I've got red hair in that pic, but that was just a temp spray Robyn tested on me. You'll be pleased to know that I'm back to my natural blonde now.

Four weeks to go!
Are you excited? Nervous? Both?
I'm all three!
Love,

L

PS. Got that other thing you told me to buy ☺
xoxo

The date meant that these weren't from Lucy. Leanne. They must be from Leanne. My heart is pounding and the whole of me is shaking. What the hell did he ask her to buy? I don't want to imagine. She sounds so young. *HNY* I only deciphered after a few minutes. Happy New Year. It's a different language.

Why on earth would a young girl want to write to a prisoner? I've read about people who write to men on death row. One woman said she was drawn to the serial

154

killer's eyes. 'I sensed a wildness in them,' she said, 'but he seemed ever so sad.' She said that she only ever wanted someone to write to, who would write back, and she fell in love with him. What did she get out of that? Her life must have been missing something. Or was it the excitement, the challenge of finding a good heart in someone evil? Perhaps she thought she could change him.

I pick out another letter – an earlier one.

26 August 2016

Dear Craig,

It's ten to three in the morning and I'm on a visit with Dad. He's wide awake, shouting at the telly, even though it's only one of those weird casino programmes. Why do people watch them? I know he hasn't any money to be gambling on it – I've seen his bank statements (he doesn't care about anything any more, just leaves shit around – not literally, that would be gross, but saying that, I wouldn't be surprised by anything he does these days).

I managed to nick one of his ciders. It tastes disgusting, but it's helping a bit.

I know you said you had a terrible time because you never knew your dad, but I suppose we've both had it shit in different ways. If you had my dad, you would probably think that nothing is better. But we can't swap, can we? I'd probably shit myself being where you are (and I've seen some pretty bad things in my life).

Least you still have your mum. Mine was a bit wild, but she was my mum and I loved her. I cry at night sometimes, but don't tell anyone. People forget after a few months and think you're just meant to get over it. If anything, time makes it worse.

Sorry for being so depressing! Last thing you need probably.

OK, so here's a joke to cheer us both up:

A guy is sitting at home when he hears a knock at the door. He opens the door and sees a snail on the porch. He picks up the snail and throws it as far as he can. Three years later there's a knock on the door. He opens it and sees the same snail. The snail says: 'What the hell was that all about?'

Love,

L xxx

I hold the last letter in my hands.

Leanne said that he had talked about me – she hinted she knew details about his background. It can't have been from one conversation.

She's so young, though, and the letters go back a couple of years.

How could he say that about his upbringing? Did I really make his childhood that bad? I wish I'd been the one he'd told these things to.

I keep trying to pinpoint the time when things went so wrong; I keep thinking about how he used to be, when he was so pure, innocent. Like when he was only three years old, covers up to his chin, in this very bed I'm sitting on.

'I don't want to leave home when I'm a man, Mummy,' he said. 'Can I marry you?'

'I'm afraid not, love. But you don't have to leave if you don't want to.'

Then he burst into tears.

'What's wrong, love?' I said, my heart melting and breaking at the same time.

'I never want to be a daddy. I saw Mark's dad at playschool and he told Mark off because he spilt juice down his front.'

'But mummies tell kids off too.'

'But ... but ...' He wiped his face with his covers. 'You don't shout as loud as he did. And if I was a daddy, I'd have to meet another mummy and I just want *you*.' He started crying again.

I realise that I'm crying too, now.

I go to the window and there's no sign of my son outside. If I looked everywhere, there would be no sign of the little boy that once cried himself to sleep because he loved me too much. That boy is long gone.

I'd half hoped that by snooping, reading these letters, it would've jinxed Craig into coming home. When I used to smoke and lit one waiting for a bus, it always used to come. But, no. No sign.

I carefully put the letters back and go downstairs.

I get my phone from my handbag and select Craig's number.

'Craig? It's me, your mum. Are you there?'

Sounds like static coming down the line, then a strange sound as though a car is going under a series of tunnels.

'Craig!' I shout louder; he might have answered it by mistake in his pocket or something. 'Can you hear me?'

I press my mobile to my head, so it squashes my ear flat.

Faint music. A car radio maybe.

'Craig!'

There's a noise like someone's throwing the phone against a hard surface. 'Shit!' A man's voice – it doesn't sound like Craig. And then the phone goes dead.

My heart's pounding. What if someone's out for revenge? What if Brian's kidnapped him to punish Craig for taking Lucy away from him? Or it could be Jenna's dad, angry that he hasn't seen justice for his girl.

I open the front door and walk out onto the pavement, looking left and right. It's quieter than it normally is, but there's a car parked at the top of the street; two people in the front seats with their heads down. It's not a new car. Craig used to tell me that drug dealers always had flash cars, so they can't be dodgy. But surely the police would have nice cars too. If Craig was in trouble, they wouldn't be just sitting in the car like that, they'd be straight through my door.

I go back inside and pace the living room.

I could call the police, but it would sound silly: my son didn't answer his phone properly. I haven't seen him for almost two days; his supervising officer didn't mention anything like this – or I wasn't listening properly, there was too much to take in. Leaflets. They gave me some leaflets. I search the kitchen drawers and I can't find them.

No, no. I can't call anyone. I don't want to get him into trouble if he was doing nothing. Though if he's with Jason, then I doubt they're doing nothing.

The world seems to have gone quiet. No voices on the street, or jazz music from next door. I'm sure I can hear the ticking of the grandmother clock in the dining room. These four walls feel like they're closing in, laughing at me. It was better when I knew where he was, that he was safe. It's a terrible thing to think, but I've felt so unsettled these past six days – even compared to the days and nights the house was targeted. The police were no use then either.

I go to the kitchen and splash my face with cold water.

When that first lit newspaper came through the door, I was fast asleep on the sofa when the smoke alarm went. I dialled 999 after putting it out myself with the water from the kettle. I know they say not to do that, that you have to get out and stay out, but it was only small. It was more of a smoulder than a fire. Whoever put it through my letterbox obviously hadn't put enough petrol or whatever they used on it. It would've done more damage had I left it. 'Get a landline put in upstairs,' the fireman said, five minutes after I called. 'It's lucky you've wooden floors and no curtain behind the door ... curtains plus a carpet would've gone up like that.' He'd made a *whooshing* sound while sweeping his arm through the air.

I splash my face with water again.

Jason. I need to contact Jason.

But that would mean asking Denise for his phone number.

I grasp the edges of the kitchen counter and look to the calendar. I've underlined the nineteenth of February. I don't know why I always do that – it's not as if I'd forget. Thirty-nine years this year since my mother died. Where does it go?

Last Monday is circled in blue ink and I even wrote a little exclamation mark and a smiley face. It's been seven days today since Craig was released. What planet was I on then when I drew that – what did I think it would be like? I shouldn't have lied to Adam last night on the phone. It can't be like it was back then. If he's in trouble then they'll have got to him by now, but he's out there somewhere and he might be hurt.

I walk back into the hallway and open my address book. I kept that reporter's card; I knew I had. I could tell him all about my son and how it couldn't possibly have been Craig and now he's in trouble. I'll let him know that I'm still searching for a man called Pete Lawton who was with Craig when Lucy was murdered. I keep checking, but there's been no reply from the one who opened my message on Facebook. It's like I'm chasing a ghost, someone who doesn't exist.

I hold the card as I walk into the living room. I grab the remote and switch the television on to have a

comforting sound in the background. I don't wan
hear my voice echoing in this house.

The local news is on. Before I press the button to
change the channel a familiar face is staring back at me.
The photograph fills the screen. A pretty, young girl in
a school uniform: Leanne.

17

Luke

Following his talk with Rebecca Savage this morning, Luke is now convinced that Erica Wright has been covering up for her son regarding Jenna Threlfall's murder. But why would the police believe an alibi from a relative if it weren't true? Perhaps it's because the murders seemed to differ.

Several aspects of the police investigation have remained under embargo: pieces of evidence that couldn't be made public but were leaked to a member of his office.

There were key areas in which Lucy and Jenna's cases were different. Lucy was found hidden, crudely and amateurishly, in woodland. There was a rudimentary covering of leaves, earth and sticks that were perhaps pawed away by the dog that found her. Her clothes were on her person and there was nothing missing from the body. Jenna, on the other hand, was found in a place one couldn't miss – she'd obviously been moved post-mortem and her skin had been crudely wiped with bleach, presumably to rid the body of foreign DNA. While Luke believed that the treatment of Jenna's body could be perceived as different, it still seemed naive to use household bleach.

Luke types the names of Jenna's parents, Sandra and Philip Threlfall, into Google. There are hardly any results and those he finds are mentions in parish newsletters or results of cricket matches. Nothing of importance. He doubts his own parents would appear in any Google searches either.

He reads through the old interviews. Jenna Threlfall had a sister, Olivia, who was thirteen years old at the time – not that they'd been able to print any details about her then.

He types Olivia Threlfall into Facebook. There's one entry in Shropshire but with a different surname. She must have her maiden name listed as an alternative. Pictures of her and her children are there for all to see. Why do people do that? Luke had read somewhere that social scientists predicted that the next generation will be horrified at the information about themselves people put online today – that everything will reverse, and people will value privacy online.

Olivia's workplace is listed as DH Solutions Limited. Luke clicks on the link, sighing with exasperation. He found her in minutes. Before he dials, he quickly looks up her company's client list, jotting down a few names. He's pretty sure that if he were to give his true reason for phoning, Olivia wouldn't take his call.

It rings twice.

'DH Solutions. Good afternoon, Amy speaking. How may I help you?'

'Hello. Could you put me through to Olivia Threlfall, please?'

'Who can I say is calling?'

'Marc from GlobeForce.'

Silence.

'Really?'

'Yes.'

'But you're ... I mean ... You're calling on *behalf* of Marc, right?'

'Yes, that's right.'

She gives a nervous laugh. 'I thought it was some sick joke. We've just started our Christmas party, you see ... well, I've started a few minutes early ... I thought I was hearing things.'

'Christmas?'

'Yeah. We can't have our party when *normal* people have it ... but at least it's all free.' She clears her throat. 'Putting you through now.'

Luke listens to two minutes of 'Black Velvet' – she almost catches him singing along.

'Olivia Threlfall.'

'Hello, Olivia. My name is Luke Simmons.'

'Are you a relative of Marc's?'

'No.'

She sighs. 'Thank God. Reception mumbled something about hearing the voice of a dead person. I'd have hated it if it were a relative and we'd totally offended them.'

Shit.

'You're safe. I'm Luke from the *Chronicle* in Preston.'

'Oh. Really.'

'I don't think the receptionist was listening properly – she seemed preoccupied.'

God, he hopes he doesn't get Amy fired.

'I suppose it's that time of year ... I mean for us. Anyway ... sorry. I'm not with it myself.'

'Not a problem,' he says.

'This is about Jenna, isn't it?'

'Yes.'

'I should've guessed – what with Amy thinking she'd spoken to the dead. I'm not always this ditzy, you know.'

'It's OK,' says Luke, partially glad he's caught her in a distracted mood.

He'd seen a picture of her when she was thirteen, though she'd looked even younger than that.

'You've got one of those voices, I guess,' she says.

Luke *guesses* that Amy isn't the only one to start the party early. He clicks on the calendar on the bottom right of his screen. Yep – still Monday, still February. Though he does spot a random bauble tucked behind his monitor. Great – that'll have to stay there all year now, bloody superstitions.

'Hello? Are you there?'

'Yes,' says Luke. 'Sorry. I was hoping to ask you a few questions about the release of Craig Wright.'

'What am I meant to say to that? That I'm glad I don't live anywhere near Preston, that I can't believe he'd have the nerve to go back there? That's what anyone would say, and they're not even related to us.' She sighs heavily. 'You're not allowed to print anything about Craig Wright in connection with my sister, though, are you?'

'No. But I wanted to put Jenna's name out there – get her in the public eye again. See if we can jog someone's memory.'

There's silence down the line.

'Are there any comments you want to make about your sister?' says Luke.

'I read your article from that Facebook link. All those angry people who never even knew my sister that commented about her. I'm surprised they weren't deleted. It helps, you know – when people you don't know comment like that. I don't feel so alone. For years I felt that everyone had forgotten – that my sister didn't really exist, and I'd made her up. No one talked about her every day any more. I don't mean Mum and Dad – they spoke about her every time I went round ... and to be honest it got a bit much. Until they divorced, that is. It's like they reminded each other of Jenna – she had different features of both of their faces, you see. They couldn't get past that. Once they were apart, they moved on, in some kind of way.

'So, what I'd like to add is that Jenna was a lovely sister. I know I'm meant to say things like that because she's dead. It must've been the age difference. Had we been closer in age, we'd have probably fought all the time. Mum wasn't much of a talker ... I mean, you know. I learned everything from Jenna. She took me to town when I saved enough pocket money and I got my ears pierced. Mum found her voice when we got home, though, I can tell you that.' Olivia gives a half-hearted laugh that peters out. 'There are loads of things I could tell you about Jenna. What angle are you going for? You've already done a piece about that man's release.'

'I was thinking of putting a still-not-found-the killer piece, like I said. Her last known movements. And if we get quotes from you and your parents? People want to read about those left behind – it brings the humanity back into a cold case.'

Luke kicks himself for the clichés he's coming out with.

'Oh yes,' she says. 'Of course.'

'Do you think either of your parents would be willing to talk to me?'

Olivia sighs heavily down the line.

'Depends what mood you catch Mum in.' She relays her mother's email address. 'I'm only giving it to you as she doesn't go online that often. No offence.'

'That's fine,' says Luke, rolling his eyes.

'My dad's just moved. It's all been a bit rushed. I'm surprised he even wanted to go back up north. Anyway – he changes his email address every time he forgets his password, and I don't want to give out his mobile number without checking with him first.'

Luke grits his teeth. 'That's fine.'

'You could try contacting him on Facebook messenger. He's always sending spammy GIFs on there anyway.'

'I couldn't find him on Facebook.'

'I should've known you'd already tried. He's called Panhead McPhil on there – don't ask – and his profile picture is of a Harley Davidson.'

Luke clicks on Olivia's list of over a thousand friends. He finds her father's profile and clicks on to his photos. There's an old picture of him. Luke recognises the thick mop of hair, the bright grey eyes. It's dated 2010, not that long ago. He doesn't look that different at all.

'Found him,' says Luke.

'It's strange hearing you say that about my dad when he's not even forwarded me his new address.'

'You don't think he's moved back to Preston, do you?'

'I wouldn't put it past him.'

There's shouting in the background in Olivia's office.

'I have to go in a minute,' she says. 'But I have some photographs of Jenna at home – shall I scan and send them over to you? It might help jog someone's memory. It's been horrific knowing her killer is still free.'

'It must be. The photographs would be great, Olivia. Thanks for taking the time to speak to me.'

'Oh – I just thought of something that always struck me as a bit strange, but he used to come round to the house a lot when Mum and Dad were out ... when Jenna was meant to be looking after me. He was kind to me, I suppose ... brought me big bars of chocolate, cans of pop, things like that. I'm sure they used to drink booze up in her room or something – I always turned the telly up loud downstairs or put my headphones on and listened to music.'

'I guess that's what teenagers do all the time,' says Luke.

'No ... I mean, yes they do. But when Jenna went missing, I thought he had something to do with it, but I was wrong.'

'Who, Craig?' Luke asked, confused.

'No,' she says. 'I think his name was Jason.'

'I spoke to Jason Bamber,' says Luke to Amanda, sitting at her desk in front of him. 'He's one of Craig Wright's close friends – a bit flash ... full of himself, but he said he barely knew Jenna Threlfall. Talked to Jason's girlfriend – who was friends with Jenna at school. She said Craig was seeing Jenna behind Lucy's back – and she saw him with Jenna the night she disappeared. She reported it to the police, but Erica Wright had given her son an alibi.'

'Good luck untangling all that, then,' she says, grimacing slightly.

'There's more. I've just spoken with Jenna's sister, Olivia, who said she was sure that the person Jenna was seeing was called Jason.'

'Shit. Did the police know about this at the time?'

'Maybe Jason was the second man questioned for Jenna's murder.'

'That sounds plausible. So what we're missing here is ...'

'Evidence. Someone knows where the T-shirt and necklace taken from Jenna are. And I've a feeling who that might be.'

'Hey!' It's Derek at his desk next to the window: the 'sports department'. 'Check out *Granada Reports*.'

Luke turns to face the flat screen on the wall as Derek turns up the volume.

'Local teenager Leanne Livesey has been missing for three days having last been seen with convicted murderer Craig Wright. Let's go over to Samia Brennan.'

It pans to a large detached house, painted a strange yellowy beige. The reporter stands outside in a beige mac under a large umbrella.

'Leanne Livesey, who is seventeen years old, was last seen getting in a car with Craig Wright, who has in the last few days been released from prison after serving seventeen years for the murder of his girlfriend, Lucy Sharpe. If anyone sees Craig Wright, the police have advised not to approach him, but to dial 999.'

'Shit,' whispers Luke.

'You can say that again,' says Amanda. 'Isn't that the kids' home on Mill Street she's standing outside? I pass that on the way to work. Why aren't we there? It's only about a mile away. Bloody *Granada Reports*, they get everything first.'

Luke grabs his keys from his desk and his coat from the back of the chair. As he's putting his arm in the first sleeve, his phone rings.

'Leave it,' says Amanda.

'It won't take a minute,' says Luke.

Amanda folds her arms as he picks up the handset.

'Luke Simmons, the *Chronicle*.'

There's a few seconds' silence before a quiet voice says, 'Luke? It's me. It's Erica Wright.'

'Erica?' Luke grabs a pen and points to the phone. Amanda gives him a thumbs up. 'How can I help?'

'I have a name that I've been researching. Pete Lawton. I hope you're writing this down. He was with Craig when Lucy disappeared. He was having work experience at the garage. Craig said it was called Anderson & Campbell in Ashton. I thought you might do a better job of tracing the man. It would clear Craig's name. It's very important.'

'Erica, have you seen the news?'

'Well, I saw the girl ... I mean I saw a girl on the news ... they mentioned Craig, but they've got it all wrong.' She talks slowly, as though choosing her words carefully. 'I know you think I'm only saying that because he's my son ... that I'm burying my head—'

'Erica,' says Luke. 'The police know he's taken a young girl ... taken her away in a car. She's only seventeen.'

There's a clatter down the line, like she's dropped the handset – or has she fallen?

'Erica!' Luke shouts down the phone. 'Shit, Amanda. I think she might've collapsed or something.'

She grabs the handset from Luke's hand.

'Erica, love. My name's Amanda. Can you hear me?' She looks to Luke. 'She's crying, wailing. She's not unconscious.' She turns to face the desk. 'Erica. Come on. Talk to me. I'll have to phone an ambulance if you don't talk to me.'

Luke watches, holding his breath as Amanda stands still.

It seems the whole newsroom is listening to the silence.

Amanda's shoulders drop and she turns to face Luke.

'Thank God, Erica. You had me worried, then. Do you want us to pop round? ... Oh really? Well, I'll let you get that. We'll come and see you in an hour or two ... check you're all right.'

Amanda holds the handset away from her ear.

'She hung up ... said there was a knock at the door.'

'Police.'

She replaces the handset. 'Well, yeah. Most likely.'

'Come on,' says Luke. 'Sunningdales, then Erica's.'

Luke walks across the office, the adrenaline pumping down his legs, his arms. This is the best he's felt in years.

18

Jenna was a lot feistier than Lucy. She didn't really want
to come out with me that day.

'Tell her we're only popping to the shop,' I said to her.

'But she's thirteen,' she said. 'I can't leave her on her
own.'

'Thirteen's fine. Kids walk home from school from eleven
years old. Listen . . . she won't know we've gone – we could
sneak out. We'll only be a few minutes.'

'But what's the point of going out if it's only for a few
minutes?'

Jenna was a loose end. She was the one who could get
me into trouble. I wanted to know if she'd keep quiet for
me.

We drove to somewhere different than I went with Lucy.
They still hadn't found her. I should've pointed them in the
wrong direction, but then I'd look like a grass, wouldn't I?

I'd put vodka in a SodaStream bottle and she'd been
drinking it on the way there.

'Don't worry, Jen,' I said. 'It's six o'clock now. Your
mum and dad will be home.'

'What? What time is it? Have I been asleep?'

'No, no.'

She sat up straight in the car.

'The police came round the other day,' she said. 'They asked about you.'

'I'm sure they didn't, Jen.'

'They know a lot about you.'

'But you didn't say anything, did you? Because I know a lot about you, too, Jen. About how you betrayed your friend. And you wouldn't want that to get out, would you?'

She shook her head, but there was something in her eyes. Back then I thought it was guilt, but looking back, it was probably fear.

'It was you, wasn't it?' she said. 'Did you take Lucy somewhere? Have you hurt her?'

'Don't be silly,' I said. 'As if I'd do a thing like that. I loved – I mean I love her.'

I almost slipped up – Lucy was only missing then.

'But what about me?' said Jenna, relaxing into the seat. 'I thought you loved me.'

It was the stuff in the vodka I gave her that made her less resistant. It didn't take as long as with Lucy.

I knew that she knew, as soon as I saw her face.

Once she got in the car, she wasn't coming out alive.

I made sure she was totally clean.

And now, I've done it again.

19

Erica

I'm still on the floor after hanging up the telephone and the thuds on the door are getting louder, stronger.

'If you don't answer the door,' a woman's voice, stern, 'we have a warrant to forcibly enter the premises.'

'Wait, wait,' I say. 'I'm here. Just give me a minute.'

She's looking through the letterbox now, and I'm sitting against the wall of the hallway.

'Are you all right, Erica?' she says. 'Has Craig hurt you?'

'What? No, of course he hasn't.'

Why aren't I moving? It's like my bottom's been glued to the wooden floor.

'We don't want to break your door, Erica,' she says. 'Can you get up? Or is your back door open? Have you had a fall?'

Those last five words seem to be louder than the others. I'm not at the foot of the stairs and I'm not bloody deaf.

'I'm getting up,' I say. 'It's just that my knees ...' I try to get purchase on the telephone table, but it's too

175

high up and the legs are too unstable. Instead, I rest my left hand on the bottom step of the stairs and the other on the floor. Jesus. When had getting up from the ground become so difficult?

I'm dizzy when I stand, but shuffle to the front door to unlock it.

As soon as I open it, about six or seven police officers dressed in black storm into my house – half go upstairs, the rest check the rooms downstairs.

'He's not here,' I say to the woman in a black suit and white shirt. Her hair is short, blonde. Her skin olive and covered in freckles. 'I heard about it. I was talking to Luke ...'

'Luke?'

'A reporter at the local paper. He said it was on the news about Craig. It can't be him, though. He hasn't got a car ... he'd have had to tell his supervising officer if he bought a car ... I found the leaflet ten minutes ago—'

'Well,' says the detective – I presume she's the detective as she's not in uniform. There's a man behind her that I've only now noticed. Young, in a smart suit that must have cost a few bob. It doesn't have that sheen that cheap suits have ... that's what *he* used to tell me. 'He won't necessarily have told them if he'd borrowed one, will he? When did you last see your son?'

'On Saturday ... he's been spending time with his friends.'

'He's meant to be staying here, though, isn't he? Has he been in contact with you since?'

I think about the phone call I made to him, the strange banging and the swearing. But it could be nothing – he won't be stupid enough to take a young girl away – not straight after getting out of prison.

'No. I didn't want him to think I was checking up on him.'

She raises one eyebrow.

'That's not a bad thing ... considering. Is it?'

Smart alec.

'I've been trying to find Pete Lawton,' I say. 'I've asked the police countless times, but you've only got back to me once. He's out there somewhere – he can prove my son's innocence. No one can just disappear like that.'

'Ah,' she says, briefly glancing upwards. 'The elusive Mr Lawton. No, Mrs Wright, there is still no trace of the Peter Lawton who worked in a garage. No one recalls him ever working there. You do know that, don't you?'

She thinks I'm making him up, doesn't she? I hear the others upstairs, opening and closing wardrobes and then I remember the letters from Leanne. The blood rushes from my head; I grab hold of the end of the banister.

'Which friends has he been hanging around with?'

I take a deep breath – does she register my hesitation?

'I'm sorry,' I say. 'I don't know their names.'

'Male? Female?'

'Male probably ... he's been going to the local pub, I think.'

Am I saying too much, or not enough? I feel I'm being pulled apart, my conscience examined.

'Boss.' It's the young man in the sharp suit. 'The car's been found ... near the docks.'

'And?'

He shrugs. 'That's all they said.'

The detective tuts, briefly looks to the ceiling and mumbles, 'Give me strength.'

'Craig's not there, is he?' I ask, but she ignores me.

The five officers from upstairs come down empty-handed, but my heart is thumping.

'To the docks,' the detective says, and they leave as fast as they barged in.

I close the door and slowly walk to the living room, holding the walls then the settee for support. I look through the gap in the curtains. They quickly get into the three police cars and speed off. I look to the houses around and see a silhouette of someone in the house opposite. I don't know the name of the person who lives there, but it's a man – early thirties. He's looking at me, I can sense it.

I pull the curtains fully closed, take a few breaths to help stop my shaking, and go upstairs to Craig's bedroom. The wardrobe doors are open, but his drawers are shut. Was it a manhunt then? His bag's still there. I grab it and fling it on to the bed, lifting up the flimsy plastic base to retrieve the letters. They're innocent enough, but what would the police read into them? That he was grooming her, probably; a phrase that's used a lot these days.

Seventeen! What the hell does he think he's doing? Doesn't he realise how young she is? I hope she lied about her age to him – otherwise I don't know what to think.

I take the letters downstairs into the kitchen, laying them next to the cooker. The back door is standing open where they checked the shed in the backyard – its flimsy lock is pulled to pieces. They'd have found nothing quickly in there as it's empty. I go out to pull the shed door to, to try to fix the lock, and see that there *is* something inside.

I step on the flimsy wooden floor; it gives way slightly under my feet. Who would put tins of paint in my shed? The police ignored them – they're items usually found in outdoor buildings. They probably thought nothing of them. I lift them and they're not heavy. I shake them and something lightweight hits the metal inside. I try to prise the lid off, but my nails are too weak. I grab the other and step out, kicking the shed door closed with my foot.

I glance up at next door. Mrs Eckersall is standing at the bedroom window. Her gaze is unwavering. I don't nod, smile or wave; she doesn't either. I feel a shiver down my spine. She obviously saw the commotion outside and now I'm creeping around with cans of paint.

Inside the kitchen, I place them on the counter and lean against it, steadying myself from the dizziness. My chest feels tight; I can barely breathe.

I shouldn't have lied to the police today. I should've learnt from my mistakes all those years ago. I should've told them that Craig only has one friend: Jason. And they would both do anything for each other. Where will that loyalty take them both? I recall the conversation I overheard before Craig went missing: Jason said, 'Don't worry ... We've all got our little secrets.' Did he mean himself or Craig – or was it both of them?

I grab a butter knife from the kitchen drawer. The tins of paint are rusted around the rim, so I easily prise open the first one. The smell hits me first: pungent, earthy. The leaves are dried and in lots of little bags.

I hold one up: cannabis.

I open the rest. There are three tins crammed with the drug.

If the police were to come through the door, I'd be guilty as charged. *Always the quiet ones*, people would say. *Did you know Erica was a drug dealer?* they'd say. *I'm not surprised in the least*, Pamela Valentine would reply.

What am I meant to do with it? I can't burn it like I did the T-shirt – the whole street would smell of the stuff – a red arrow pointing to my chimney. I could put it back where I found it, pretend to be oblivious to it.

I grab the three handles and take them upstairs to the bathroom, placing the tins in the sink. One by one, I open the little bags and shake the contents into the toilet.

20

Luke

Luke stops his car a few doors down from Sunningdales where a white van is parked outside.

'Oh bollocks,' says Luke. 'It's that twat Damian Norris. He was on my journalism course – I thought he'd moved to Leeds ... got a job at *Look North*.'

'You sound jealous,' says Amanda.

'Of him being a twat? No.'

She wrinkles her nose and opens the car door. 'Come on then, Lois Lane. Let's see what we can find out for our wonderful readers. I've had to change my Facebook name, you know. I got twenty-five private messages last week after reporting about that football scandal. Didn't read most of them after opening the first couple. The rage targeted at me!'

'You never know,' says Luke, slamming the car door, 'the person of your dreams could've been in your inbox.'

'Just because I'm single, doesn't mean I'm looking – or desperate.'

They make their way to a man with gelled hair

straight out of the eighties. Luke's surprised he's not wearing a casual white blazer and a pink T-shirt but concludes that it's too cold for that get-up – even for Damian.

'Lukey boy,' he says. 'The force still with you, eh?'

Damian gives a wheezy laugh – he's on the fags again by the sound of it. Same old smug bastard he always was. Luke feels a strange urge to kick the other man's knees.

'Did I ever tell you, you look nothing like a Luke?'

'Countless times,' says Luke. 'Thought you'd moved to Yorkshire.'

'Yeah,' says Damian. He looks around, but no one else is listening. 'Thought there was more action back in the North West ... turns out I was right.'

Damian frowns for an instant and Luke recalls the awful events in Rotherham. They would've been covered on Damian's patch; the guy's putting on a front. If Luke remembers rightly, Damian has daughters himself.

'So,' Luke says, nodding towards the reporter preparing for camera. 'What happened to Geoff? Didn't he used to do most of the OBs. Samia Brennan, eh? Poached from the BBC?'

Damian shrugs.

'Not just one person reporting any more, Lukey boy. Gotta keep up with the times. Have to include the fairer sex in everything now.'

'Oh, for God's sake,' says Amanda. 'What a chauvinist b—'

'It's lovely to meet you, too,' says Damian.

'So, what's happening here?' says Luke. 'Know anything more than they're reporting?'

'Not much. CCTV picture of what appears to be Craig Wright in a red car ... bit of a banger ... old Peugeot, I think. Leanne Livesey gets in the back seat. But all we have to go on is a shit, grainy picture.'

'Why would she get in the back seat?'

Damian shrugs.

'Does Leanne live here?' Luke gestures to the brightly coloured building behind Damian.

'Yeah ... has been here a few years from what I gathered from those kids over there. Haven't made that official, though, as children aren't the most reliable of sources ... as you well know.'

'Think they'll talk to us?'

'They'll talk to anyone ... they're loving it. Think one of the matrons – or whatever you call them – is over there, so perhaps clear it with her first. Don't want you to get into trouble.'

'Well, obviously I wouldn't take what they say as fact ... I'll check before printing.'

'Yeah, course you will. "*A source close to the missing girl*" ... we all know that means we're making it up.'

'I'm a serious journalist.'

'I know that for a fact.' Damian salutes him. 'Good write-up of Bombay Spice last week ... though I'd recommend the Jalfrezi.'

'Fuck off, Damian.' Luke smiles and pats Damian's arm, before walking towards the low wall where about ten kids are sitting. 'See you around, mate,' he shouts behind him. You need to keep on the good side of everyone – Luke never knows when he might need Damian again, unfortunately.

'Just so you know,' Amanda says from the corner of her mouth, 'I'm not very good with kids.'

'Don't worry ... they're like normal people but smaller ... and more honest.'

Luke approaches a woman in an oversized skirt and cardigan. Her hair is short and grey, which makes her enormous orange butterfly earrings more prominent.

'Hello, there,' says Luke, holding out his hand. 'I'm from the *Chronicle*. Are you OK to talk?'

The woman looks at his hand before shaking it. Her hand is cold and dry. She folds her arms and bites her bottom lip.

'I'm afraid I won't be of much help,' she says. 'I can't talk about Leanne – she's only seventeen. And a young seventeen at that.'

'Is it all right if I have a chat with the older kids? We want to try to help get Leanne found ... we can put something on Facebook ... get a wider audience ... a lot of people don't watch the news these days. We'd only ask the same questions as they would ask.' Luke gestures to the crew, and bets this woman was swayed by the famous face of Samia Brennan.

'I suppose ... if you could run everything past me first before printing? I can't have any of the children named, or any sensitive information printed.'

'I'm only going to ask them if they saw this man.'

Luke gets the iPad from his inside coat pocket and

taps an icon on the home screen to bring up the mug-shot of Craig Wright.

'They think it might be him who was driving when Leanne was taken.'

'OK,' she says. 'I think that should be all right. You'll take everything you hear to the police, won't you? Every minute counts. That's what they say, isn't it?'

'It is. Thank you . . .'

'Fran. Fran Harrison.'

'Thanks so much, Fran.'

'You bloody lick-arse,' Amanda whispers in Luke's ear as they move towards the wall.

'It worked, didn't it?'

'Isn't it every *second* counts?'

'As if I was going to correct her.'

Luke's still holding his iPad.

'Afternoon,' he says to the kids lined up on the wall, his pulse quickening at the thought of speaking to streetwise teenagers. 'I was wondering if you recognise this man.'

'Well, fuck me,' says a lad of about sixteen. 'Are you some paedo showing little kids dirty pics?'

He nudges the younger lad next to him who gives a fake laugh. Luke knows it's fake – he used to do it all the time with his mates when he was the same age.

'I'm Luke Simmons. I'm from the *Chronicle*. It's a local newspaper.'

The lad runs his eyes from Luke's feet to his face.

'I know what the *Chronicle* is. I'm not stupid. I'm well versed in current affairs, don't you know.'

His mate gives a genuine laugh this time. 'Nice one, Dec,' he says.

'Dec?' says Luke. 'Is that a nickname?'

The lad's not laughing any more.

'No,' he says, his face contorted as though smelling something putrid. 'It's short for Declan.'

'Oh ... right.'

Luke used to feel as though he could mix with people of any age. He remembers being a teenager, thought he'd be approachable, empathic to anyone under the age of eighteen, but clearly he has no street cred at all (and they probably don't even call it that these days).

'If you could take a quick look at this photo,' says Luke. 'It could help find Leanne.'

Declan reaches into his pocket and pulls out a pair of glasses – his face is transformed in an instant. He takes the iPad and Luke feels slightly apprehensive. Just because he wears glasses doesn't mean the lad wouldn't thieve a £500 gadget. Luke scolds himself, again, for being so judgemental.

'Yeah,' says Declan. 'I saw him. He doesn't look like that any more. Hey, Jaden.' He shouts to the smaller boy sitting at the end of the line. 'Didn't you get a picture of that bloke the other day – the one that was talking to Leanne?' Declan looks at Luke. 'Jaden loves taking pictures ... everyone who comes here.'

Jaden, who looks to be about eight or nine, walks over to the older lad with a digital camera covered in scratches.

'My memory card only holds about a hundred,' he says to Declan.

'Give it 'ere.'

Jaden does as he's told, and Declan scrolls through the pictures.

'That's him.'

He gives the camera to Luke. Amanda peers over his shoulder to get a look.

'Bloody hell, Craig's changed,' she says.

The man in the photograph seems twice the size of the man Luke remembers in the courtroom − the same man he saw on the street corner. He's wearing jeans, a plain black T-shirt and a bomber jacket.

Luke takes the iPad from Declan and brings up a photograph of Jason.

'Have you seen this man, too?' Luke asks.

Declan shrugs. 'Nah. Not seen him before. But you do get a few dodgy blokes hanging about this street. If Franny McPhee over there caught them, they'd soon fuck off.'

'Why would they hang around here?'

'Why do most weird blokes want to hang around young girls?'

Luke looks up at Declan, surprised at the frankness and wisdom that just came out of his mouth.

'Did Franny Mc— I mean Fran. Did she never report anything to the police?'

He shrugs. 'Must've done. That's why they're searching for Leanne.' He takes off his glasses. 'She's all right is Leanne. She helps Jaden a lot ... he likes animals, you

187

see. They make him feel safe at night. She helps him clean out the cages and stuff, doesn't she, Jaden?'

The little kid sniffs and wipes his nose.

'Can I have my camera back, please?'

'Course. I'll just try to take a picture of this on my phone.'

Luke hands the camera back to Jaden.

'There's been another bloke driving past ... only the past week or so,' says Declan. 'Really slow, like a proper kerb-crawler. Must think we're so stupid that we don't notice. But this bloke was older ... about forty ... or sixty ... It's hard to tell when people are that old.'

'I'm nearly forty,' says Luke.

'Oh right. I thought you were about fifty,' the lad says, looking at Luke's belly.

Amanda covers her mouth, but her shoulders shake.

'Thanks, Declan, Jaden,' says Luke.

'Sorry, I shouldn't have laughed,' says Amanda as they head back to the car.

'Just because I'm a bloke doesn't mean things like that don't hurt.'

'Come on, he's only a kid.'

'Yeah, whatever,' says Luke, opening the car door.

When Luke pulls out on to the road, Amanda's still looking at the kids sitting in a row on the wall.

'You weren't lying when you said you weren't good with kids, were you?' says Luke. 'You didn't say a word to them. You weren't scared, were you?'

'A bit.' She gives a little laugh. 'But admit it. You were afraid, too.'

'Yeah. Ant or Dec was a bit intimidating, wasn't he? I wasn't that confident at his age – I was slightly terrified of grown-ups I didn't know.'

'Luke, you're not even that confident now.'

'Can't hear you.'

'Can you believe what Craig looks like now?' she says. 'I wouldn't have recognised him. He looks so different ... so intimidating.'

'I don't think those kids know that Craig's a convicted murderer. Can't see them being that blasé about the bloke if they knew that.'

'Maybe. Where to next?'

'Erica's. I want to check she's all right.'

21

Erica

The dining room door is still open from when the police barged their way through it. I walk in, bending to resurrect the wicker laundry basket that's on its side. They didn't move the small chest of drawers in front of the fireplace; they wouldn't think to look there – why would they? I doubt there are any remnants from the burnt clothing anyway.

When I found the blood-soaked blue T-shirt in Craig's dirty laundry, I washed, dried, and hid it. It was only a little thing – it must've shrunk in the wash. I ironed it as flat as I could and zipped it flush under a cushion cover.

They searched the whole of the house after Craig was arrested for the murder of Lucy. I stayed with Denise while they did it. Afterwards I went back, and it was as though someone had taken a demolition ball to the place. The contents of every cupboard had been taken out and thrown back in, leaving the floors clear for them to pull up the boards. Jenna Threlfall was still missing, you see. They didn't know where she was. I shuddered at the thought of her being hidden in my house – I've often had dreams about a body hidden somewhere. But those nightmares are nothing compared to what her parents will have gone through ... are still going through.

Why is this happening again? Am I being punished for what I did?

I move a few bits at the side of the chest of drawers then push it out of the way so the fireplace is clear. I take the letters out of my pocket and kneel before it.

I run my fingers through the ash in the hearth (why on earth didn't I get rid of it?). I shake it off, rub my hand on the rug I'm sitting on. Does blood turn to ash or does it evaporate? Whose DNA would be on my fingers if it lingered in the remains? The thought of it appals me. When had I turned into this person – a person who burned potential evidence? But then I realise that I've always been that person, a person who would do anything to protect her child. I didn't think he would be capable of such dreadful deeds, but I can't bury my head if it happens a second time. What's that phrase ... *Fool me once, shame on you. Fool me twice...* The shame. An emotion I'm familiar with – so familiar it's there from the moment I wake.

There's a pile of newspapers next to the hearth – they'll have been there for years. I reach for the top one; it's dated *Monday, 21 December 1981*. Its headline reads: *In 70 minutes, the lives of these brave men SHATTERED*.

I'm working on autopilot as I grab a sheet from it and scrunch it into a ball. Soon, half the newspaper's turned into a little pile of boulders. I pick out pieces of kindling from the basket at the side – surprisingly, it's still dry after Lord knows how long in this damp room.

I grab the box of Cook's Matches, take one out and strike it three times before it powers into a small flame. I throw it on to the newspaper and it gradually lights. I strike another, and another, spacing them out so soon all the paper has taken alight. The kindling begins to glow, then steadily starts to burn.

I unfold the first letter, but it's one I've already read. Should I read them all before I cast them to their grave? Would it be disrespectful not to?

I should stop acting like this is some sort of sacrifice. No one has been found; no one is dead. Not yet.

I throw it onto the burning fire – but there are no logs, nothing substantial: this fire won't last long. I watch as the letter glows around the edges before crumpling into black.

Some of the smoke is coming back to me – the chimney's not been swept for years. The smoke hurts my eyes. I cover the hearth with a sheet of newspaper, but that makes the fire erupt fuller into life.

'What the hell are you doing?'

I turn to see Craig in the doorway.

'I didn't hear you come in,' I say. 'Where have you been? I've not seen you for days!' I get up from the floor, grabbing the mantelpiece to pull myself up. I must stink of smoke. 'I've had the police round here looking for you ... that young girl's missing – the one who came round the other day.'

'I heard on the radio,' says Craig.

He's not looking at me – he's staring at what's in my hand.

'They say she got into your car.'

'I haven't got a car, Mum. Don't you believe me?'

'I didn't say I didn't believe you, I said it was what *they* said. And you wouldn't be here if you were with her, would you?' I snap.

'What have you got there?' he asks, stepping closer to me.

He snatches the letters from me – an edge of one of them cuts into my skin. He seems to tower over me. 'Have you been going through my things?'

'It's better *me* finding them than the police, don't you think?'

'The police wouldn't be interested in these.'

'But they would, Craig. She's only young. Did she tell you her age?' My voice shakes, and my hands are cold, sweating. He's looking into my eyes now, glaring at me. There are beads of sweat above his top lip.

'Stop it, Craig. You're starting to scare me. I'm only trying to protect you.'

'You really shouldn't have gone through my things, Mum.'

'Everything will be OK if you tell the police the truth.'

He gives a short bark of a laugh. 'Like I did last time. No fucking way.' He takes a deep breath, then steps away from me. 'I only came home for a few things.'

'You need to stay here. They'll recall you to prison if you don't stay here.'

He bangs a fist on the wall.

'Will you stop it?' His voice is loud; his eyes are bloodshot, wide. 'All your interfering didn't help me last time, so why don't you just keep your nose out. I already had an alibi for Jenna. A concrete one.'

'What do you mean?'

'That I was with Lawton at the garage, but you lied for me.' He steps closer to me. 'Did you think I meant something else?'

'I ... I ...'

He grabs the top of my arms.

'You're squeezing too hard,' I say. 'Why are you doing this to me? I'm on your side – you're not thinking straight.'

'What did you do?'

'You're not making sense.'

He shakes me once.

'I'm your mother – you shouldn't be doing this to me. What's happened to you?'

'Tell me what you did!' he shouts.

'I burned that top ... seventeen, eighteen years ago ... the one in your laundry basket with blood on it. I panicked ... Lucy was missing ... I'd never known you to have nosebleeds before ... so I took it out ... washed it ... hid it, then burned it after the police didn't find it.'

He lets go of my arms.

'What are you talking about? What top? Why are you talking about nosebleeds?'

'It was a blue top ... a plain T-shirt ... one you bought

194

with your own money. You were acting so strange that week. When Lucy and Jenna went missing I didn't see you for days ... then you—'

'But that could've helped me.'

'What do you mean?'

Slowly he brings his face closer to mine. I can't stop shivering; the tears are pouring down my face, dripping on to the floor.

'You don't know what you've done,' he hisses.

He walks backwards into the hallway, through the kitchen and out of the back door.

I grab the door handle for support in case my knees give way under me.

I don't know what just happened, and I'm shocked to realise that I'm relieved he's gone. I don't know what he's capable of any more. It's not normal to be afraid of your own son.

There's a bang on the front door.

The letterbox flaps open. Whoever it is can't have seen Craig leave. I'm going to get rid of that blasted letterbox.

'Erica,' says a man's voice. 'It's Luke Simmons from the *Chronicle*. Just wanted to check you're OK.'

22

Luke

Luke remembers the first time he stood outside this door. He had sat in his car, sometimes Claire sitting next to him, sometimes Amy, the work experience lass at the time. When he'd knocked on the door, there had been no answer, even though he knew she was in. She never went out, not since the trial, not that he'd seen. 'I thought you might want to give your side of the story,' he'd said. She hadn't replied, hadn't opened the door. He knew he had some cheek after printing that interview with her 'best friend', but that was his job. Denise Bamber – that was her name. Shit. Why hadn't he realised? She must be Jason's mother.

He doubts that the two women are still friends. Erica probably never spoke to Denise after that – and she'd not even been paid for it. He often wondered what drove people to take stories to the papers. OK, the nationals sometimes paid for kiss-and-tells, ratting on someone famous, but the local news? That's different: more personal.

He knocks again.

'She's probably gone out,' says Amanda.

Luke turns to her and raises his eyebrows, putting a finger to his lips.

'She hardly ever goes out,' he whispers. 'She can hear us.'

Amanda rolls her eyes.

Luke opens the letterbox.

'It's Luke, Erica,' he shouts. 'Are you all right in there?' He straightens back up. 'I think I saw something,' he says quietly.

'Let's have a look,' says Amanda, bending down.

He elbows her shoulder gently, trying to signal her to be quiet. She stands straight.

'She's there,' she says, softly this time. 'She's closed the back door and she's walking towards us.'

The front door opens.

Erica stands behind it; one arm on the door, the other behind her back. She looks at Luke, then Amanda.

'I'm a bit busy at the moment,' she says.

'You phoned me,' says Luke. 'Did you want to talk?' He tries to look over her shoulder. 'Is Craig in there with you?'

Luke feels a little braver with Amanda next to him, though his heart pounds at the thought of seeing Craig. But if he has Leanne Livesey, he's hardly going to pop home, is he?

'No, he's not here. The police have already been.' She looks to the ground. 'Didn't tear the place apart like last time, though.'

'Can we come in?' says Amanda. 'We only want to see that you're all right.'

Erica narrows her eyes at his colleague.

'This is Amanda,' says Luke. 'She works with me at the paper.'

She holds her hand out to Erica, but the older woman just looks at it. Her face looks the same as Luke remembers, perhaps a little fuller in the cheeks, but there aren't the many wrinkles he'd expect from a smoker. Her skin is pale, though – almost grey. Her thick hair – once light brown – is peppered with grey, still in the same old-fashioned hairstyle with the thick fringe that might be considered trendy again.

She's wearing a black jumper and dark blue jeans that look as though they might be elasticated around the waist. Helen has some of them, but they're tighter and she calls them jeggings; they're probably different things. Helen's make her arse look fantastic.

Luke looks up at Erica's blue eyes, blushing at the incongruous thoughts running through his mind.

'Are you OK, Erica?' says Luke. 'You don't look well.'

'I have to go and lie down,' she says. 'I've had a strange day, that's all.'

'Have you any idea where Craig might be?' he says.

She shakes her head.

'His picture's all over the news ... it's an old picture, though. Can we come in and talk about it?'

He sees her hesitating – it's not a no.

Come on, Erica, he thinks. Let us in. He's wanted to

see inside this house for years, often imagining what's it's like.

'OK,' she says. 'But only for a few minutes. I'm not feeling too well.'

Luke steps over the threshold. To the right is a curtain-less window, frosted glass like a bathroom window. On the sill is a large vase, full of water, but no flowers. Next to that is a black-and-white photograph of a woman sitting at a table with a cigarette in her hand. She's wearing a paper hat – one you get in a Christmas cracker. She has a light smile on her face, but a sadness in her eyes.

'Is that your mother?' asks Luke.

Erica seems surprised when she looks at it.

'Yes,' she says. 'I forget that's there.'

Luke looks at the wooden floor and is reminded of Pamela Valentine's words. He imagines the woman in the photograph lying at the bottom of the stairs, and makes a mental note to get a copy of her death certificate.

'Come on through,' she says. 'It's warm today, isn't it?'

Amanda raises her eyebrows at Luke as Erica walks them through to the living room. It's nearly minus one outside – and it's freezing in this house. Luke smells something burning, but the fire in the living room is electric. It's one of those that has bars, but on top there are faux coals that glow when switched on. It must be from the sixties.

'I can smell burning,' says Amanda.

'Oh,' says Erica. 'We've a fireplace in the dining room. Sometimes you can smell other houses' smoke come down our chimney. Can I get you a cup of tea?'

'Yes,' says Luke. 'That'd be great, thanks.'

She gestures for them to sit down before walking slowly out of the room. Amanda chooses the armchair next to the fire. It's part of a three-piece suite that must've been all the rage over forty years ago: brown fabric. Luke can't tell if it's bobbly through age or design.

Luke leans towards Amanda.

'Erica looks terrible,' he whispers.

'I expect she's anxious about her son,' says Amanda, looking around the room.

The old-style television in the corner is huge. Luke's surprised it can still receive a signal – he'd thought big TVs were obsolete these days. Or is that something manufacturers tell us? On top of it is a silver set-top box and two framed photographs. One is of a baby, so tiny it looks premature, fragile – the hat on its head seems far too big. The other is of a schoolboy, around nine or ten, with his fringe cut straight across, but the hair is shiny golden brown. There's a gap where the tooth next to his canine should be – it must've been late coming, poor kid. Luke wonders when it all went wrong for Craig, for Erica.

In the cabinet under it is a DVD player and a line of films. Luke spots *The Notebook, Heaven Can Wait* and *Jerry Maguire* among them. *The Notebook* is one of Helen's favourites, though she can't even watch the beginning now without crying.

At the end of the settee that Luke's sitting on is a bookcase. He recognises the spines of the rows and rows of Mills & Boons. His gran loves them – Luke's mum still asks the charity shop to save them for her. Luke didn't have Erica down as a romance fan and she's at least twenty years younger than his grandmother.

Erica's always seemed so calm, together, apart from the tear she shed after the sentencing. He wonders how many times she's cried over her son since then.

There's a laptop in the corner on a metal computer desk. He goes over to it; the screensaver is on: a picture of a cottage made of stone surrounded by trees.

Erica brings through a tray and places it on the coffee table in the middle of the room.

'It's in the Lake District,' she says. 'It's always been a dream of mine to live there.'

There are only two cups. Erica stands next to the television, her hands clasped in front of her.

'Please help yourself to milk and sugar.'

Luke walks to the coffee table, puts sugar in a cup and pours the tea. The metal pot burns his fingers, but he tries not to yelp.

'What do you use the laptop for?' says Luke, sitting back on the settee.

'You think because I'm over sixty,' she says haughtily, 'I wouldn't know how to use a computer?'

'No, no. I didn't mean it like that.'

There's a brief silence.

'It's all right,' she says. 'I use it to talk to my friends. They've been through the same thing I have. It's good to feel connected, isn't it? Especially when everyone around here hates me.'

'Why didn't you move?'

She sits down on the other side of the settee, plucking a tissue from the box on the table and dabs her forehead.

'I'm beginning to ask myself the same question. At first, it was because I wanted to be near Craig. Then he was moved to another prison – they're always moving them, aren't they? Anyway, the longer time went on, Craig always said how good it would be to get back home, back to this house. I've lived here nearly all my life.'

'Do you see much of Denise these days?' says Luke.

'No.'

She says it in a way that tells Luke not to enquire further, almost hurt that he changed the subject so abruptly. She's held the grudge against Denise for almost twenty years, but then Luke supposes he would, too, if anyone so much as said a cross word against his daughters, let alone gave an interview to the local press.

'Like brothers, they were,' Denise had said. 'Thick as thieves. Even though Jason was a year older. Like family, Craig was.'

But why would Denise say all that other stuff about someone she considered family? Her son wasn't perfect either. But he wasn't a murderer.

'That name I gave you. You haven't got back to me about it yet. Did you find him?'

Luke glances at Amanda. He's heard the name Pete Lawton before today – the police couldn't find the man.

He can't believe that Erica's still going on about this. Doesn't she realise he can see straight through her?

'No,' he says. 'I can't find any trace of him.'

'I've been searching for him for years. There must be CCTV or something, but the people I've contacted about it have all either blanked me or sworn at me.'

'I doubt there would still be CCTV from that long ago.'

'Do you have any idea how frustrating this all is?' she says. 'I know he didn't do it.'

Luke hears a waver in her voice when she says that. Is she changing her mind now that Leanne Livesey is missing? Surely she can't cover for her son again.

He needs to take a tentative approach with Erica.

'What was Craig like as a child?' asks Luke.

'Oh, you know,' she says quietly. 'Same as any other boy, I expect. I suppose you could call him a mummy's boy ... though I don't think he is now. Don't print anything like that, will you? He wouldn't like people knowing that about him.' She puts a shaking hand on her forehead as if checking her own temperature. Her skin has gone from pale to flushed in minutes. 'He always wanted to be on the football team, bless him. He rehearsed for the team ... not rehearsed ... what do you call it? Anyway, they even gave him a place, but the bullying ... the name-calling ... got too much. You try to protect them from all that, don't you?'

'And you told the police that Craig was with you the day Jenna disappeared?'

She frowns, seemingly confused at his change of direction.

'Is this why you're really here?' she says, standing. 'I was questioned at the time. Craig wasn't charged with the murder of Jenna.'

'I know,' says Luke, glancing at Amanda. 'It wasn't mentioned in the press before, but there were items missing from Jenna's body. Did you know about those?'

He can feel Amanda's eyes burning into him. He knows he's probably not meant to give this information away, but it's been buried for nearly seventeen years and that's not helped anyone.

'What items? What were they?'

He can't read Erica. Her face is blank, but her eyes glisten with tears, or rage, he can't tell which.

'A blue T-shirt and a necklace with a daisy on it.'

She gives a sharp intake of breath.

Luke knew she would know.

'Have you seen them, Erica?'

'No, I haven't.' She says it quietly, not meeting Luke's gaze. 'I wouldn't withhold items I thought would be evidence.'

'Not even to protect your son?'

She stares at Luke then finally shakes her head again.

There's a bang from outside. While he's never considered himself a coward, Luke doesn't have the bravado some of his mates have. What if Craig comes through the door and threatens him and Amanda?

'How long were the police here before?' he asks Erica.

204

He's half surprised she hasn't already thrown him out. It must be the shock.

'Only a few minutes ... said they'd found a car on the docks matching the description of the one on the news.'

She's looking at the carpet, not meeting Luke's eyes.

'Did they find anything?'

She shakes her head.

There's another bang.

'We ought to get going, Erica,' he says, standing up quickly. He feels nauseous, jumpy. Why did he think it was a good idea to come here when Craig's a wanted criminal? The man could use the pair of them as hostages to keep himself safe. Fleetingly, Luke thinks this would make a great story, but his wife would bloody kill him, putting himself in the way of danger. 'Come on, Amanda. Let's check out the docks.'

Amanda stands, rubbing the tops of her arms from the cold.

'One other thing,' says Luke. He pulls out his phone and shows Erica Jaden's picture of the man who took Leanne. 'Is this Craig?'

Erica steps towards him – the top of her arm brushes against his; her head is near his shoulder. As he breathes in, he smells nothing, not even shampoo.

'It's not clear. It's taken from too far away,' she says. 'I can't be a hundred per cent sure.'

The woman doesn't take the phone for a closer look but leans over so Luke can see the back of her neck, and a gold chain that he hadn't noticed from the front.

'No, I'm sorry,' she says. 'I don't recognise him. It could be anyone.'

'Thanks anyway,' says Luke.

'Bye,' says Erica quietly.

Her front door closes behind them as soon as he and Amanda step outside.

In the car, Luke automatically turns the radio on to hear the local news, but Toto's 'Africa' is playing.

'Erica's not how I thought she'd be,' says Amanda as they pull away from the house.

'What did you expect?'

'I don't know. I thought she'd be older, I guess. Her skin has hardly any wrinkles ... apart from round the eyes.'

'Well, they do say sun accounts for most ageing of the skin. She doesn't go out much.'

'She's lying though, isn't she?'

'Yes. It's clearly Craig in that picture. And she knows something about Jenna's belongings.'

'We have to tell the police.'

'They'll have searched the place at the time. Erica wouldn't still have them in the house. They could be anywhere.'

'So, we'll probably never know where. We can't print anything on a hunch. I can't see Erica incriminating her own son by telling them now.'

'No,' says Luke. 'Neither can I.'

'Well, we can check out the car on the docks. Perhaps Craig will be there.'

'I doubt that.'

Luke expects that Craig will be long gone. He won't make it easy for the police this time. If he's convicted of kidnapping Leanne, Craig will never be a free man again.

23

Erica

I close the front door behind them, resting against it.

I should've known about that top.

But I did, deep down, didn't I? That's why I burned it. The necklace. I need to find that necklace – the one that's in Craig's drawer upstairs. How long had it been there, though? The police searched the place twice – they would've found it – it wasn't hidden.

Unless it's only recently been placed in there.

I go up the stairs and into his room, walking straight to the drawer. I pull it open, closing my eyes. Willing it not to be there.

I open my eyes, and it's gone.

I rifle through the other items, open and search the rest of the drawers. I can't have imagined it in there. Someone must've taken it. I kneel on the floor, exhausted. Is that why Craig came back earlier?

I take a few deeps breaths and then I stand.

There was banging outside earlier, when the reporters were here. If Craig is hiding in the shed, then he can answer my questions. It's time for us to be honest with each other.

I step outside, my feet are cold and damp from the paving slabs as I reach the shed. It's empty. The back gate is pulled to, but the bolt hasn't been pulled across. I open it, but the alley is clear – it's not bin day, so there are no wheelies for him to hide behind.

A coldness runs through me as I close it and pull the bolt across. If he had nothing to hide, why would he run?

I walk slowly back to the house. There are no faces at the neighbours' windows; no one is watching me. I thought I was doing right by Craig, staying here – always in easy travelling distance for his weekly visits, always waiting in case he was released. I need to speak to Anne Marie – she'll know what to do. She's my best friend now and I've never even met her. I can talk to her about anything, but it's not the same as speaking face to face, knowing what someone is thinking without them saying a word. Like what I had with Denise.

Why did she say those things about Craig? Why couldn't she have just been there for me?

I lean against the inside of the back door as it clicks shut.

Come on, Erica. There's no point crying now. I blink quickly, even though there's no one here to witness if I cry or I don't.

I go through to the living room to clear up the tray after the visitors. Luke seems a nice sort, even though he did print those lies Denise told about Craig. But he was only doing his job.

I pause.

If I can forgive a stranger so easily, why can't I forgive Denise? She's knocked on the door a few times over the years. She even carried on sending me birthday cards after – though she's not done that for the past three years. She sent me a letter a few years after the newspaper article came out, but I burnt it. I wish I hadn't. I remember a few of the lines: *Not a day goes by when I don't think about you. Remember the time we caught the bus to Morecambe and got straight back on the bus home because the place was full of old people ... The night before my wedding is still the best night of my life ... It's been so hard living without you as my best friend.*

And then I recall why I haven't forgiven her: because she didn't ask for my forgiveness. She has never said she was sorry. I thought remembering that would strengthen my resolve, push her further away from my mind, but it doesn't. I think about her every day, too. My old best friend.

But I can't be sentimental about it; I must keep my resolve.

I go to the bookcase, and in between *The Lives and Loves of a She-Devil* and *Watership Down* is Denise's article. I unfold the now-yellow newspaper.

INSIDE THE MIND OF A KILLER

Denise Bamber, once a close family friend of Craig Wright, has today revealed the secrets behind Preston's most hated man.

Craig Wright, 20, was jailed last week for the murder of Lucy Sharpe, after dramatically changing his plea mid-trial.

A source close to the family has revealed she knew he was capable of murder.

'He was quiet, and you know what they say about those,' said Denise, 44, also from Preston. 'My son was friends with him, but it all went wrong when Craig turned to drugs.'

Ever-present and loyal during Craig Wright's trial was his mother, Erica.

'He never knew his dad, though,' said Denise. 'In fact, no one did. She didn't even tell me, and I'm her best friend.'

I don't need to read any further. I put the article back in its place and wipe my hands as though they're covered in filth.

I grab the cup and saucer from the arm of the chair. Lipstick all over the rim. That Amanda could've at least wiped it with a tissue from the box on the table – or even her finger, for goodness' sake.

I wanted to scream out when Luke showed me that photograph on his mobile. The words wouldn't come out that it *was* Craig.

I'm sure they'll figure it out for themselves soon enough. They probably didn't believe me when I said that it wasn't.

I try Craig's mobile phone but again there's no answer. It's ten past five – teatime. I can't even remember if I have any food in the house and I can't go outside, not today. Not when the police are probably watching the house and I've just flushed all those drugs down the toilet. I washed the tins with bleach and put them back in the shed, but there still might be a trace of it on them. And probably my fingerprints, too, as I didn't think to wear gloves.

I should go and wipe them again, but all motivation has left me. It wasn't me who'd grown the stuff.

In the living room, I pull open the curtains. I've nothing to hide – I've done nothing wrong. All I've done is protect my son.

I go over to my laptop. I haven't been on the forum for a while. I log on to find three messages from Anne Marie, and one from Trevor.

AnneMarie2348: Hi, Erica. Wondering if you were OK after the other night? x

AnneMarie2348: Send me a quick message, will you? I'm worried after what you said about being afraid of Craig x.

AnneMarie2348: I've seen the news online. Please message me ASAP. He looks so different now compared to the pictures you showed me. Can you give me your phone number? Can't believe we haven't spoken. Lots of love xx

TexanDude: Hey there, Erica. Anne Marie contacted me. Said your boy's in the news over there. I know how you're feeling. Shane was arrested three days after he was released, but they had the wrong guy. Let us know you're ok, hun.

I wish he'd stop calling me *hun*.

But it's nice they're thinking of me; it makes me feel less alone.

NorthernLass: Hi both. I'm fine, just. Craig came home about half an hour ago, so that means he can't be with the girl, doesn't it? He wasn't himself, though (I'm wondering what that actually is these days). He was so angry, but I don't blame him. I made some bad choices years ago and now they've come back. I think some journalists already know what I've done. I should contact the police and tell them what I know, but I might make things worse for him.

I stand and walk towards the living room window, resting my hands on the windowsill. The message to my friends was probably too rambling, it won't have made sense to them, but I can't put too much on there. If the police were to seize my computer, then it will incriminate me as well as Craig. It's what I deserve, anyway.

There's nothing outside to the left, but there's a car slowly crawling along the road from the right.

I will myself to stay there and see who it is. My shoulders are tight, tense, my legs feel unstable – I hope my knees stay strong. The car's getting close. I inch my face forward, so my nose touches the net curtains.

It's him.

Oh God, it's him.

I haven't seen him in over thirty-five years. I didn't know he was out. I turn quickly away, sliding down to the floor, the sill scraping the whole of my back as I do.

He can't have seen me properly through the nets, but he knows where I live, he's always known. He's not in the same car, of course. He wouldn't be seen dead in an old banger unless it was a classic.

I close my eyes and I can still see inside that rusty brown-coloured Cortina; I can smell the leather seats, my legs stuck to them in the heat.

It was the beginning of March 1979 and I was wearing a dress, because he'd told me to wear one. It was yellow, and it skimmed my knees and was made of a stretchy, jersey fabric. He drove us to Southport and along the road that runs beside the beach. The evenings were getting lighter so Blackpool Tower was visible over the water. I yearned, right then, to be with Denise, and for us to be teenagers when the days seemed to last longer.

I was twenty-three, then. I didn't feel twenty-three; I felt fifteen. But there I was, with him, parked up in a car park surrounded by sand dunes. He flicked the radio off – even though I was enjoying listening to 'Hopelessly Devoted to You'.

The silence after that felt charged. He twisted in his seat to face me. I looked out of the window behind him, but it seemed we were suddenly alone. I wanted to shout out of the window or run away, but I had chosen to be there, hadn't I? I'd got myself ready that evening, knowing what was about to happen. Denise had told me all about it. She said that it would hurt at first and that she bled a bit, but it was good to get it over and done with. She hadn't wanted to be a virgin forever and neither did I. But she was married now, it was different for her.

I'd waited for him at the top of Brindle Street near the library.

'Will you pick me up from my house next time?' I said to him after I closed the passenger door. 'My mother would love to meet you.'

I don't know why I said that because an introduction to my mother was the last thing I wanted. But I was curious to hear his reply. If I was about to give myself to him, then I reasoned I could ask him anything and he'd have to give an answer.

'You know that's impossible, Erica.'

'But why? I know you said not to mention I was seeing you to anyone – and I haven't – but I want to know that you care about me ... that we have a future.'

We'd been courting for nearly three months, but our meetings were infrequent: sometimes once a week, sometimes fortnightly. 'Maybe he's a spy,' Denise had said a few weeks before, but I didn't like talking about him – it didn't feel right. I felt my loyalties were with him, however misguided. Maybe that was when our friendship began to be tainted.

He reached over and slid my thick fringe to the side.

I hated that – my forehead was small compared to the rest of my face; it was mine to hide.

'Let's not spoil the evening,' he said. 'Do you remember that time when I took you to see *Watership Down*? Even though you knew I thought it was a kids' film. I did that for you, didn't I?'

He said it as though it were years ago, not weeks.

'Yes,' I said. 'But I wouldn't show that to a child. It made me cry.' I laughed.

Sometimes I could be myself with him, at other times I felt shy, self-conscious. He seemed much older than me but, at twenty-four, it was only a year's difference.

'Look,' he said, 'the sun's setting. Bet you've never seen that before.'

Of course I have, I wanted to tell him. From my bedroom window. I can see the sunset every day in the summer because we live on a hill and I can see the water at the docklands. It's prettier than it is now, in Southport, I wanted to say, because I can't see the sea here for the sand dunes – they're ugly and dry and covered in that grass that almost cuts you when you walk past it at the wrong angle.

Then I looked into his eyes and it was like in the books that I read. His eyes looked deep into my soul and it was only us right then; we were alone in the world and then he kissed me.

After a few minutes (I wanted it to be longer) he said, 'Let's get into the back. I can get closer to you there.'

He'd laid a blanket on the back seat; he'd come prepared.

216

'We should get engaged,' he said as he put his hand on my thigh; I was sitting in the middle – he was behind the driver's seat.

'You'd have to meet my mother, then. Wouldn't you?'

'I've heard a few things about your mother,' he said. 'She's quite a character in the town, isn't she?'

'No,' I said, taken aback that he'd even heard of her. 'Why would anyone want to talk about my mother?'

He shrugged. 'They say she's loaded – has money tucked under the mattress, so to speak. I overheard one person say she had an affair with a millionaire ... that he paid money for you and your brother's upkeep.'

'That's ridiculous,' I said. 'People have obviously got nothing better to talk about, so they make up stories. My dad ran off when I was born ... they were married, you know.'

He shrugged again and looked out of the window. I gazed at his neck and his ears while he wasn't looking. His skin was so smooth. He reached into his pocket.

'I got you something.'

He handed me what looked like a ball of navy blue tissue. I peeled it open, and inside was a gold chain with a matching heart about half an inch in diameter. I couldn't decide if it was really expensive, or really cheap.

'Does it open?'

He took it from me and pulled the hearts apart.

'You can put two pictures in it,' he said.

'I don't have a photograph of you.'

While I was holding my hand up to admire it, he put his head on my lap, facing away from me. His fingers stroked my ankles, brought them up towards my knees and slid his hand up my skirt.

'What are you doing?'

'It's time, don't you think? We've been seeing each other for ages. I feel like I've known you all my life.'

'You feel that, too?' I said.

He sat up and gently pushed me down, so I lay on the back seat. I knew what was going to happen. I'd been worrying about that moment since I first knew it existed. I thought it would be in a bed, though. I thought people got naked to do it, but he just slid my knickers off and put his trousers around his ankles. It hurt so much I thought there'd be lots of blood when he finished, but I couldn't see any. It must have sunk into the tartan blanket – it was red after all. Perhaps that's the way he planned it. It only lasted a few minutes and I kept waiting for the passion to take over, but I barely felt anything but pain.

He laid on top of me, his full weight almost crushing me, as though he were dead.

'That was amazing, Erica.' His breath was hot against the sticky sweat on my neck and I wanted to run out of the car and into the sea to get cool and clean again.

'Yes,' I mumbled, anyway.

'Maybe next time you could go on top. You might enjoy it more that way.'

I didn't reply, but his words made me realise this wasn't his first time.

We saw each other for a month more after that, until he suddenly turned to me on the back seat and said, 'How come you've never said no?'

'What do you mean?'

And he said, 'Your period.'

I'd never heard a man say it out loud like that and so frank. Even Mother called them *the monthlies*. I blushed even more (the vodka that he always brought gave me flushes). He took his hands away from me and said, 'I need to get you back home.'

The look in his eyes, then, I thought, was pure hate.

He probably still hates me. I wrote to him at his workplace when I found out I was expecting Craig but got no reply. I couldn't very well turn up at his house or his office. He'd abandoned me when I was at my most vulnerable – couldn't he see that? I felt so alone, especially after what happened with my mother.

Is this the first time that he's driven down my street, or is this the first time I've caught him? Why would he be coming here after all these years of no contact? He doesn't deserve to have Craig in his life – I've done all the hard work. How dare he come back now!

There's a knock on the door. A shriek comes out of my mouth; I cover it with my hands. My shoulders are tight as I lean closer to the wall; I feel rooted to the floor, shaking.

Why won't people leave me alone? I just want to be left alone. Please don't let it be him.

A tap on the window above my head.

'I know you're in there, Erica. I can see your feet

under the windowsill. It's urgent. I need to speak to you about Craig.'

It's Denise.

24

Luke

It's not far to the docklands from Erica's house. Usually, if anything has happened – a body in the water, say – the police will erect a white tent that's visible from the roadside, but today, Luke can't see anything that resembles a crime-scene tent along the waterfront.

'Do you think she misheard the police?' says Amanda. 'Looks like there's nothing here.'

'I'll drive all the way round. There's that road just off the marina ... leads to the estuary.'

Luke turns the car around, eyeing up the burger van in the car park, but ignores his growling stomach. He's tempted, but this is the most excitement he's had at work for months, maybe years.

They pass the boatyard on the right and immediately after see four or five police cars near another car that's smoking. Luke turns down the road. There are houses on the left that overlook the water. He parks alongside the barriers and they both get out.

Amanda pulls out a scarf from her inside pocket and wraps it around her neck. The abandoned car has been driven up a hill where the road ends. It's a maroon 2001 Peugeot 406. Luke hasn't seen one of those on the road for a few years.

'Looks like someone tried to set fire to it,' says Amanda. 'But they didn't do a very good job.'

'All right, Mands?' says a policeman leaning against the railings. He's warming his gloved hands by breathing into them. 'Never thought you were a hotshot reporter. Thought you just checked what was trending on Twitter.'

'Too funny, Steve,' says Amanda. 'Call that proper police work? If you weren't just standing around, you wouldn't be so cold.'

'I'll have you know that standing around is one of the most important parts of the job.'

'Is this the car Leanne Livesey was seen getting into?'

'I'm fine, thank you. How are you?'

She rolls her eyes. 'Well?'

Steve shrugs. 'I reckon there aren't many of these about any more. Surprised it still runs.'

'Was there anyone or anything inside?'

It seems Amanda is far more comfortable questioning police officers than children.

'You know I can't answer that.'

'It was worth a try.'

'No sign of Craig Wright, then?' asks Luke.

The copper shakes his head, but Luke reckons he's the last person Steve would be telling.

'Whoever it was did a shit job of setting it on fire,' says Amanda.

'They didn't try to set fire to it,' says Steve, breathing another load of hot air into his hands. 'It was the engine . . . it overheated.'

'Come on, Luke,' says Amanda. 'Let's go and have a look around.'

'Hey, hey.' Steve reaches out a hand. 'You can't just go wandering round. There are officers searching the area. Unless you fancy answering a few questions yourself.'

Amanda rolls her eyes and tuts.

Luke looks over at the Peugeot. The bonnet's up and the smoke, on closer inspection, is just steam. There must be signs in it that Leanne has been in there – DNA, hair strands. He knows Craig's behind this. It's how it was with Lucy: the police found the empty car first.

'Come on,' he says to Amanda.

As they turn around to walk back to his car, Luke spots a man in a car at the top of the road. He gets out. He's tall, dark-haired; his hands are in his pockets. From here, he looks too old to be Craig, but there's something familiar about him.

He stops at his own car door.

'Open up then,' says Amanda. 'What are you waiting for?' She follows Luke's gaze. 'What's he doing, staring like that?'

Luke narrows his eyes. It seems the man hasn't seen them watching him.

'Maybe he's a rubbernecker.'

'That's all *we* are at the moment,' she says. 'There's no story here.'

'We've got a burned-out car.'

'I thought you never lied in your articles.'

'It's not lying. It's true.'

'Yeah, but you're stretching it a bit. We don't know for sure if it's the same car and it overheated – it wasn't burnt out.'

Luke presses the fob on his keyring; Amanda opens the passenger door.

'I might go and ask him if he's seen anything,' he says.

The man is about fifty metres away. Luke pretends to look around, at the houses, at the boats over the water in the yard – anywhere but into the man's eyes. He wants him to think he's not approaching him; he doesn't want to startle him. He's only ten metres away now, and Luke chances a glance at him. Definitely too old to be Craig.

Shit. The man saw him looking. He jumps back into his car.

'Hey, wait!' shouts Luke. 'Can I just have a quick word?'

The car starts; Luke bangs on the window. He feels the adrenaline running through him, making him braver than he thought he could be.

'I'm not police ... I only want to ask if you know—'

The man presses on the accelerator, and the car screeches off.

Luke runs back to his car.

'What the hell, Luke?' Amanda says as he gets behind the wheel. 'You're not bloody Ross Kemp. What if that guy had a knife or something?'

'I didn't really think about it,' he says, trying to catch his breath from the short run.

He feels his heart pumping, endorphins making him feel alive.

'Bloody hell though, Mandy. That was amazing.'

'Come on, then, T.J. Hooker.'

They fasten their seat belts. Luke starts the ignition and executes a perfect three-point turn.

'Let's see if we can find him,' he says, turning right at the end of the road.

'OK. But, Luke ...'

'What?'

'Don't ever call me Mandy again.'

'Come on, Luke,' says Amanda. 'We've circled the docks twice.'

'Hang on. Look over there.'

Luke pulls into the car park and stops the car near the Mexican restaurant.

'What?' says Amanda.

'There's his car.' Luke squints into the distance. 'He's sitting on a bench near the water.'

'How the hell did you see him there?'

Luke gets out and starts jogging towards him. The man on the bench has his head in his hands.

Luke stops running as he approaches.

'Excuse me,' says Luke.

He looks up and stands.

'Wait. I'm not police. I'm a friend of Craig's.'

The man sits back down.

'Really?'

'Yes.' Luke sits down next to him. 'I haven't seen him for days and he owes me a pint. I'm worried – the police are looking for him.'

'I know.'

'My name's Luke.'

'I'm Alan. Alan Lucas. You've probably heard of me if you're a friend of Craig's.'

'Of course.'

Luke senses he's said something amiss; the man is looking at him intensely, taking in every feature of Luke's face.

Shit. He doesn't even know who this man is. He could be dangerous, violent. The reason he might seem familiar to Luke is probably because he's seen a mugshot of him.

'They're looking for the wrong person,' says Alan. 'Craig didn't take that kid.'

'What?' Luke jerks his head back, feels a fluttering in his stomach at the thought of an inside story. 'How do you know that?'

'He's been staying with me.'

'But ... doesn't he have a curfew? He has to stay at his mum's.'

'At Erica's? Nah. The police have been there already. Craig won't stay there, not for long.'

'If Craig doesn't have Leanne, then why doesn't he go to the police? It'll be obvious that he doesn't have her if he's at the station.'

'*The station*? Who *are* you?'

'I said. A friend. I'm looking out for him, that's all.'

'Well then, you'll know that if a body turns up, Craig will already be where they want him. In the *station*.'

'Have you known Craig for a while?' says Luke.

'Not as long as I'd have liked. Life was complicated thirty-eight years ago.'

'Have you known him that long?'

'No. I've a lot of regrets.'

'Actually,' says Luke, trying to read the mind of the man in front of him, 'if I'm honest, Craig has never mentioned an Alan Lucas.'

'No, well he wouldn't have done. I thought you were taking the piss earlier. Pretending to be his friend when you weren't. I've only just got in touch with Craig. Saw him on the news. I didn't see it the first time round. Too much going on. Wasn't even in this country.'

'Are you a relative?'

'Yes,' says Alan. He looks across the water, narrowing his eyes. 'I'm his father.'

25
Erica

'Come on, Erica,' says Denise. 'I don't want to be shouting in the street. You know what they're like around here.'

'Shouting in the street's not as bad as running to the local paper to yell about it.'

'Your neighbour opposite's looking out of his window,' she says. She must be leaning close to the glass because she's not shouting any more. 'Come on, love. Let me in. We can talk properly.' There's a gentle thud on the window, like she's leaning against it. 'I miss you.'

I slowly stand and turn to face her.

She's looking as old as I am, but she probably dyes her hair as it's still blonde and I can't see any grey from here. The shade's too harsh for her, now; it makes her face look too pale.

She still wears blue eyeliner, even though I told her it stopped being fashionable when the eighties ended. She still tilts her head to the side when she's sorry; her lips still purse together when she knows she's wrong and wants me to forgive her. We were friends for over thirty years before she did what she did.

I walk to the front door, my legs like jelly.

I open the door. She seems smaller, somehow. She was always such a presence – a firecracker, my mother called her; she really liked Denise, even though they never spent much time together.

'Come in, then,' I say.

I stand aside and close the door behind her.

'Go through to the living room.'

I follow her, and she stands in the middle of it, looking around.

'It hasn't changed a bit,' she says. 'Except you've more Mills & Boons than I've ever seen!'

'I ... well ... it's escapism.'

'I'll bet.'

'Do you want me to take your coat, or aren't you stopping?'

Whatever I might think of her, it's comforting to have a familiar face in my house when all I've had is strangers these past few days. She takes it off, walks out of the room and hooks it on the back of the under-stairs door.

'Did you get my letters?' she says when she comes back in. 'The cards?'

Does she regret doing what made us spend all these years apart? I look at her and I want to take her in my arms – it's like no time at all has passed. I feel an ache in my chest for all those moments we never shared over the years. She could have made my life so much better than it was, had she not done what she did.

I perch on the edge of the settee. 'I did.'

She sits on the chair and places her handbag on the floor next to her feet.

'Why are you here now?' I ask.

She looks up from the floor and into my eyes. Hers are swollen – the blue eyeliner disguises the redness underneath.

'I haven't seen Jason for days. His wife hasn't seen him either.'

'He's married?'

She shrugs gently. 'It was a few years ago. They went to the registry office, just the pair of them ... Drunk probably, but what can you do? He's a grown-up. Even though he hardly behaves like one.'

'Have you tried his mobile?'

She looks at me and raises her eyebrows. Of course she's tried his mobile.

'Thing is,' she says, 'I put this tracker thing on his phone ... I know that's wrong of me, but he lost his old phone the other day ... my contract was running out, so I got a new one ... gave him my old one, but before I did, I put that location thing on – Find My Friends, or whatever.'

She gets her phone out of her pocket.

'I like to know where he is ... After the last time he was in prison, I wanted to be sure he wasn't up to anything. But now ... '

'What is it? Where is he?'

'I don't know where he is now, but before his phone was switched off, he was at that old house ... the one

230

on Inkerman Street. Do you remember we found Craig there, when he was having a hard time at school?'

'Yes ... I was just thinking about that place the other day,' I say. 'Did you go round there to check?'

'There was nothing there — empty. I darted around the back, but the place was boarded up with steel shutters. I couldn't budge them.'

I pause then say, 'Do you think he's got anything to do with that missing girl? You've seen the news. Did you see the picture of the car that the girl got into?'

She types into her phone and holds up the CCTV photograph that's been on the television.

'This one?' She holds the picture closer to her face, then puts it face down on her lap.

'It's not Jason's car, is it? He gave me a lift the other day,' I say. 'That's a different car. But he was with that girl on Saturday. He brought her round here — can you believe that? She's only seventeen. She told me she was nineteen.'

The colour seems to have run from Denise's face, making her blue eyeliner look even more ridiculous against her pale skin, pale hair.

'Have you seen Craig?' she says. 'Have the police been round looking for him?'

I shake my head. 'No.'

She betrayed me, once; I'd be a fool to tell her the truth now.

'I remember when it was Craig they were looking for,' she says. 'You came round to ours while they ransacked this place. Do you remember?'

'Of course.'

'It's like it's happening all over again.' She shifts to the end of the chair. 'They must be together, Erica. This has never happened with Jason ... it's only since ...'

'It's never happened that you *know* of,' I say, almost shouting. 'From what I saw when he brought the girl around, they were quite familiar with each other. She must have been in that car before. It didn't look like she was forced into it.' I sigh. 'Craig always hung around with Jason ... even when those terrible things happened. Did you tell the police about the house on Inkerman Street?'

The colour returns to her face, there are patches of red in the middle of her cheeks.

'No,' she says. 'No, I didn't.' She takes a deep breath. 'I'm sorry,' she says. 'I know this might be too little too late, but you have to believe me when I say I'm sorry.'

'You always said Craig was family to you. Why did you do it?'

She looks to the floor.

'Everyone used to stop talking when I went out ... I heard them speaking about Craig, but Jason's name was mentioned, too. They started to ask, if Craig didn't kill Jenna, then who did. I wanted to protect my son ... to stop the rumours, that's all. I'm sorry, Erica. I didn't mean for them to print those things I said about Craig. He twisted my words. The police had been sniffing around Jason ... everyone thought my son was the one who killed Jenna, after they couldn't link it to Craig.'

I don't know what to say to her. I had certainly heard

Jason's name pop up – the articles in the newspaper about Jenna could never legally mention my son in connection with Jenna. They must've realised that that was the truth, started looking elsewhere for the killer.

'I overheard Jason and Craig the other day,' I say to her. 'Jason said, "We've all got our little secrets."'

'That could mean anything,' she says. 'You know what they're like.'

'Jason's hiding something.'

'What are you getting at?' she says, angrily. 'Are you trying to make me think that it was Jason? That it was my son all along who did ... those awful things?'

'I don't know what to think, Denise. I was only making conversation.'

'No you weren't.'

I should throw her out of my house, but she's going through the same thing that I was. Only her boy hasn't already been inside for murder. What if it *had* been Jason? It would make more sense. At twenty, Craig was still so impressionable, gentle – in awe of his best friend, however foolish that was.

'What's the matter?' she says.

'Nothing,' I say, rubbing my right side. 'I've got that kidney pain again.'

'You should make an appointment at the surgery. I remember how bad you were when you were expecting. You phoned me in the middle of the night, do you remember? You thought you were dying. You had a fever and thought you saw your mother at the end of your bed. That was when you were still in your single bedroom. It took you years to move into her old room, didn't it? But that night, you were almost delirious. You said the strangest of things about your mother. Peritonitis, it was. They left you with antibiotics and not even any painkillers. It's a wonder you didn't go into labour sooner than you did. The stress of everything you'd been through.'

'I can't believe you remember,' I say. 'I had no one else to call.'

Denise looks at me that way again; I've had it often from her over the years: pity. Did it make Denise feel better in herself to have a friend less fortunate – did it make her feel like the lucky one?

'Oh, Erica, love. How has it come to this?'

'You know how.'

'Yeah. I do.' She sighs. 'I always felt for you. On your own. I know you didn't get on with your mother, but at least you weren't alone when she was alive.'

'She wasn't that bad. And perhaps I deserve to be on my own after what I did.'

'What do you mean? Are you talking about Craig's father ... because he was a married man?'

'No,' I say, and I can tell Denise doesn't believe me. I've lied about it for so long I don't even blush. I don't want to linger on the subject of my son's father. 'How's Caroline getting on?'

'Good. She's good. I still can't believe she's living so far away. I've five grandchildren now. Can you believe that? When did I become old enough to be a granny?'

I was going to say how I wish *I* could say that, but I don't want to be that person.

'You don't look old enough to be a grandmother,' I say, instead.

'Do you want to see some pictures?'

'Go on then.'

She slips on to her knees and walks on them towards me. I can't believe she's so agile. My knees started going in my forties; I might be able to walk on them, but I couldn't get up without leaning on something and looking twice my age.

She flips open her mobile phone again.

Denise hands it over to me and four children's smiling faces beam at the camera.

'They look ever so sweet.'

'They have their moments, I suppose. That's Ellie,' she says, pointing to the youngest – her blonde hair's in need of a brush, but it's clean, shiny. 'She's just turned two. The eldest is nine. I don't know how Caroline does it.'

I pass the phone back to her and she clicks the home-screen to black.

'Won't Jim be wondering where you've got to?' I say.

'I don't think he'll notice.' She gets up easily from the floor and sits back on the edge of the chair. 'It's like we live separate lives. I don't think we've much in common these days. Don't know if we ever did.'

'But you love him, don't you?'

'I suppose. Whatever that means.'

235

She stands and reaches for her handbag and I follow her to the hall cupboard where she retrieves her coat.

'I guess we've all done things we regret,' she says. 'And now they're coming back to haunt us.'

'What do you mean?'

Her back is to me as she puts on her jacket. She turns to face me.

'Did you always believe Craig when he said he didn't do it?'

'Yes. I did.'

She pulls her jacket close around her without doing it up. She used to do that as a kid, a self-comforting habit.

'What is it, Denise?'

'You see ... when you say that, it makes me feel terrible.'

'Why? What would my words change?'

'I mean as a mother. You're meant to think the best of your kids, aren't you? We're meant to see past everything.'

'Come on, spit it out. What are you trying to say?'

'You said you can't picture Craig doing those things, but I can imagine my Jason hurting someone. I've seen him with Rebecca, his wife ... such contempt.'

My knees almost give way; I grab hold of the phone table.

Blue eyeliner mixed with tears runs down either side of Denise's face.

'But the police didn't think he killed Jenna,' I say. 'Did they? They wouldn't have dropped it for no good reason.'

'Oh, God. You'll never forgive me ... I shouldn't have come here, but I thought ... I don't know what I thought, or why I've picked now, after all these years ... It's that new girl ... that one from the telly.'

'Leanne,' I say. 'Her name's Leanne.'

'It can't happen again,' she says, her voice trembling. 'Not after last time.'

'Denise, for heaven's sake. *What*?'

'The reason the police dropped it ...' She takes a deep breath, tears still running down her cheeks, '... was because I gave Jason an alibi.' She looks down at her hands. 'I didn't think he'd take it a step further, actually *kill* someone ...' She pauses for a moment, taking a tissue to dab her face. She scrunches it and puts it up her sleeve and finally looks me in the eyes. 'I got one of the old blokes from work, Charlie Sumner, to tell the police he'd seen us ... that Jason had helped us at work all day. I think Charlie had a bit of a crush on me, so I used it to my advantage. But when the police couldn't find anything on Craig about the second girl, well.'

'What?' I want to grab her by the shoulders and shake her. 'You mean you gave him an alibi for Lucy? Why the hell didn't you admit it then? Denise, how could you have kept something so important quiet? It's my son's life we're talking about.'

She looks to the floor, and I stand.

'Don't think I'm going to feel sympathy for you just because you're sorry *now*. It's too late for your tears, Denise. Do you even understand the enormity of this?'

I go into the living room, pacing the floor, but it feels

237

as though I'm not really here. I lean against the mantel-piece – the room is spinning; it's far too hot in here.

Denise sniffs, retrieves the tissue and wipes her nose. She's standing at the doorway.

'But ... you see,' she says, finally, though barely audible, 'I was thinking about *my* son.'

I consider my lie – my lies: plural. The top that I burned, the things I told the police years ago. But I can't tell her about that now. It's what I've had to live with. Now isn't the time for my confession, to trump hers. This might be some kind of trick. She might be recording our conversation on that fancy phone of hers.

I go back into the hall, to the front door and open it.

'You'd better go,' I say.

She walks out of the door in silence. I close the door and reach over for the telephone, but I stop mid-air. I can't ring the police, can I? Because, when they asked where Craig was when Jenna died, I gave my son an alibi too.

26

Luke

The kids have been asleep for an hour, so Luke reaches into the fridge for a beer, thinking it's the perfect reward. He shouldn't really be drinking on a school night but it's not every day he chases down someone on the street for a story.

Alan Lucas, he said his name was. He must have heard about the abandoned car at the docklands too. Luke can't believe his luck that he stumbled across Craig's father, assuming he was telling the truth and didn't give a false name – it wouldn't be the first time that'd happened. No one else in the press has delved into Craig Wright's paternity – or if they have, they've been as unsuccessful as he was. Luke has never dared to ask Erica who her son's father was. It's such a personal question if you're not on *The Jeremy Kyle Show*.

When Luke questioned Alan after his revelation, he admitted that Craig hadn't known who his father was. Alan had made contact with his son after seeing him all over the news. It seems that Erica is very good at keeping secrets.

He opens his laptop on the dining room table, placing his bottle of beer on a coaster. Helen's shift doesn't finish until ten, so he has a couple of hours to kill. He types in the name, then clicks on the most recent article:

27 July 2002

MEN JAILED FOR SERIES OF ARMED ROBBERIES

Two robbers armed with imitation firearms who targeted seven petrol stations during a three-month period have been sentenced to nine years in jail. Alan Lucas, of West Derby, formerly of Preston, and Lee Traynor, also of West Derby, were sentenced after pleading guilty to five charges of robbery, two charges of attempted robbery and seven charges of possession of an imitation firearm.

Luke scans the rest of the Google articles, but none are a match for the Alan Lucas he's interested in.

He leans back in his chair.

Jesus Christ. No wonder Erica didn't want to tell her son who his father is – an armed robber!

So this Alan Lucas can't be trusted any more than she can. He'll be trying to protect his son, too, after abandoning him and Erica.

Luke knows he can't run with this story. He would need actual proof that Alan Lucas was Craig Wright's biological father. Would Erica confirm it? Luke seriously doubts that she would, but it might be worth visiting her again.

On Genes Reunited he types in Craig Wright's name and year of birth. The transcript results only show the name of the mother. The father isn't listed. He'd have to order a copy of the birth certificate, which would cost over twenty quid – and there's no guarantee it will tell him anything.

The front door clicks gently shut. Luke glances at the clock. Shit, it's twenty-five past ten already. Helen walks into the kitchen, clutching a bottle of white wine.

'Hi, love,' she says, weary from a fourteen-hour shift. 'Thought we deserved a drink since we've been so good with our diet.' She reaches into the cupboard for the glasses, still in her coat. 'Though it looks as if you've started without me.'

'Guess what happened today,' Luke says.

He's been dying to tell her all day. He even contemplated ringing her at work, but she's never happy about that these days. Far too busy.

Helen takes off her coat, hanging it on the back of a chair.

'Give me a second,' she says, sighing. 'I've had a shit day today.'

After pouring the drinks, she flops on to a chair. Her hair's scraped back off her face in a ponytail. Luke likes it better when it's down, but he doesn't say things like that to her any more. She's liable to assume he's criticising her.

'Go on then,' she says. 'What is it?'

She doesn't sound as interested as her question suggests.

241

'I think I met Craig Wright's father today. I've been trying to check the birth certificate online, to see if he's named on there, but you have to order—'

She rolls her eyes. 'Craig Wright again? Sorry to burst your bubble, but there's no way you can confirm who his father is unless you have DNA samples.'

'There was talk that Erica might have had an affair with Denise's husband.' Luke pauses, rubbing his chin. 'Actually, until today, I've always thought that made sense. If Denise had suddenly found out, that would explain why she gave me the story about Craig. Revenge.'

Helen stifles a yawn. 'I've no idea who these people are.'

'The kids from Sunningdales recognised Craig from his mugshot as the same man who kidnapped Leanne.'

'You're talking in riddles, love. Craig's paternity, now random kids you've been talking to.'

'Pamela Valentine must've rubbed off on me.'

'Now that sounds more interesting.'

'Glad you're secure enough in our relationship not to be jealous.'

'Hah! You don't half talk some bollocks when you're pissed.' She laughs.

He hadn't meant it to be funny. He's slightly stung by her implication that other women wouldn't find him attractive. OK, the woman in question was in her eighties, but still.

'Are you going to be on there all night?' she says, pointing to his laptop with her glass.

'Give me half an hour, then I'm all yours.'

She doesn't reply but gets up, grabs a massive packet of crisps from behind the tins and goes into the lounge. He says nothing about her choice of snack.

They used to watch television together every night when Helen wasn't working a shift. Most nights, she would get into her pyjamas as soon as she came home, then they'd settle down with a box set and a buffet of snacks. No wonder they'd got into the mess they're in now. He doesn't know if it's his own physical shape or the state of their marriage that he's most concerned about.

It's been years since he was this interested in a story, and his wife is already pissed off. She's been telling him for months that he should get more involved with life. He can't win.

He turns back to his laptop, frustrated. He shouldn't really message people when he's had a bit to drink, but he clicks on Denise Bamber's Facebook profile and fires off a quick note. She might give him more information about Alan Lucas, her son, Jenna ... Denise spoke to him last time – with a bit of luck she'll do it again.

27
Erica

Denise is long gone, but I can't bring myself to go to bed yet, not while Craig is still out there, and not while Leanne Livesey isn't home safe. I've been lying on the settee for what feels like hours. I keep thinking I'm about to vomit, but I've managed to hold it down. I try to lift my head to get a better view of the telly, but it feels like too much of an effort.

They'd announce it on the news straight away, wouldn't they – if they'd found her? The news report an hour ago said that she lived in a home for Looked After Children. What must that be like? Denise told me, when we were about fifteen, that a friend of a friend of her cousin, or something equally questionable, gave birth at one of those mother-and-baby homes. It was the early seventies and she was unmarried. Denise said that the girl cried for three whole weeks after they took the baby from her. She'd been with the baby for a fortnight before that. It sounded horrific, barbaric. She said the child would be six now and the woman was counting the days, the years, till that child reached eighteen and might contact her.

When Craig was growing inside me, that story preyed on my mind. I began to feel so close to him – that I was placed on this earth to be his mother.

It might not even be true about that distant acquaintance giving away her child. Denise said her mum told her to tell me, too. It might've been to encourage us to keep our legs closed, hem down, and knickers up. Didn't work, though, did it?

The loneliest time of my life wasn't when Craig was in prison, it was when I was pregnant with him. After my mother died, I worried about how I was going to cope as a single mother in a community that was less than forgiving (which was rather short-sighted of them, considering most of them went to church on a Sunday). It overtook my grief for my mother. Denise suggested lying to everyone – I could say I'd had a shotgun wedding and he'd scarpered. 'People would believe that,' she said, 'because it happens all the time.'

'No, it doesn't,' I said. 'Not enough times for it to be normal.'

I kept thinking about Mrs Delaney who lived near the chippy. She had four kids to bring up on her own. She was always working somewhere (the post office, the local pub). Her kids were looked after at various neighbours' houses. She always seemed so exhausted; that was my future.

Perhaps it was because my mother had not long died – and her being so well known in our town – but no one said anything to my face about my situation. If Denise heard anything, she didn't let on.

The kids at Craig's school years later were different. They had no filter from the brain to the mouth and usually accepted what their parents told them as gospel.

'What's a bastard?' Craig asked me one day after school. 'Someone said I was one of those.'

'Who called you that?' I said, shocked at the word that came out of his mouth. I stopped in the street, the rage building inside me but wanting to hide it from my little boy. He was only four then, so I couldn't tell him off for swearing; I didn't know what to say. I thought times were changing, but there was still that stigma in some people's minds about children born out of wedlock. I wanted to run back to the school and find the little brat.

'Kelly Winters.'

I took several breaths and forced a smile.

'I think you must have heard her wrong, love.'

Denise was right earlier today, though – about mothers and their children. It's what we're here to do: shield them. She'd told a lie to protect her son, years ago, and I had done the same.

It had come so easily, the lie.

The third of January 2000: six days after his twentieth birthday and Jenna was still missing.

'Craig says he was with you on the first of January for the whole day, but on the thirtieth of December, you were working. Is that right?'

'I was only in work for a few hours – did the early

shift. But he was definitely with me on the first. He was hungover from the night before.'

'Did you leave the house? Were there any other witnesses to this?'

'Next door ... she came in for a cup of tea ... was here a few hours.'

'Name.'

'Mrs Eckersall.'

I said that even though Mrs Eckersall was only sixty-five, she was a bit hard of hearing and often got her days mixed up. Made her sound a bit senile and eccentric.

The fact was, she hadn't dropped by at all. Yet my lie came so quickly, so easily.

When he arrived home from the police station a few hours later, his voice was quiet, and he stood in the doorway seeming half the size he was before he left. His T-shirt was dirty, his hair greasy. He held his denim jacket limply before letting it drop to the ground, looking so much like the little boy whose hand I held walking home from school.

'I love you, Son,' I said, my voice shaking, but he said nothing in return.

A single tear ran down his face.

But that was then. He's different now. Stronger. Quicker to lose his temper.

There's a noise from the rear of the house. I stand and realise I'm sitting in a darkened room. I go into the kitchen and open the back door. It sounds like there's a car in the alley, which isn't that unusual, I suppose. The gate rattles, then opens.

A shadow of a figure.

'Craig? Is that you?'

It *is* him. He rushes at me. I jump but he's moving past, almost pushing me aside as he pounds up the stairs. I close the back door and follow him up quickly. I stand on the landing as he pushes his bedroom door open. He grabs his holdall and starts packing what little he has.

I rush into his room, trying to snatch away the bag, but he tugs it from my hands.

'What are you doing?' I shout. 'You can't leave!'

'I can't stay here, can I? The police will be back for me soon, and I've stuff here that ... won't look good.'

'Where have you been?' I say. 'I've been worried about you.'

'Walking around ... clearing my head.'

'What will I say if the police come again?'

'Tell them you haven't seen me.'

'I don't know if I can keep on—'

'Lying?' He's scowling at me. 'You didn't have to lie for me. It didn't help then, and it won't help now.'

'Denise was here earlier,' I say to him, calmly, trying to remain unaffected by his anger.

He looks up quickly.

'What did that cow want?' He almost spits out his words.

'Don't call her that!'

'You've changed your tune, haven't you?' He's shouting louder at me now, his face is contorted. 'Whenever I've mentioned her in the past, you've stuck your nose in the air – said you wouldn't have anything to do with her, after what she said about me.'

'I haven't changed my mind,' I say quietly. 'I just don't like name-calling.'

There's a slight shake of his head. He never used to shout at me.

'She seems to think Jason's got something to do with the disappearance of that young girl. Is that true? Denise said she lied about where he was the night Lucy disappeared.'

He doesn't answer but gets up to grab a few towels from the airing cupboard.

'Jason can look after himself,' he says eventually, brushing past me so quickly I almost fall.

'I had a reporter round this morning,' I say.

My voice feels as though it's getting quieter every time his gets louder. Didn't he notice that he pushed me?

'Don't tell me – it was that wanker who printed Denise's story.'

'How do you know that?'

He shrugs.

'A friend told me about him. Said he spoke to him earlier,' he says, sounding slightly calmer now. 'I saw him driving past the other day. What's his fucking problem?'

'He showed me a picture – wanted to know if I recognised you in it.'

'He should keep his nose out.' He thrusts the towels into his bag with such force, he's almost punching them. 'How would he like it if a member of his family was front-page news? Someone needs to teach him a lesson ... he's got a family ... I looked him up online.'

'Did you?' I linger at the doorway. I don't want to get in his way again – not while he's like this. 'Why? I didn't think you held a grudge against him. He was only doing his job.'

'Yeah, and so were the police who fitted me up in the first place. That Luke Simmons better watch himself.'

'You're not going to do anything stupid, are you?'

He zips up his bag and hoists the strap on to his shoulder.

'I've never done anything stupid, Mum.'

There's the slam of a car door outside.

He stands, grabs his deodorant from the windowsill and bounds down the stairs.

'Craig, please, don't do this.' I say. 'You're safer here with me!'

But there's no reply.

28

Luke

Helen was still in bed when Luke left the house this morning. He brought her a cup of tea, but it was untouched when he went up to say goodbye. He felt the effect of the few beers (and two glasses of wine) that he'd drunk last night. He's drinking too much, he knows that, but can't fathom if it's down to what's going on at work, or because he feels lonely in his own home.

Thankfully, his daughters got themselves ready for school. He remembers as a kid that his own mother used to do everything for him in the morning: lay his uniform out on his bed, hand his bag to him as he opened the front door. How easy life was then.

His eldest, Megan, usually gets her and her sister's uniforms out of their chests of drawers and loves to pour the cereal into bowls. He's trained them well; Luke wonders how long that'll last.

'We're walking today, girls,' he shouts from the hallway, 'so we need to leave five minutes earlier.'

They both appear at the door from the lounge.

'Alice says she doesn't like walking,' says Megan.

'She says she doesn't know if her legs will take her all that way without hurting.'

'Has Alice got something wrong with her mouth?' says Luke. 'Come on, get your coats on. We're going to be late. Alice, your legs will be fine – it's only a ten-minute walk.'

He hands them their coats, bending down to zip up Alice's.

'I can do it, Daddy,' she says.

'No time,' he says, standing up and opening the door. 'Come on, come on.'

'Daddy must've had too much beer last night,' says Megan to her sister. 'That's what Mummy says when she's up in the morning and Daddy's still in bed. I don't think Mummy drinks beer, though. She likes wine.'

Luke makes a mental note to advise Helen on the disadvantages of speaking so honestly in front of their children. Megan's teacher looks at him strangely as it is; what on earth has his daughter been revealing to her?

He breathes in the fresh air – somehow it seems sweeter in the mornings. It's bloody freezing, though – none of them have gloves or hats. Tomorrow, he'll make sure he's more organised.

'Stick your hoods up, girls. And put your coat sleeves over your fingers,' he says, moving between them so he can hold hands with them both. 'We can swap hands as we go.'

Alice's teeth are chattering.

'Come on,' says Luke. 'If we walk faster, we'll warm up.'

He feels like today is a turning point, for him and the story. He needs to check whether Denise has replied to his Facebook message, then prepare a list of questions for her. He can say he's running a piece on the cold case of Jenna Threlfall – see if she remembers anything from that time. That way, he could slip in a few questions about Erica and Craig. She must know who the father of her best friend's child is. Ex-best friend. That might come in handy. No loyalties on Denise's part. Perhaps that would work in Luke's favour with Erica, too.

Writing a cold case appeal for Jenna Threlfall isn't such a bad idea, he thinks.

At last they're at the school gates, having swapped hands at least seven times, but Alice is almost in tears because she's *too freezing*.

'It'll be lovely and warm inside,' says Luke, rubbing her arms. 'And I've made you your favourite sandwiches.'

'Peanut butter?'

'I didn't know you changed favourites. I made you jam.'

Her lip wobbles.

'I'll make you double peanut butter tomorrow. How does that sound?'

She nods, her little bottom lip sticking out in an effort to stop the tears, and wraps him in a hug.

'Come on, Alice,' says Megan, taking her sister's hand. 'We don't want to miss the register.'

'Bye, Daddy,' says Alice, before Megan tugs her gently away.

'See you later, girls,' he shouts after them. 'I'll be picking you up from after-school club today.'

Megan lifts her arm in a wave without turning around. When did she get so grown up? He's been asking himself that a lot lately. Is it because he's been so distracted these past couple of days that he's not been there to do the little things for them? He didn't know that Alice doesn't like jam sandwiches any more. But he does his best; that's all anyone can do.

He watches as the teacher beckons them into school. At least they're not late today.

He puts his hands in his pockets, feeling warm from holding his daughters'. He stops to cross the road, at the place where the lollipop man helps the children to cross, and feels a bit ridiculous when he's the only person waiting.

'Cheers, mate,' he says to the man who always has a smile on his face. What's his name again? Mr Bailey, that's it.

The car that stopped to let him cross is still there, even after Mr Bailey reaches the other side of the road. The man in the driving seat is looking at Luke. Luke can feel his eyes on him.

The man's hair is short and Luke recognises those eyes. Is it Craig? Luke doesn't want to stare but he's sure it's the same man he saw at the end of Erica's street last week.

The car is an old Renault Clio, dark red. It's only a few feet away.

Luke stops.

What's Craig doing here? Has he followed Luke? Alan Lucas will have told him that Luke was asking about him. And now they will both know that Luke lied about knowing Craig to get information.

Shit. He must've seen him with his children. Luke feels dizzy, like he's going to be sick. He rests his legs against the garden wall on his right.

Car horns sound from behind the Renault.

Craig shakes his head at Luke.

Luke sits fully on the wall. His hands are shaking as he gets out his mobile phone, taking a picture of the car as it screeches away.

Oh God, thinks Luke.

Now Craig knows where his children go to school. He might even know where they live.

Luke is breathless by the time he almost collapses through his front door.

'What happened to you?' asks Helen. She's standing at the bottom of the stairs in her dressing gown, a cup of tea in her hands. 'Are the kids OK?'

'Yes, yes. They're fine. Got to school fine.' He walks to the kitchen and sits on one of the chairs, breathing hard. Helen follows him. 'I saw Craig Wright.'

'He's up early.'

'It's not funny, Helen. He stopped at the crossing ... looked straight at me. That girl's missing and he was at our daughters' school.'

'There can't be anything in it, though. It's a coincidence, that's all. What would he want with you? If he

255

went after all the reporters who covered his story, he'd be busy for the rest of his life.'

'But I was at Erica's house yesterday, and he could know that I lied to his father to get information. I said I knew him.'

'OK, OK, calm down. Well, it's not as though you've done much wrong. I bet this whole town is talking about him. You're too invested in this case, but the man probably doesn't even know you're writing a story about him.' She pours the cold tea down the sink and refills the kettle. 'Listen. Phone the police and tell them what you saw. Perhaps you could hang around the house for a bit, just in case. You were up until two last night on that laptop. I'd say that more than makes up for having a few hours off this morning and the sleep will calm you down.'

She's putting on a brave face, he can tell. Trying to stay calm because she's trained to. Or is it because she doesn't care? *Too invested*, she said. Isn't it right that he should put all his efforts into getting the best story he can?

Luke opens his laptop and brings up the police non-emergency number. After several minutes, they answer, and he gives the details of what he saw.

'Shall I email you the photo of the car?' he says.

'Just the description of the vehicle and its registration, please, and I'll make sure it gets to the relevant person.'

Luke gives the woman his details before hanging up.

'It's like she wasn't really interested,' he says to Helen.

'People report sightings all the time and they turn out to be nothing.' She sighs as she pours boiling water into a fresh mug. 'I bet they've had hundreds.'

Luke walks into the living room, going straight to the window. He waits for several minutes. He almost jumps when he hears a bang, but it's only the couple from next door leaving the house for work. They do everything together, those two.

'No, you're probably right,' he says. 'There's no one out there.'

But Luke can't shake the feeling that he and his family are being watched. He's seen those cold eyes close up now. Craig is capable of anything.

29

Erica

I need to go outside today. I can't just lie around while my son has gone off God knows where. I haven't spent so long waiting for him to let him get into trouble again. Perhaps Denise knows where he is – Craig tells Jason everything.

Sleeping has made me feel so much better this morning. The pain is still there, but it doesn't seem as bad. The only knocking last night came from the house opposite. About midnight, there was someone banging on his door for about ten minutes – didn't even glance in my direction when I peeked through the curtains.

It made a change for there to be goings-on with someone else. Perhaps Jason was true to his word and he's made sure that no one bothers me at this house. There has been nothing through the letterbox, no bricks through the windows. I can only conclude that people are afraid of my son.

I knew Craig wouldn't return last night. I don't want to think about what he's up to, but I have to face it. Like Lucy, I've met Leanne Livesey. It changes everything.

She's not just a pretty, silent face in a photograph. She's a living, breathing human with problems of her own, and by the sounds of it she's had a terrible childhood. She must have suffered, too, in her seventeen short years. Life can be so unfair.

I've tried ringing Denise's landline, but there's no answer. I don't have her mobile telephone number, so I have to go round there. I must be brave.

I get my coat from the back of the under-stairs cupboard. I haven't been to Denise's since the day the police searched my house. She sat me down, made me cups of tea that she had laced with whisky and sugar. They helped, then. I've nothing to bolster me now. I should've taken to drink years ago. I wouldn't be going through this – I probably wouldn't be here at all.

I grab the packet of co-codamol from the cupboard, taking two out of the blister packet and washing them down with a handful of water. They should keep the pain away for the next couple of hours.

The sky is clear; I think it's cold because some of the cars have a dusting of ice, but I can't feel it. I don't need my scarf, though the ends of my fingers catch the icy breeze.

There are no cars outside Denise's house. Jim must be at work. He must have a good position now. If I were in their situation, I'd have moved from here years ago.

I knock three times, but there's no answer.

Their letterbox is at the bottom of the door and I'll be damned if I'm kneeling on the ground to shout through.

I put my ear to the front window and there's a faint

murmur from the television. I tap gently on it – it doesn't take much to make a lot of noise.

'I know you're in there. It's me, Erica. Can you let me in?'

A figure stands, walks out of the living room. I wait at the front door, the footsteps getting closer. It opens, but it's not Denise who answers: it's Jim.

'Erica!' he says. 'What are you doing here?'

'I'm looking for Denise.'

He leaves the door wide open and walks back into the lounge. I step inside, closing it behind me. They've changed the carpet in the hallway. It used to be dark brown, the hardwearing type. Now it's laminate – all the way through to the kitchen. It's the same layout inside as mine, but it seems bigger. On the window sill at the bottom of the stairs is a glass vase with real flowers in. They don't look fresh. Some of the white ones are browning; petals litter the base. Next to it are five, six photos in paper frames of numerous children in their school uniforms.

I'm waiting for Denise to appear when Jim shouts, 'Come through!'

I walk through to their living room. It's so modern, with its flooring and red rug near the wood-burning stove. The television's on low, it's a wonder I heard it. At least there's nothing wrong with my ears.

'Will Denise be down in a minute?' I say.

'I doubt it,' says Jim.

He's sitting on their plush grey sofa that looks as though it's made of velvet. He's wearing a denim shirt and black jeans. I can see that underneath his slippers, his socks don't match.

'What do you mean?' I say.

I don't think we've ever talked alone. He hardly ever looked me in the eye then, and he seems to be avoiding my gaze now.

'I think she's having an affair,' he says. 'She didn't come home last night.'

'She wouldn't have an affair ... that's not like her.'

'How would you know?' He's staring at the television. He looks so tired; there are shadows under his eyes. 'You haven't seen her for God knows how long. You wouldn't know her at all, now. She's not like she was back then.'

'What makes you think she's having an affair, though? What if she's in trouble – she might've been in an accident.'

'I've spent all night phoning the hospitals, even driving round them. Preston, Blackpool – even bloody Blackburn, on the remote chance she was unconscious and wasn't able to give her name. I've rung round her friends and no one has seen her. She's been acting weird since that new bloke started at work a few weeks ago ... he's moved on to your street, as it happens. You haven't seen her hanging around there, have you?'

'No. She came by yesterday, but I didn't see her go into another house.'

'She visited you? Out of the blue like that?' he snaps. He leans forward, his hands on his knees as though ready to stand. 'I bet she was covering her tracks.'

'Did she say who it was that'd started at her work?'

He's frowning, looking at the floor.

'What?' He shakes his head. 'No ... I didn't pay much attention. She's always yakking about something. Wish I'd listened now, though. Not that it would make any difference to you – you wouldn't know him even if I gave you his full name, address and date of birth. Not up to mixing much, are you? What do you do there in your house all day? Why the hell stay round here when you get treated like shit by everyone? I've never understood that. It's like you wanted it, like you felt you deserved to be treated like that. If it were my Jason, I'd have been long gone ... and I wouldn't have visited him in prison like you did. Fuck, no. Not if he were capable of those things.'

Jim used to be such a quiet, brooding man. This is the most I've heard him talk since their wedding night, when he'd drunk too much whisky.

'I've got friends!' I say, sharply. 'You can't possibly know anything about my life! And you don't know how you'd react about things until it happens to your son.'

'I can imagine. Look, I'm sorry, Erica. I didn't want to be shouting at you. I've been up most of the night worrying ... Maybe she's not having an affair after all. You say you saw her yesterday?'

'Yes, because she was worried about Jason – he was seen with that missing girl, Leanne Livesey.'

Jim stands and grabs the remote control from the side of the television and switches it off.

'That bloody lad.' He puts a hand through his hair.

'He's going to be the death of me. He's been sent to prison three times. Three times! You'd think he'd learn. Can you imagine what that's been like for me at work? Bloody shameful. I seriously thought of changing my name at one point. People don't care about talking about it – even when you're right there and they know you can hear them.'

'I know.'

He sits down again.

'Shit. Yeah, of course you know.' He stands again and walks to the shelf in the right alcove. He takes a bottle of whisky from it and pours himself a glass. 'Want one?'

'No, thank you.'

He downs it in one, refills his glass and replaces the bottle on the shelf.

'I remember when Jason and Craig were lads, I used to take them both fishing at the canal ... nearly every Saturday.' He sits back down. 'Good memories. I think Jason might have preferred it being just him and me sometimes, but ... you know.' Jim glances at me. 'I didn't mind, Craig was a nice lad.' He swirls the drink in his glass. 'Denise thought Craig could do with a father figure ... She worried about him more than Jason sometimes.'

'Really?'

'Did you ever tell Craig who his father is?'

My back stiffens. 'Pardon?'

'You heard me.'

'No, I haven't. What business is it of yours?' I pull my coat around myself. 'Anyway, it wouldn't do him any good – if anything, it'd make him feel worse.'

263

'Hasn't he been curious?'

'I said I didn't know his name – that it was a one-night thing.'

'Ah. So that means that the opposite is true, eh?'

I just nod. I owe him nothing – I don't want to talk about Craig's father any more.

'You know,' he says, 'people thought it was me! As if I'd have had a chance with you.'

'Enough! The subject's closed.'

My face flushes. It feels uncomfortable sitting here with Jim talking like this; a dream, unreal.

He holds one hand up, the one not clinging to his large glass of whisky.

'OK, OK. I didn't mean any harm by it.'

I need to leave. I feel cold – the tablets must be starting to work and the fire's not on in here.

'Get us, eh?' he says, obviously enjoying the sound of his own voice. 'We've probably said about five words to each other in the past, and now we're having a proper heart-to-heart. Who'd have thought it?'

I stand and do up the buttons on my coat.

'Stay a while longer, love,' he says. 'We can have a right good catch-up.' He steps closer to me and holds the top of my arm. 'I've always liked you, Erica. You've kept your figure, too. Even though you hide under those middle-aged clothes.'

'You're drunk, Jim. And you're trying to get back at Denise. What if something's happened to her?'

'She'll be fine … she's a tough one … can look after herself.'

He's slurring his words and I can smell the whisky on his breath.

'But something might be wrong. Can I have her mobile number?'

He's still holding my arm. For a few moments I think he's not going to let go, until he sighs and almost stomps into the hallway.

'This is her card,' he said, grabbing one from the pile on the window sill. 'Her cleaning business on the side ... she got a load printed.' He grabs a pen and writes on the back. 'I'll give you my number, too. Let me know if you hear from her.' He hands it to me. 'And let me know if you change your mind,' he says, winking at me.

So that's where Jason gets it from.

'Thanks,' I say, not wanting to antagonise him.

I open the door myself and close it behind me, relieved to get out of there.

I carry Denise's card in my hands all the way home. I can't lose it. It's not like Denise to be gone for the whole night. But Jim's right: seventeen years is plenty of time to change.

When I step inside my hall, the telephone starts to ring. I almost dive on it.

'Denise, is that you?'

'No. It's Luke from the—'

'Oh, Luke. I can't find Denise.'

'What do you mean?'

'I've just been round to her house. Her husband said she didn't come home last night – he's checked all the hospitals.'

'Do you think she might be with Jason somewhere?'

'Maybe, but I didn't think they went anywhere together these days. Not that I'd know much about that.' I lean against the wall. I can't think straight; there's a nauseous feeling in my stomach that's not going away, and I don't think it's my nerves. 'Do you think she'll be all right?'

'I hope so.'

'Why did you call?' I say. I can't stand here chatting all day.

'I wanted to know if ... Has Craig got a new car – a Renault Clio?'

'He hasn't got a car. I'd know if he had a car, wouldn't I?'

'I was just checking. I saw him early this morning—'

'Early? It doesn't sound like Craig, then. He hasn't been getting up before ten since ...'

Since I can't remember when. When did he last sleep here – was it Saturday? It can't have been that long ago.

'Erica!' shouts Luke. Why is he shouting at me? 'Listen, I saw him outside my children's school – he was looking at me ... it was as if he knew where to find us. Has he mentioned me at all?'

'I can't remember now. I'm so tired ... too tired. I felt OK when I got up this morning, but all this is getting to me. Is there any news on that missing girl?'

He sighs down the phone; it almost hurts my ears.

'Not that I've seen – and I've had the news on since I got into work. We've had no updates from the police. There is talk, though, that this isn't the first time Leanne has run away. They seem to think she'll come back of her own accord.'

'They shouldn't think that,' I say. I feel breathless; I'm talking too much and need to sit. 'I have to go, Luke.'

'What do you mean: *They shouldn't think that*?' he says. 'If you've got information that'll help find Leanne, then you have to say.'

'I only meant that ... I'm worried about history repeating itself.'

'Erica, what do you know? What has Craig told you?'

'Nothing about Leanne. I'm always the last to know. Will you let me know if you hear anything?'

'Erica, please—'

'You'll let me know?'

'Yes.' He sighs.

I replace the handset, thinking that he probably won't keep his word. He'll have more important things to do than update me. But for those few moments we were chatting, it was almost like talking to a friend.

I sit on the downstairs step to catch my breath. I'm too old for this.

Craig is a stranger to me. It's like he wants to break my heart all over again. And Jim was right. Why am I still here? I get to my feet, and shuffle back to the phone table.

I open my address book and find his number.

30

Luke

Luke spent the rest of the morning thinking about Craig Wright being outside school. He imagined seeing Megan and Alice in the distance, waving as they held the man's hands. No matter how fast he ran, he could never reach them.

After ringing the school and, at the risk of sounding like *one of those* parents, reiterating that under no circumstances are they to let his children leave school without it being him or Helen picking them up, he set off to work.

He resisted passing Erica's on the way there – he was already a few hours late as it was.

Now it's midday, and the more he thinks about it, the more he feels it can't have been a coincidence. He replaces the handset after speaking to Erica.

'What's your face like that for?' asks Amanda, sitting opposite him.

Luke had told her about seeing Craig that morning and she'd been the only one so far not to think he was going insane.

'I've just had a weird conversation with Erica Wright,' he says. 'She was going on about losing Denise. I asked her if Craig had mentioned me, but she couldn't remember. I'm sure she knows more than she's saying.'

'What do you mean, she lost Denise?'

'I've no idea. Do you think Denise has gone missing?'

'We're like dumb and dumber here,' says Amanda. 'We've obviously no idea. And we can't go round there again – not when Craig followed you after we interfered the last time.'

'She didn't sound well.'

'I expect she's having a stressful few days,' she says. 'Son released from prison for murdering a girl, another girl seen with son goes missing. I'd say that makes for a shit week.'

Luke remains silent while he thinks.

'Look,' says Amanda, 'there's nothing we can do from here. The police will be doing what they can. You gave them the details of the vehicle Craig was driving. Plus, you didn't see the girl with him this morning, did you? It might be Jason Bamber – or someone we don't even know about – working alone. There's nothing we can do but wait.'

'Wait for another girl to turn up dead?'

'It's not like we can hunt them down, Luke, is it?'

'No.'

But he knows he'll get little work done this afternoon. As soon as it gets to three o'clock, he's going to wait outside the school until his children are out and safe.

*

Luke feels calmer now that Megan and Alice are safely tucked up in bed. He's set up his laptop in his small office upstairs so he can keep an eye on them.

'Not on the beer tonight?' Helen shouts from their bedroom.

She's trying on yet another black dress for a work do. Luke's positive she hadn't mentioned it before. She's done her hair too; it's up in a twist, with bits hanging round her face. Luke hasn't seen her dressed up for months.

'I need to keep a clear head,' he says.

'So what do you think of this one?' Helen says from the landing.

'Looks great,' says Luke, thinking it looked exactly the same as the last one. 'Who's leaving again? And since when did going out for an office party on a school night become a thing?'

'Eh?' she says, slipping her feet into two-inch heels. 'What are you talking about?'

'Just someone I spoke to yesterday at work. Jenna Threlfall's sister was having her Christmas party on a weekday. Anyway.' Luke waves his hand, batting the subject away. 'Do you remember she had a sister?'

'I don't remember much about Jenna, let alone her sister.'

'What time will you be back?'

'No idea. I'm not working till six tomorrow night, so it might be a late one.' She kisses the top of his head. 'You'll hardly notice me gone, Luke,' she says. 'You've barely spoken to me in days. You've become obsessed

270

with that case. You know you're not some kind of detective.'

'I'm not obsessed. It's giving me a focus. Last month you said I'd lost my drive, now you're complaining because I found it.'

'Hopefully that girl will come home safe and everything can get back to normal.'

'Her name's Leanne.'

'Bye, love,' she whispers loudly from the top of the stairs.

He rushes to the landing.

'I was in the middle of talking to you!'

She stops halfway down the steps, turning around slowly.

'You will wake the kids,' she hisses.

'So? What do you care?' He shouts, knowing that the volume will piss her off even more. 'You're hardly ever here – and when you are, you take no notice of me.'

'Have you heard yourself?' She's leaning towards him, her eyes narrow. 'I hardly ever go out for actual fun. In case you hadn't realised, when I am out all hours, I'm bloody working!' She turns and stomps down the rest of the stairs. She stops as she reaches for the door handle, looking up at Luke. 'We can talk about this tomorrow.'

The door slams shut. She didn't bloody care about waking the children then, did she? Luke is shaking. What's wrong with her? Can't she see how much it hurts him to be dismissed all the time?

Luke hadn't heard a cab waiting for her outside. Did

she actually mention where she was going? Fuck it. Helen's a grown woman – she can look after herself.

He briefly checks on the girls before returning to his office, slumping onto his chair. After a few deep breaths, he turns to face his computer.

Luke clicks on Olivia Threlfall's email and scrolls through the pictures she sent him. He stops when he comes to one that's obviously been scanned – the photo is slightly bent in the top right corner. It's one of Jenna that Luke hasn't seen before. In it, Olivia is sitting on her older sister's knee. Jenna has her arms wrapped around her sister; their heads are level, with Olivia's long brown hair resting on Jenna's shoulders.

Luke can't stop thinking about what happened today. He thought that Craig was alone in the car, but who knew. Maybe Alan Lucas – who might not even *be* his father – is an accomplice and was with the girl that morning.

And what about Jason? Have the police asked him questions in connection with Leanne Livesey? Rebecca Savage said she saw Craig Wright with Jenna, but he also remembers her parting words to him: *We've had this hanging over our head for years. I want it to go away.* It would've been better to have said 'I just wanted the truth out there' or something. Maybe it's not Erica who's lying after all.

But Luke can't speculate in his articles about Leanne Livesey and Jenna Threlfall. If he's honest, he's a bit fed up of thinking about Craig Wright. He must research the facts.

31
Leanne

He left me on my own. He said it would be fun.

But it's not.

I really trusted him. I'd written all those letters, told him everything about me, and for what? Nothing.

This room is rank. It's like one of those places you see on those reality crime shows where someone's been murdered, but all that's left are the stains. Franny McPhee loved those types of programmes. When I couldn't sleep sometimes, I'd go downstairs. She said I shouldn't watch them, but I told her I'd only watch them on my iPad anyway.

She forgot that I didn't have an iPad.

People don't remember the little things about you when they don't really care. They never do. Mum remembered, before. When she cared. She used to record *Made in Chelsea* for me when I wasn't in – without me even asking. When I was feeling down about something, she'd make me cheese on toast with pepperoni on it.

I just want someone to know that I only drink a milky coffee when there's half a sugar in it, or that sometimes, in the morning, it takes me five minutes to come round and to actually speak. I want someone to know that, when I care about them, then I'll always have their back.

But what if it ends here, in this shitty, stinking room?

I've never felt so alone. And that's making me think too much, you see.

I thought *he* cared about me. But everyone's the same, aren't they? They all want something. They probably think I'm stupid.

Now, I'm sitting on a sofa that's probably been here for years, covered in stains from people that might be dead.

I'm so cold, and it's so dark in here. The electricity's not working and there are no candles.

I pull my knees towards my chest and wrap my arms around them, as though I were hugging someone else.

32
Erica

I'd only intended to have a short rest on the settee, but I slept all night. I kept the twenty-four-hour news station on and briefly woke at midnight and again at three in the morning, but there was nothing about Leanne.

I'm so exhausted. I can't tell if it's from the pain or the worry. It's February – surely it can't be this hot outside; I'm drenched in sweat.

I hadn't expected Craig home – he hasn't stayed here in days. I pray to God that he's not done something stupid. Perhaps he's taken her somewhere nice – she probably hasn't had a holiday in a few years.

Why am I thinking this? Of course he won't have whisked her away on some jaunt. I'm doing it again. My head's in the clouds, not wanting to see what's right in front of me: the truth about my son.

I can't move from the settee. Perhaps if I take two or more of these pills, then I can close my eyes and never wake up. I've never been that brave, though. Never had the courage to end it all. I feel too ashamed about what I've done. And I've done it for nothing. Everyone else was right and I was wrong.

I wish I could go back to the day everything changed – the day my mother died. If she were here, then everything wouldn't have turned out like this. She would've been there for me, helped me bring up Craig so I wouldn't have made the same mistakes.

It was a few days before she died that she noticed there was something not right.

'You've not used your monthly supplies in the bathroom,' she said. 'I bought you some more and the others are still there.'

I used to like that I never had to worry about things like that – perhaps that was my laziness, but right then I hated that she knew things that were so personal to me when I wanted to hide everything.

I was sitting against my bedroom door, wrapped in my quilt and reading a book to take my mind off a problem I didn't know how to fix.

'I bought my own, Mum,' I said.

'You did what? You didn't buy those tampon things, did you? You're not married yet, you shouldn't be using objects like that.'

I pulled my quilt closer around me. Who called tampons 'objects'? She had silly euphemisms for everything.

'You've not been out gallivanting, have you?' she said. 'Pamela Valentine said she saw you and Denise's Jim driving past her on the high street. I don't want you to get a name for yourself. You're a good girl, Erica.'

'Pamela Valentine's a nosy old cow,' I said, the strongest words my mother would allow.

'She's younger than I am, Erica,' said Mother. I heard a noise behind the door, like she was sitting down against it. 'I know you think you know everything, that I've never been young, and I've always been this old, but I'm only looking out for you. I wouldn't want you making the same mistakes I did.'

So this was where we were going to have this conversation, I thought. Divided by a door, like a priest and a sinner in a confessional box.

'He's been giving me a lift when I finish at five,' I said. 'Denise gave him earache about leaving me at the bus stop.'

'Well, so long as that's all it is. I wouldn't want you to get into trouble.'

While we were being so open about things, I chanced a question I'd always wanted to know the answer to.

'Do you know where my dad is now?' I said.

There was silence behind me. Were those few words all I was going to get from her?

'No,' she said quietly. 'The last I heard, he got divorced and moved to Scotland.'

'Divorced? He married again?'

She started drumming her fingers on the carpet – she always fidgeted when she was thinking.

'No, Erica,' was all she said before I heard her get up from the floor.

When I heard her go down the stairs, I realised that the conversation was finished. It was the last serious discussion we would have. She didn't question my lack of periods again, so I made sure to take the supplies she bought me and hide them.

I had misunderstood what she said, back then, about my father. I didn't think about it much afterwards; I had too many other, more important things to worry about. I hear her words now, as clear as I did then: 'He got divorced.' Why would she say that if she'd meant he ended their own marriage? She'd have said *we* divorced.

She lied. She hadn't married my father at all.

I pick up the remote control from the floor and turn the television off.

I put my hand underneath the settee and bring out my folder. All the pictures I've collected. There's a cottage that has views of Lake Windermere. The photo I cut from the holiday brochure shows it covered in snow. It's truly beautiful. I could spend the day reading, making hot chocolate. Maybe I could even write my own stories – I've often dreamed of doing that.

My brother, Philip, assured me that the money would be in my account today. An advance that he'd deduct from the house sale, of course – he never was the generous type. He sounded surprised to hear from me last night; it wasn't that late.

'What do you want this time, Erica?' he said, sounding as weary as he always does with me.

'Good to speak to you, too, Philip,' I said. 'I wanted to take you up on your offer of arranging everything, but I might need some money to get away for a while. Just until everything's finalised.'

278

He sighed in the way he always did, like he was being strangled.

'Right you are. Is that everything?'

'Yes, thank you, Philip.'

I hated the way I had to talk to him, to appease him. As though I owed him something for letting me stay in the house we jointly owned. I suppose I should be grateful that he hadn't forced me out in the first place. That surprised me, but I suppose he did owe it to me.

I hear a noise coming from upstairs.

I sit up and put my folder back underneath the settee. The pain's not as bad this morning – all those pills must be doing their job. I swivel my legs to the floor and stand. When I reach the hall, the noise stops for a few seconds before starting again.

I climb the stairs – my ears tingling, listening to try and track the source of the sound.

Craig's bedroom. It's the mobile phone I bought him.

It stops again, just before I pick it up.

Fifteen missed calls.

I press select and see that the person who's been ringing my son is Leanne. I almost collapse on to his bed with the relief of it. She's alive; she's fine. And Craig's not with her.

I'm looking to the ceiling, almost smiling when the phone beeps again.

Three New Messages, it says on the screen.

I press select again. They're all from Leanne.

I open the oldest one.

279

Where are u?

I press the exit button and click on the second.

Too dark in here. I'm freezing. The toilet doesn't work.

My hands are shaking by the time I open the third.

She keeps crying. You have to get me out of here.

I stand, clutching the phone in my hand, and rush to the bathroom. I lean over and retch into the toilet bowl; yellow bile is all that comes up. I flush it, close the lid and sit down.

Oh, Craig. What have you done?

I'm shivering worse than ever now. What am I supposed to do? I can't phone the police on my own son.

When I try calling Leanne's number, there's no answer. It only rang a few minutes ago; she must be all right.

Denise.

I'll try Denise's mobile again. Her card is in my cardigan pocket.

Dee's EZ Cleaning Services.

I dial the number. It rings seven times before it's answered.

'Craig?' A woman's voice.

'Denise? Is that you? It's me, Erica. Thank God you're all right.'

'Erica?'

'Denise? Where are you – why's your voice echoing?'

'It's nothing . . . I'm fine, I'm fine.'

'Are you sure? You don't sound fine. Jim said you didn't come back the other night. I've been worried about you.'

I'm trying to make out the background noise. Chatting, as though people are in a café.

'I had to get away – needed time to think about everything.'

'Have you seen Craig?'

Silence.

'Not for a while. Listen, I've got to go. I'll phone you tonight, yeah?'

'Wait, Denise. Do you think Craig might have gone to the house on Inkerman Street? Only I've seen some texts from Leanne Livesey. She says it's dark and the loo doesn't work. Do you think we should go round there?'

'No. No. Don't go anywhere near that house.' She coughs down the line. 'Sorry. I've not been feeling too well. Everything will be fine. It'll all be fine. Bye.'

'OK. Bye then, Denise,' I say, but she won't have heard because the line has already gone dead.

A door downstairs bangs closed.

'Craig!' I shout. 'Is that you?'

There's no reply. I walk to the top of the stairs, listening for any movement from below.

Footsteps from the kitchen, along the hall.

Then he appears at the bottom.

He's coming slowly up the stairs. There's a strange look in his eyes, wild and dazed. Instinctively, I take a step backwards until I'm against the landing wall. There's a smell to him: something sickly sweet mixed with stale whisky – the same scent of Jim yesterday. Hadn't *he* washed in days either? Craig walks towards me; an odd smile on his face.

'Son? What's got into you? Why are you looking at me like that?' I press my back further into the wall, but he's getting closer. My breathing's rapid; I can't stop shaking.

'Hello, Mother,' he says, looming towards me. 'I hope you've not been snooping around again.'

33

Luke

Luke wakes three minutes before the alarm, but already senses that there's something wrong. Helen's not in bed next to him. He'd managed to stay awake until eleven last night, after his wife had texted him to say she was going to a colleague's house for more drinks. He grabs his phone – whose house did she say?

He reads the message again; it's filled with typos, which is unusual for Helen.

Perhaps she fell asleep on the sofa downstairs and he didn't hear her come in.

He gets up, rushing to check his daughters are safe. He usually can't sleep until his wife gets in from a night out. How did he sleep so deeply last night? He gently pushes open the door. Thank God. They're both sound asleep.

He goes quietly down the stairs, opens the lounge door, but she's not there.

He feels the panic rising in his chest. No, it'll be fine – she'll be OK. She said she was going to Amelia's house. She probably fell asleep there, though she's never stayed overnight somewhere and not contacted him first – not because he's possessive; it's simply a courtesy.

He tries Helen's mobile, but it goes straight to voicemail. His hands feel too clumsy as he searches for Amelia's number.

'Hello?'

'Hi, Amelia, it's Luke – Helen's husband. I was wondering if she was there.'

'I ... what time is it?'

'Sorry, it's early, and I know you were probably up late ...'

'No ... I went to bed about ten ... I've been off sick for two days.'

'Oh, OK.' He's talking in his work voice. 'Sorry to wake you ... hope you feel better soon.'

Adrenaline and suspicion course through Luke's body. He looks out of the lounge window. His car's on the drive – she's not asleep on the back seat.

'Where's Mummy?' says a little voice behind him.

It's Alice, holding Ted by the arm so he dangles at her side.

'She's staying at a friend from work's house.'

Yes, that must be it, thinks Luke. She'll have been too drunk to type properly – the predictive text got the wrong name. It always happens to Luke.

'Like a sleepover,' says Alice.

'Yes. Exactly like that. Let's get you some breakfast. Is your sister up yet?'

'Yes,' says Alice. 'She's having a poo.'

284

'Nice,' he says. 'Glad you're keeping me informed.'

Unlike his wife.

He gets the Rice Krispies from the cupboard and pours some into two bowls. Alice hops on to one of the dining chairs as he gets out the milk.

'Can I pour my own today, Daddy? Megan never lets me do my own.'

Luke opens his phone's messages – 'Yes, yes. Go on ...' – and types a few lines to another of Helen's colleagues, Simon. He always got on with Simon – well, he used to. Luke hasn't been out for a pint with him for ages.

He stares at his phone, waiting for *Delivered* to turn to *Read*, but it doesn't.

It doesn't change after the kids have eaten their breakfast and gone upstairs to get dressed.

If he still hasn't heard from Helen after the school run, then he'll ring Simon, then Helen's work to see if he can find out about this night out. He doesn't want to come across as some jealous husband. He'll tell them that a man's been following them and he's afraid something terrible might have happened to his wife.

Megan wouldn't stop talking about Helen all the way to school.

'Mummy said last night that she was taking us this morning.'

'I doubt she said that,' said Luke. 'Not if she knew she was going to a work party.'

'She never told me she was going to a party.'

285

'She probably forgot.'

But Helen never forgets things. The calendar on the kitchen wall is what she lives by. Her shifts are marked with colour-coded sticky dots on the relevant days. Nights out and day trips are planned at least four weeks in advance. Luke looked this morning and there was no entry for anything yesterday.

By the time he gets to his desk, there's been no reply from Helen or Simon.

'What's wrong with you?' says Amanda. 'You've been standing there, staring into space with your coat on.'

'Helen didn't come home last night.'

'From work?'

'No. She went to someone's leaving do.'

'She's probably at a friend's. I do it all the time.'

'Yeah, but you haven't got two kids to take to school. And it was a Tuesday night.'

'I ... No. You're right. It does sound odd for Helen. She's usually so sensible.'

'Her phone's dead. It must've run out of battery.' Luke puts his phone on his desk, not taking his eyes from it as he takes off his coat. 'I'll ring the hospital – see if I can get hold of one of her colleagues.'

He uses the phone on his desk and gets put through to the ward.

'Staff nurse, Ward 19.'

'Hello. It's Luke, Helen's husband. Who's that?'

'Hi, Luke. It's Ivy. Is everything all right with Helen?

286

She's hasn't got that awful bug that's going round, has she?'

'No, she's fine. Actually, no. I don't know. Did you go to that leaving do last night?'

'Yeah, I only stayed for one – early shift today.'

'Oh, I see.'

'Did Helen make it back OK?'

'No, she hasn't come home yet.'

'Really?' She pauses for a few moments. 'That's strange.'

'Did she drink a lot last night?'

'No more than the rest of them, but I left early. If we've had a bad day here, we can certainly go for it in the pub.'

'Do you have any contact details for anyone else that went out?'

'I can't really give that information out. Leave it with me. I'll do some asking around and I'll call you.'

'Thanks, Ivy.'

'And try not to worry. She'll turn up. I expect it happens all the time.'

Amanda looks up as he replaces the handset.

'No joy, then?' she says, not disguising the fact she was listening to his conversation.

'I'm really worried. It's not like her.' Luke falls on to his chair. 'What if it's something to do with Craig Wright? He might have followed her to work ... watched her leave the pub. She'll have been vulnerable ... everyone is when they're pissed.'

'Didn't she contact you at all last night?'

Luke picks up his mobile and hands it to Amanda.

Hey Lukey buoy going for after party at Amelia's buck ltr loadsa luv.

'Right,' she says, handing it back. 'Does she always text like that?'

'No, but she hasn't been on a big night out for a while. I guess some of her texts in the past have been as dubious as that.'

Luke paces up and down along the bank of desks.

'It'll be fine, Luke,' says Amanda. 'She'll turn up — she'll ring you when she gets home and charges her phone.'

'I've got a horrible feeling about this. Seeing Craig outside the kids' school and now Helen's gone missing.'

Luke can't keep still. It seems wrong to sit when something could've happened to his wife. He looks around the newsroom. It's silent; everyone looks down quickly.

His desk phone rings, making him jump. He doesn't recognise the number on the display. Please let it be Helen, he thinks. He almost doesn't want to answer it. So long as it's ringing, he can cling to the hope that it's her calling.

He grabs the handset.

'Helen?'

'Excuse me?' A man's voice.

Luke's shoulders slump. He shouldn't have picked up the phone.

'Sorry. Luke Simmons, the *Chronicle*.'

'Thought I'd dialled the wrong number, then.' His

voice is deep with a broad Chorley accent. 'You say that's Luke Simmons?'

'It is.'

Luke keeps his eye on his mobile, flicking from the last message he sent to Helen and the one he sent to Simon. Neither has been read – only Simon's has been delivered.

'It's Brian here. I've never telephoned a newspaper before. I got your number from my wife.'

'Brian?'

'Brian Sharpe.'

Luke hesitates for a second. Lucy's father is the last person he'd have expected to hear from.

'Of course. How can I help?'

'I don't need anything . . . I thought I could help *you*,' he speaks quickly, with confidence. 'I know this sounds odd, but I've been keeping tabs on Craig Wright since he left prison. Not stalking, like. Just had my eye out for him when he's been out and about. Saw him talking to that young girl, though I didn't see where they took her. Bit pissed off with myself for that, to tell the truth.'

'Have you seen him since the girl went missing?'

'Yes. My wife Gillian says I'm getting a bit fixated about it all . . . but it's given me a reason to get up and out in the morning. I need to stop him before he does it again – and he will, if he hasn't already. The boy has no fear; he'll do anything he wants. Nobody can see that but me. He shouldn't have been let out. Everyone knows that he killed Jenna Threlfall, too. If he'd been convicted of that, he might not have been released.'

'I was convinced of that, too. What are you phoning me in connection with?'

'I'm ringing about your wife.'

34

Luke

Amanda wasn't eavesdropping on Luke's last phone call; she didn't look up as he replaced the handset.

'That was Brian Sharpe,' he says.

'You're joking!' She looks up from what Luke assumes is her Twitter feed. 'What did *he* want?'

'He's been following Craig Wright since he was released from prison.'

'What?' she says, frowning.

'Yeah, I know. It's all a bit strange. But he rang about Helen. He said Craig's been watching her. Brian followed him into the hospital car park, then as Helen came home.'

'Are you sure this Brian isn't some crank?' says Amanda. 'I mean, how did he know that Helen's your wife?'

'Shit. I hadn't thought of that.'

Luke rests his elbows on his desk and covers his face with his hands. What will he tell the girls if something has happened to their mother? He can't bear to think of their little faces, their tears, their lives growing up without her.

Luke sits up, wiping his eyes. He'll call the police and tell them what Brian said.

After replacing the handset, he clicks on to Facebook to see if Helen was tagged in any photos last night. Luke wonders why he hadn't thought of that earlier, but he sees none. He clicks on Helen's colleague Simon's page, and he's uploaded seven pictures. Helen is in all of them, but they're not sitting together, which is obvious if Simon's the one taking the photos. In the first few, she's sitting next to Ivy, so it must've been early. Ivy has her arm around Helen, whose hand is shielding her eyes, her head lowered. Was she crying, or didn't she want her picture taken?

Luke clicks on to his Facebook messages. There's still no reply from Denise; the message remains unread, but that might be because they're not friends and it's gone into a separate folder. He goes to Helen's profile. There's a post on her page:

U lost ur phone, hun? Missed u at work today. Give us a call when u see this xx

'Have you rung the police about Helen?' says Amanda.

She places a cup of coffee on his desk; he hadn't noticed her get up. She sits back opposite him.

'Yeah.' Luke rubs his face, trying to rid himself of weariness. It doesn't work. 'They said they'd keep a lookout for her. I don't know what else they can do — they're already looking for Craig Wright.'

'What else did Brian say?' She leans forward, resting her chin in her hands. 'He's gone to the police with what he saw, hasn't he?'

'I don't know.' Luke sighs, checking his mobile again.

'What did he say about Craig? Has he been home since the other day?'

'I didn't ask.' He throws his phone on to the desk. 'Sorry. I sound useless, don't I? I just want to know she's OK.'

'I know,' she says. 'But Brian might be mistaken. He's probably losing it. He can't be that good at following Craig or he'd know where he is now.'

'You can't say he's losing it, Amanda. His child was murdered.'

'I'm sorry.'

'How's the Jenna Threlfall piece coming on?' asks Sarah, appearing from nowhere.

She's wearing her running gear, complete with a rucksack and ear muffs that are hanging around her neck.

'How did you ... ?' says Luke.

'I just mentioned it to Sarah,' says Amanda, 'because she wondered what you'd been up to after writing your articles so quickly ...'

Fuck.

The week started so well and now it's all turning to shit.

Amanda's doing that thing with her eyebrows, where she assumes Luke's a mind reader. He guesses that she wrote the book and takeaway reviews for him and promises her (mentally, with a lift of his own eyebrow) to buy her lunch tomorrow.

'Heard from Brian Sharpe today,' says Luke. 'He's been watching Craig Wright and said that he'd been following my wife, Helen. I've telephoned the police, but I haven't heard from her.'

'Oh God,' says Sarah. 'You should get home. Are your daughters all right?'

'Yes. I phoned their childminder straight after I spoke to the police. She's going to have them until I get back, however late.'

'Shit. I assume Brian Sharpe's taken whatever information he has to the police?'

'He didn't specifically say that he'd spoken to the police ...'

Sarah puts her hands on her hips.

'OK, right. Do you want me to hang on here with you?' she says.

'No, no. I'll be fine,' says Luke. 'I'm sure it'll be fine.'

'OK, if you're sure. You'll keep me updated, won't you?'

She puts in her earbuds, covers them with her ear muffs, and jogs towards the exit.

'Hey, guys,' shouts Derek. 'Turn the news up.'

'Just seen it on Twitter,' says Amanda. 'A body's been found.'

'Oh God,' says Luke. 'Any details?'

Derek gets up from his seat; it's the most Luke's seen him move all day.

Luke turns to the television. It shows a white tent

294

in the distance, beyond the yellow crime scene tape. It looks like a picture taken from social media.

'Police have discovered the body of a female in a disused house in Preston. It is not *believed to be the body of the missing teenager Leanne Livesey.'*

There's a collective sigh of relief as the brief report ends.

'So who the hell is it?' says Luke, walking to Amanda's desk. 'Anything on Twitter about where it was found?'

'Someone's saying it was an older woman. No idea who found her.'

'Anyone mentioned Craig Wright?'

'Not that I can see.'

'Drugs maybe?'

'Don't think so.'

Amanda looks up at Luke and seems to have the same thought as he does. Luke's blood runs cold.

'What if it's Helen?'

'It won't be her, Luke. Don't worry. You'd have heard from the police if it were Helen.' She glances up at him, but he can tell she's worried too. 'Oh,' she says. 'Someone's tweeted a picture of the house the body was found in. It's on Inkerman Street.'

'I can't look. That's near Erica's house, isn't it?'

She types both street names into Google.

'Two minutes' walk between the two.'

'Oh God. What if Craig's taken my wife there?'

Luke feels like he's going to be sick; he can't breathe.

Amanda looks at him, her eyes wide.

She grabs her bag from her bottom drawer. 'Let's go.'

It's dark outside. It makes Luke worry about Helen even more. Please, God, please don't let it be Helen. He closes his eyes as Amanda drives them across town.

'It won't be Helen,' she says. 'It can't be.'

'That's what I keep telling myself.'

Luke checks his phone again: no messages. He dials his wife's number; this time it doesn't ring at all – it goes straight to voicemail.

'I think her phone's been turned off,' he says.

'It'll have run out of battery. Try not to worry.' She glances at him. 'I know, it was a stupid thing to say. Of course you're going to worry.' She slows down to take a right. 'We're about a minute away.'

They turn on to Inkerman Street and it's obvious from the blue flashing lights and the gathering on-lookers where the house is.

Amanda pulls up a few metres down the street.

'I don't think I can move,' says Luke. He folds, putting his face in his hands. 'I just want a few more minutes where everything's OK.'

He feels Amanda's hand on his back.

'Take your time. Whenever you're ready.'

He pictures his lovely wife's body in a derelict house; pale, lifeless, like the photographs of Lucy Sharpe that were shown in court.

He opens the door and vomits on to the road, retching until there's nothing left.

Then he wipes his mouth with the sleeve of his jacket.

'Oh God,' he says, though he feels as though he's choking. 'I don't want it to be her, Amanda.'

Her hand is still on his back.

'I know. Come on. Shall we?'

Luke nods.

He stands slowly, not even bothering to close the car door. His legs are numb. Amanda takes his elbow and guides him to the officer standing next to the crime scene ribbon.

'Hi,' she says. 'We're from the *Chronicle*. Any ID on the body?'

'Not yet,' says the officer.

'How old was the victim?' says Amanda.

'It's hard to say.'

'Did you see the body?'

The man nods.

'Hair colour?'

'Fair.'

'Oh fuck,' says Luke.

He feels his knees weaken. If it weren't for Amanda holding him up, he'd be on the ground. He holds up his phone and scrolls to the most recent photograph he has of Helen. He hands it to Amanda.

'Was this the woman?' she says.

The officer leans forward, taking the phone for a closer look. Luke can't take his eyes from the man's face.

He shakes his head.

'No, it wasn't her. This woman was much older.'

'Oh, thank God,' says Luke.

He bends over, his face in his hands.

It's not Helen.

Tears roll into his palms, finally released. He wipes them away, trembling, before standing straight.

'Thank you.' Amanda takes the phone from the police officer. 'Shit. Are you OK, Luke?'

He takes a few minutes to breathe. It's not her; it's not Helen.

'So,' says Amanda. 'If it's not Helen, then who the hell is it?'

35

'You shouldn't have got rid of my weed!' I say to her. 'What makes you think you can do that? Who the fuck do you think you are?'

This house is so dark that I can't tell if it's four o'clock at night or four in the morning. I can't even see the expression on her lying bitch face.

'I'm hungry,' says Leanne, lying on the mattress.

'For fuck's sake,' I say. 'You ate only an hour ago.'

'I can't help it,' she says.

'Have a sleep,' I tell her.

'Hmm.'

Good job I let her have a smoke earlier — she's a lot quieter than she was before.

She sits up suddenly.

'I can't sleep. It's too hot.'

'You can't be too hot — it's fucking February.'

'Please.'

'For fuck's sake.' I go to the window and open it a few inches. 'Five minutes ... that's all it's staying open for.'

I walk over to my mother and grab her feet, shaking

them to wake her. How can she fucking sleep at a time like this?

'Come on, Mother,' I say. 'I've given you time. If you tell me where it is, then you can go home.'

She's staring at me. Her eyes look as though they've no fight left in them.

'I told you,' she says. 'I didn't touch your things. I've no idea what happened to—'

'You're lying,' I say. 'You've always hated me, really, haven't you? Always so disappointed with how I turned out.'

'I'm not,' she says. 'I love you.'

'I don't believe you. You called the police on me last time. You didn't believe me when I said I didn't do it.'

'I wouldn't do that. I gave you an alibi.'

I kneel at her feet. 'If you just tell the truth, everything will be fine,' I say. 'You know how much trouble I'll be in when they found out I've lost it all? They'll kill me.'

'I'm sure you can sort it out,' she says.

'"Sort it out"? What planet are you living on? They'll find me ... hurt me. This is fucking serious.'

'I ... I ...'

I crawl on to the mattress, putting my arms either side of her.

'You, what?'

'I didn't know ...'

'What have you done, Mum?'

'I got ...' The last few words are mumbled – a jumble of words.

'What did you say?' I lower my face so it's only inches

300

from hers. I turn my head, my ear right above her mouth.
'Say it again.'

'I got rid of it.' She's sobbing, sniffing. Crying for her-
self. 'I'm so sorry,' she shrieks. 'I'm sorry.'

She brings her hands up to her face, her shoulders shak-
ing with her cries.

I slap her hands away.

She winces – screams – when my ring catches the corner
of her eye.

She places a hand over it, dabbing her face. She screams
again when she sees the blood.

'Shut up, Mum,' I shout, but her wails are getting
louder.

I glance at the open window and place a hand over her
mouth.

She's wrestling, struggling beneath me.

'If you promise to stay quiet,' I whisper to her, 'then I'll
take my hand away.' Her eyes are wide – almost bulging
out of the sockets. 'OK?'

She nods, quickly.

Slowly, I slide my hand from her mouth.

But she screams again. Louder this time. She heard me
open the window. Was she pretending to be asleep before?

I put two hands over her mouth this time.

'Why did you do that, Mum? Why couldn't you just
behave for me? You owe me that.'

She's struggling more than ever now. She won't bloody
stay still.

'Mum!' I shout. 'Stop it! It'll be OK if you just stop it,
stop screaming. Please, Mum!'

But she won't stop.

I press harder, but her body shakes even more, like she's having a fit.

'Please, Mum,' I whisper, even though she's probably not listening any more. 'Please stop.'

And then, she does.

I take my hand away, and there are no more screams.

When I hear footsteps on the stairs, I can't move.

He's here. I suppose he might as well be.

'Shit, man,' he says. 'What the hell have you done?'

'I didn't do it,' I say. 'You did.'

36

Erica

It was the telephone that woke me. It's so hot in here – Craig must've turned the heating on. I'm lying on my bed, too warm, too nauseous, to get under the covers. The pain is taking over my back, my side, like it's possessing my whole body. It's never been this bad before. I remember standing at the top of the stairs as he walked up towards me. There was a look in his eyes, like he'd been smoking that wacky baccy stuff.

'Hello, Mother,' he said, the way he used to greet me at visiting time. 'You don't look so well.'

He kept walking towards me – like he'd forgotten about personal space. But I shouldn't have been thinking that about my own son, wanting him away from me.

'It's my kidneys again,' I said. 'I'll make an appointment with the doctor in the morning.'

He went into the bathroom and I waited on the landing while he splashed water on his face. He came out patting it dry with a towel.

'I've been inside for too long,' he said. He took hold of my hands and guided me towards my room. He sat next to me on my bed. 'I just need to check something outside.'

He went downstairs, and I must have fallen asleep.

'Craig?' I try to shout the words, but my mouth is dry. There's a tumbler of water on my bedside table, so I take a sip. 'Craig! Are you there?'

He walks into my bedroom.

'Have you seen Leanne?' I say. 'It's been all over the news. And Denise? Jim said she didn't come home. It's been such a long day, Son. What time is it?'

He's pacing the short space between my bed and the wardrobes.

'It's late. I've seen Denise. She said she hid Jason's supply in our shed ... that she put it into empty tins of paint. Jason didn't believe her ... he said that she's always on his case. He said that she grassed him up the last time she found drugs in the house. Is that true?'

'I don't know anything about how they are now,' I say. 'He was always a wild one.'

'Did Denise put the tins in the shed?' he says, sitting on the edge of my bed.

'I don't know who put them there,' I say, feeling so ill, so tired, so fed up with all the lies. 'But I flushed it all down the toilet.'

'Fuck!'

I shouldn't have trusted the kindness in his question.

He leaps up from the bed and begins pacing again, grabbing at his hair.

'Mum, why did you do that?'

'The police had just been round.' I prop myself up with my elbows and reach over to touch him, but he's too far away. 'Please, Son. You have to understand: I didn't want you getting into trouble. I was trying to protect you. I thought *you* put it there.'

He kneels before me, wiping the tears from my face that I have no strength to hide.

'No, Mum. It wasn't me.' He lowers his head, laying it on my stomach. He's shaking. 'You should've left it there. It would all've been fine then. He wouldn't have hurt Denise.' He stands, slowly, and strokes the side of my face. 'He hated her, Mum. He hated the way she treated him. And this was the last ... Oh shit. What a mess.' He sits next to me again, his arm resting on my shoulder. 'If he knew you were the one who got rid of it, he'd probably ...'

I grab hold of his hand, squeezing it tight to quell both our trembling.

'Has he got Leanne, too?'

'Yes.' He stands again, rubbing his hands through his hair. 'Well, he *had* her. God knows what he was going to do with her. But she managed to escape. I had to help her, Mum. She was only a kid. I'm a lot stronger than I was before, but the punch I gave him won't have knocked him out for long. It's like Jason's someone else – he's changed ... or he's been like that all along ... I don't know. It's like he hated me too. I mean *always* hated me. The police'll be there soon. They'll find Denise. Shit, this is such a mess!'

'What's happened to Denise, Craig?'

He goes to the window, lifting the net curtains. He looks for a few minutes before standing at the end of my bed.

'Didn't you hear me?' I say. The dread of his reply gives me the strength to sit up. 'What has happened to Denise?' Then it dawns on me. 'You said Jason *hated* her. Did you mean to say that in the past tense?'

He's rubbing his face with his hands – like there are insects crawling under his skin.

'I think he's killed her. I couldn't stop to check. I had to get Leanne out of there. I phoned the police as soon as we left. I'd gone to Inkerman Street to show the necklace to him and tell him about the top that you found. He admitted it was him – and that he planted those things in our house. How could he have done that to me? I thought he was my friend.'

'What? Jason?' My hand goes to my mouth. The room is spinning again. I can barely breathe. 'I don't understand ... You're his friend! You were like brothers.' I wipe the tears from my face, though my hands don't feel as if they're mine. This can't be real. 'There must be some mistake. He wouldn't do that, would he? Let you go to prison for so long.'

'But he did.'

'I can't believe this.' I swing my legs on to the floor. 'Denise, Lucy ... I can't—'

'Everything will be all right, Mum.'

It's as if our roles have been reversed.

'But it's not going to be all right!' My heart's beating too fast. I've a fever. I could be delirious, hallucinating.

306

I dig my nails into my palms, but I feel the pain. 'How can it be – Denise is dead!'

'I know ... I know.'

There's a bang on the front door.

Craig puts a finger to his lips. I sit up slowly.

'I know you're in there, Craig!' It's Jason, shouting outside. 'You'd better fucking come out now.'

Craig leaves the bedroom; I hear him tread slowly down the stairs.

I manage to make it to the top of the stairs, but I don't trust my knees not to collapse under me, so I sit and shuffle down them one at a time.

'I can see you both,' says Jason through the letterbox. 'If you don't come out now, Craig, I'm going to pour petrol in and throw in a match. Is that what you want?'

The pain in my side is overwhelming. I think it's spread to my middle, to my neck. It feels like I'm either going to pass out or be sick. I sit on the bottom step.

Jason bangs on the door again.

'If you don't open up, I'm going to knock on every door in this street and tell them all to come out.'

Craig steps towards the front door. He looks back at me.

'He wants to frame me for killing his mother. But I'm stronger than he is now.'

'Don't go out there with him, Craig. Phone the police! Please!'

He opens the door and Jason's hands reach in to grab my son.

I stagger to the front door.

307

Jason is shoving Craig towards his car; it's as though my son isn't fighting back.

'Craig!' I shout. 'You don't have to go with him. You're stronger now, remember!'

'I'll be fine,' says Craig, looking into my eyes. 'Trust me on this one.'

Jason scowls at me as he walks to the driving seat. It's like his face is someone else's – someone I don't recognise.

'Craig!' I raise my hand, reaching out to him.

His eyes are locked on mine as they drive away. He looks afraid, and my heart is breaking all over again.

37

Luke

As they drive away from Inkerman Street, Luke's mobile phone beeps. It's a message from Helen.

Thank God, he thinks, swiping it open.

'Sorry about last night. Had a really bad day at work yesterday and had to let off some steam. Battery ran out on phone. Stayed at a friend's. Am heading to bed. See you later.'

'Who's that from?' asks Amanda.

'Helen.'

'Jesus. Thank God.'

'She didn't put any kisses on it. And she didn't say where she stayed last night.'

'It'll be a mate from work.'

'I guess.'

Luke clicks on Helen's contact details and presses *Call*.

It goes straight to voicemail.

'Hi, it's me,' says Luke. 'Just wanted to make sure you're OK. Had a strange call this morning saying a car was following you last night. Make sure all the doors are locked, will you? Give me a ring when you get this.'

He ends the call and selects the number for the house landline.

It rings countless times, there's no answer.

'Something's not right,' says Luke. 'She wouldn't sleep through the landline, would she?'

Amanda shrugs. 'It's likely, if she's had a heavy night.'

He checks the message he sent to Simon. It's been read, and Luke sees the dots as the other man types out a message. It's intermittent. Simon's taking his time to find the right words perhaps. Is he trying to get his story straight? Maybe Luke was worrying about the wrong thing – Helen could be having an affair. He's overdramatised what might have happened to his wife when the truth is much simpler. They haven't been as close as they were. They go to bed at different times, barely talk about anything that doesn't involve the kids or work. Luke's face feels hot at the thought and he hopes Amanda won't ask any more questions about Helen.

After several minutes of composing, two lines of text appear:

Sorry, phone was dead. Helen stayed at ours last night – just dropped her home. Simon.

Is that it? He's been worrying the best part of a day and that's all the explanation he gets?

There's silence between him and Amanda. Luke doesn't want to ask her opinion on what it all means.

'Anyway,' she says, moments later. 'I'm going to make a quick detour.'

She turns into Erica Wright's road.

Erica's standing in the street, hands in her hair, screaming. People are opening their front doors and staring at her.

'Shit,' says Luke. 'What the hell has happened now?'

They pull up and he jumps out of the car.

'What's wrong?' he says, rushing to her. The poor woman is shaking uncontrollably. 'You look awful.'

'He's taken Craig!' She reaches for Luke, taking hold of his hands. 'We have to find them ... Jason ... It was Jason. He killed his own mother ... Inkerman Street.' She's tugging at his hands. 'But there's no time. Will you help me find them?'

Luke can barely take in her words – she's not making any sense.

'Come on,' says Amanda, snapping Luke from his thoughts. 'You get in the back, Erica.' She stops at the car door. 'Are you just going to stand there, Luke?'

The canal is only twenty minutes away. Luke thinks it's a pointless journey – why would Jason drive Craig to a place they went fishing as children? Isn't that too obvious?

'But he went back to the house on Inkerman Street,' Erica says. 'With Leanne. He'll go to familiar places – where he knows he can't be seen. And he knows that canal – it's so dark at night. Not many people would go walking down there at this hour.'

Luke doesn't know how Erica's managing to sit upright. He's never seen someone look so ill and not be in hospital.

'I took a picture of Jason's car and number plate,' says Luke, 'when I was outside his house the other day.'

'I'm impressed,' says Amanda with a smirk.

Luke wants to tell her to fuck off, but with their passenger within earshot that would be inappropriate, not to mention unprofessional.

'We're here,' says Amanda, as they pull into a pub car park. 'We'll have to go the rest of the way on foot.'

'I can't see the car,' says Luke after getting out.

'They've probably parked further up,' says Amanda. 'I can't see him dragging Craig through a car park.' She opens the passenger door. 'Do you want to wait here, Erica? I could stay with you.'

Luke almost protests – he can't chase after two convicted criminals alone.

'No, no,' says Erica, almost tumbling out of the car. 'I need to be there for him.'

'But he might not ...' Luke begins, but Amanda cuts him off with one of her looks.

They each take one of Erica's arms and guide her along a footpath that's lit with one solitary lamppost. Luke tries to bury his fear, but he can't stop the nausea rising in his stomach. What if Jason *is* here? The three of them are hardly tough opposition.

After they've been walking for ten minutes, Erica stops.

'There!' Her voice is louder than it's been since they

312

saw her on the street, but barely more than a whisper. 'I can see something over there.'

Oh God, thinks Luke. He's not prepared for this at all.

38

Craig

'Where are you taking me, Jason?' I say.

I glance at him. He's sweating ... out of control. He's driving too fast and it's only a thirty-mile-an-hour zone. He's going to get pulled over, but that's probably too much to wish for. He's barely said a word to me.

'Why would you want to frame me?' I ask him. 'What have I ever done to you?'

He turns to look at me; his eyes are wild, filled with hatred.

'Keep your eyes on the road,' I say.

'Don't tell me what to do,' he says, but he turns to face the front.

His knuckles are white where his hands are gripping the steering wheel so tightly.

'Being killed in a car wreck would be better than what I've got planned for you,' he says, almost laughing. 'You're such an idiot, Craig. When I asked you to pick Leanne up from Sunningdales, you did it, no questions asked.'

'Why would I have asked questions?' I say. 'You're my— you *were* my friend. I can't believe . . .'

I turn to look out of the passenger window. Seventeen years of my life I've spent in prison. There were times I wondered whether I could have hurt Lucy and then erased it from my memory. All those years at the beginning when I was beaten nearly every day. I'd recover, then I'd be punched again. The years spent with no hope, with only my mother visiting me. I should've known that Jason visiting me towards the end was about *him* more than me, but why would I suspect my best friend of something like that? I wouldn't have believed it if someone else had told me. We've been through loads together. It was all fake. I thought we'd grown apart when I was inside. I'd come to terms with that. Then this past year when he got back in contact, I thought everything would go back to how it was.

But he was never there for me, not when it mattered. I heard nothing from him after I was arrested. I should've remembered that.

He's a murderer.

Cold. Sociopathic.

Some of the most hard-hearted killers I met in prison could instantly turn on the charm to get what they wanted. He's no different to them.

I've seen Jason with my own eyes, with his mum and Leanne; he's capable of so much more than I ever was.

I turn to face the front.

'Come on, Craigy boy. Man up! Are you crying, eh? All those years inside and now it's all going to end. You

315

should've been convicted for Jenna's murder as well. I've had that hanging over my head for years ... people whispering about me. The police should've fucking found her necklace, the top ... bloody incompetent pricks.'

'Hanging over your head? But *you* killed her!'

He bursts out laughing; he sounds like a maniac. He *is* a maniac; he's insane.

'Seventeen years of my life!'

'Seventeen years ... blah, blah, blah. You're like a stuck record. What have you got to live for anyway? You've come back home, and no one wants you there.'

'I loved her,' I say.

'Which one?'

'Lucy,' I say. 'I barely knew Jenna.'

'Yeah, whatever,' he says. 'Well, your Lucy soon forgot about you, I can tell you. I can't believe she agreed to meet me.'

'She wouldn't have been up for it with you,' I say. 'She hated you. That's why you killed her, isn't it? She wouldn't let you do what you wanted to her.'

'Fuck off. You don't know anything about that night.'

I can't shake the picture of him on top of her – him with his hands around her neck. 'I thought you were my friend,' I say, wiping my face.

'Right. And my friendship had nothing at all to do with the fact my precious, darling mother told me I had to keep an eye on you. She always preferred you to me when we were growing up. Do you know how that felt? I couldn't spend time with my dad either, without you tagging along. When you were getting bullied, my mum actually paid me to protect you. Did you know about that? But after you were sent to prison, she came to her senses. She betrayed your mother – her best friend – to protect me. She gave me an alibi. It was all too easy. Especially as I managed to plant a few traces of you on Lucy. And I don't know how I've managed to keep a straight face while your mother has been banging on about Pete Lawton all these years. That wasn't even his real name. It was my mate, Gary. Your mum really believed you were innocent, didn't she?'

'Of course she did. She was right to.' I glance out of the passenger window. I know where he's taking me. His head's stuck in the past. 'How could you kill your own mother?' I say.

'I didn't mean to kill her. It was an accident – she wouldn't keep quiet.' He looks at me, shakes his head. 'She shouldn't have taken my stuff. That weed was worth thousands – and it wasn't even mine. Do you know what they're going to do to me when they find out? I've got a family.'

Rain begins pounding on the windscreen. The wipers are going full speed, but it's all I can do to see the road ahead. Shit.

'I don't believe you,' I say.

'And I don't give a fuck what you think.'

Suddenly, he takes a hand off the steering wheel; I only feel the first two punches, then everything goes dark.

*

'Wake up, you piece of shit.'

I can't move. Where am I? Hands grab my jacket by the shoulders and I'm thrown to the ground.

'Get up,' he says, kicking me.

I turn onto my stomach, using my hands to push myself up. The pain in my right temple is throbbing, but I need to find my strength. I've had worse beatings than this one. Never show that you're hurt, that's what my friends inside used to tell me.

'Give me your phone,' he says.

'What?'

He pats across my jacket and pulls the mobile from my pocket.

'You're going to record your confession,' he says, looming over me, his breath stale in my face. 'You're going to tell everyone you killed Jenna Threlfall. Then you're going to tell them that you can't live with it any more and you're gonna say goodbye.'

I look around. We're by the canal. Jason's dad used to take us fishing here in the summer as kids. Should I have suspected that Jason was jealous of my presence back then? I thought he was happy to have his friend come, but he probably wanted his father's attention for himself. Jim always treated me like a son.

'I'll tell it to the police,' I say, but my words don't come out right.

'It's not going to happen like that,' he says. 'They sent you down for Lucy. Most people think you killed Jenna as well. No one will question it — they won't know it was me.'

He grabs my elbow and yanks me towards a gap in the railings, sitting me against them.

I look up, but I can't keep my head straight.

He slaps me across the face.

'No,' he says. 'You need to be here. I'm not going to make it easy for you.'

'I want to go home now,' I say. I can't think properly. 'I'm going to be sick. My mum'll be waiting for me. She worries, you know. I think she'll know where I am.'

He slaps me again.

'We're going to practise,' he says. 'Repeat after me: I killed Jenna and Denise. I'm sorry.'

'Repeat after me,' I say.

'No!'

'I'm sorry,' I say. But I can't remember what I'm meant to be sorry about.

'No, no, no!'

'I'm sorry, Mum.'

'For fuck's sake.'

'She's coming,' I say.

'Who's coming?'

'My mum.'

He bends over, laughing.

'I've heard it all now,' he says. 'Your mum isn't going to save you. She couldn't help you all those years ago – she's not coming to save you tonight.'

He kneels before me, holding up my mobile phone.

'*I killed Jenna,*' he says. '*I'm sorry*. That's all you have to say.'

'Son!' A voice in the distance, or did I imagine it?

319

'Shit,' says Jason.
He puts his hands around my neck.
'What the hell do you think you're doing?'
A woman's voice.
It's my mother.

39

Luke

'What the hell do you think you're doing?' says Erica.

She stops when she's only two metres from them.

Jason has his hands around Craig's neck, whose head is only inches from the edge of the embankment. There's blood pouring from his nose and mouth; he looks barely alive.

From the corner of his eye, Luke sees Amanda on her mobile. He's holding his own up, recording what's in front of him. He hopes there's enough light from the lamppost behind them.

'Police,' she whispers. 'We've found Craig Wright and Jason Bamber.'

Luke wished she'd said it louder, but he wants Jason to think the police are already on their way. His face is sweating but cold. It's only just stopped raining and the pathway is slippery. It might only take one small push to shove Jason into the canal.

Jason looks up at Erica. His clothes are soaking. He's wearing the same white shirt Luke saw him in the other day. It's filthy.

'What does it look like I'm doing?' he shouts.

Jason laughs; it echoes in the tunnel nearby. Eerily wicked. Luke has never heard a sound like it – not in real life.

Amanda steps forward, standing next to Erica.

'The police are on their way,' she shouts. 'Get off him.'

Jason narrows his eyes.

'Well look who it is.' He's staring at Luke. He takes his hands from around Craig's neck, grabbing the man's collar and shoving his head hard on to the ground. 'Hiding behind two women, eh?'

Luke walks towards Jason, his heart pounding. He doesn't know what to do. He's never hit anyone before.

Amanda grabs his arm.

'No, Luke.'

'I've recorded you,' says Luke. 'I know it was you who killed Lucy and Jenna.'

Craig whimpers; Jason slaps him hard across the face.

'No you haven't,' he says. 'You've only been there a minute.'

Where are the sirens? The police can't be far away – it's not far from town. There's a manhunt for Craig, they should be here by now.

Then Luke sees them.

Four officers dressed in black behind Jason. Luke tries not to look at them again.

'Erica!'

Amanda rushes towards her as the older woman's knees buckle, grabbing her arm. Luke takes hold of the other. Erica is so light, but she's almost a dead weight.

'I need to lie down,' she says. 'Lie down.'

The police officers run towards Jason and Craig. Jason doesn't put up a fight as they handcuff him. Craig is motionless, his eyes closed.

'We're going to need two ambulances,' says one into the radio.

Luke kneels on the ground next to Erica, collapsing with relief. He wants to burst into tears.

There are two paramedics kneeling over Erica. She wanted her son to take the first ambulance, not that it had been up to her. She closed her eyes after seeing police officers take Jason away.

'Stay with us, Erica,' they're shouting. 'Come on, love.'

Blinking slowly, she turns to face Luke as though she knew he would be there.

'Is that you, Craig?' she says.

'No,' he says. 'It's Luke.'

'Oh, yes. That's right. Luke.'

The paramedics bring out a wheeled stretcher.

'Will you come with me, Luke?' she says, her voice hoarse, breathless. 'I don't want to be alone.'

He looks over to Amanda. There are tears in her eyes.

'Go on,' she says.

He climbs into the ambulance after Erica and one of the medics.

'Is it OK if I come?' says Luke as he sits on one of the fold-down seats, but the man in green ignores him.

The doors slam shut, locking them in.

'Luke?'

'I'm here, Erica.'

'Has she been ill for long?' says the paramedic. 'Did this come on suddenly?'

'I barely know her,' says Luke, to the man's back.

He immediately feels guilty for saying it. He *does* know Erica: she doesn't have any friends; she hardly ever goes out; she reads romance novels to escape reality; she'd do anything to protect her son.

'She said she hasn't been feeling well,' says Luke.

The medic sits on the chair next to him. Erica tries to sit up.

'Are you there?' she says.

Luke glances at the man next to him; he nods.

Luke kneels next to Erica, holding the rail under her bed to stop himself falling when the ambulance turns a corner.

'Everything's going to be all right now, isn't it?' she whispers, her eyes closing longer than they're open.

'Yes,' says Luke. 'We know it was Jason. You were right about Craig.'

She opens her eyes fully.

'I think I'm going soon,' she says. 'Tell him that I love him.'

Luke moves away from the stretcher.

'You have to help her,' he says.

'We're nearly there. They're waiting for us. If you could stand clear, please, sir.'

Luke does as he's told. He watches as the double

doors are opened and they drag the stretcher from the back. He steps out of the ambulance; he doesn't know what to do now.

He goes through the doors to Accident and Emergency, but they've taken her away.

She might have been confused, but Luke knows that Erica has been right about her son all along.

40

Erica

We're moving, but I'm lying down.

It's like my mother's standing over me now.

Am I dying? Is this what it feels like?

She's standing over me and she's saying, *It's all right, Erica. Everything's going to be OK.*

But that can't be my mother, can it?

The day she died, she found my sanitary towels in the outside bin. She banged on my bedroom door.

'You hid them,' she said. 'I knew you were up to something. We can do something about it. It doesn't have to be the end of the world. You can still do something with your life.'

I stood up from my spot behind the door and opened it.

'No, Mum,' I said. 'I'm going to keep it.'

'But I don't want you to end up like me ... bringing up children alone.'

'What do you mean?' I said. 'Do you regret having Philip and me?'

'No of course not,' she said. 'I've always loved you, haven't I? You've always felt loved?'

I nodded.

'Do you think he'll marry you?'

'No,' I said. 'He can't marry me. Because he's already married.'

She looked at me, then, like she didn't know me.

'Oh, Erica.'

Her knees went from beneath her. It happened so slowly, her balancing at the top of the stairs. I reached out my hand to her, but she didn't take it. Our fingertips brushed and before I could stop her she fell backwards.

The sound of her head on the floor was something I'll never forget.

There was no movement from her; she wasn't breathing. I should've phoned the ambulance, but I was in shock. I knelt next to her, put my head on her belly and lay there until she started to feel cold. I should have done so much more.

I'm picturing Denise now. She's standing over me, holding my hand.

'Your mum says it's OK,' she's saying.

I'm fading somewhere, I think. I don't think Denise or my mum are really here at all.

It's so bright in here, I can see it even with my eyes closed.

'We're losing her,' someone keeps saying.

But I'm still here, can't they see that?

I told him I didn't want to be alone. I think he's

somewhere; he came in with me. Nice young man. Was it Craig?

No, no: Luke.

It was Jason all along, wasn't it? He had us fooled and we didn't deserve that. We were worthy of a better life.

Craig was always so precious to me. I hope he understands that now.

I hope he'll be OK, my boy. He can take care of himself, I know that. I hope they give him justice – he's paid too high a price for being naive, loving, confused, frustrated.

I hope he knows that I never stopped believing him. I always said that I couldn't imagine him doing something like that, and that was true. He was such a loving little boy – that had to mean something. A mother knows these things.

They're putting something on my chest now, pressing down on me.

I always wondered who'd come for me when I died, though I don't really believe in all that nonsense. I can't see anyone, but I can sense something. It feels as though my mother and Denise are right next to me. My hands are tingling, like when you know someone's close to you – as though the tiny hairs are standing on end.

I'm not afraid of dying. I never have been.

I can see my son now, with my eyes closed. It's perhaps two or three years in the future. He's with a woman and she's expecting their first child. It's a little girl, I think.

'She's gone,' says a voice.

They might call her Erica.

328

41

Luke

The taxi drops him off outside his house. After paying the driver, Luke sits on the wall of their small front garden. Looking up at the clear sky, the stars seem closer than they usually do. It's as though he could reach out a hand and touch them.

His mobile phone beeps. He takes it from his pocket and opens the message from Amanda.

No word yet on Craig or Jason, they're still questioned. Leanne Livesey also at the police station. Any news on Erica?

He doesn't want to reply. He can do that later.

'What are you doing, sitting out here?' It's Helen at their front door. 'It's nearly ten o'clock. I've been worried about you.'

Luke could counter that he knows how it feels after she didn't come home last night, but it doesn't seem fitting.

She walks across the grass in bare feet and sits next to him on the wall.

'Is everything OK?' she says. 'I heard they found a

body.' She rests a hand on his shoulder. 'Was it some-one you knew?'

'Vaguely,' says Luke. 'I interviewed her nearly two decades ago.'

'Denise Bamber?'

He looks at his wife.

'I didn't think you were paying attention when I was talking about it.'

'I'm sorry. I've been distracted.' She takes hold of his hand. 'So why are you sitting out here?'

'It's been an eventful day,' he says, rubbing his eyes.

Helen rubs his back.

'Have they found the girl? Leanne, is it?'

'She's safe, from what I gather.'

'Thank God for that.'

'Yeah.'

'What happened to you last night?' says Luke.

'Let's go inside,' says Helen, standing. 'I'll make us a hot drink. It's freezing out here.'

He follows his wife into the house.

'Why are you avoiding the question?' he says, clos-ing the front door quietly.

She walks into the kitchen and flicks the kettle on. Luke pulls out a chair and sits at the kitchen table. He watches as she makes the tea and brings it over, sitting opposite him.

'I'm not avoiding the question,' she says finally. 'I had an awful day yesterday. There was a nine-year-old girl brought in. She had the same hair as Megan. At first I thought it was her, but then her mother came in after her. Sylvie Billington her name was. Such a lovely name.'

'*Was?*'

Helen nods, not looking up from her mug.

'And then it was the night out. I was putting on a brave face, as I normally do, but after a few drinks, and everyone trying to be jolly, I think I began to question the meaning of everything. How could we be sitting there, drinking, chatting, when a little girl had just lost her life?'

Luke reaches a hand across the table as her tears begin to fall; she places her hand over his.

'Simon brought his wife, Carly. She's a therapist.'

Helen wipes the tears with her other hand.

'I don't want to be a nurse any more. It's too hard. I'm hardly ever home and I feel so anxious every time I step inside the hospital.'

'You might change your mind.'

She shakes her head.

'I won't. I've been feeling this way for months, maybe years. But you were always so down. I had to keep going in case you got worse.'

'Was I that bad?'

'You weren't bad, no. But I had to be the strong one, sorting the girls when you couldn't get out of bed on a Sunday.'

'I'm so sorry, Helen,' says Luke. 'I didn't realise.'

'It's OK,' she says. 'We're talking about it now – not skirting around it any more.'

'Telling me I had no drive was hardly avoiding the topic.'

She laughs.

'I'm sorry.'

Luke stands and walks around the table. He puts his arms around his wife's shoulders and pulls her towards him. She's supported him for years, and he's never thanked her for that. He's going to be here for her now.

After tonight, Luke feels as though he could deal with anything.

42

Luke

Luke's sitting near the back of the church, holding a single daffodil in this hand. Craig is sitting behind Denise's husband and daughter. Luke can't imagine what they're going through. A son taking his own mother's life. It will take them years, if not a lifetime to get over. Will they go to Jason's trial, like Erica attended Craig's? Perhaps they believe Jason's innocent, even with Leanne as a witness.

Luke's phone vibrates in his pocket. He checks no one is looking before taking it out.

Wish I could be there. Send my love.

It's from Erica. She thought she'd be out of hospital by now, but the doctors didn't think she was strong enough for such an emotional event. She almost died herself. She said she sensed her mother and Denise next to her when she was being resuscitated, saying that she'd never believed in the afterlife until now. Erica said it's left her with a sense of peace she's never felt before.

She was right about Craig all along. How lonely that

must have been, to be the only one. Luke has, of course, written an article demanding justice for Craig. He wants to do his part in helping to get his conviction for the murder of Lucy Sharpe overturned.

There was no Pete Lawton though. Jason had set up some work experience for Craig on the days that Lucy and Jenna were taken and killed. He'd told Craig the mechanic's name was Pete Lawton, but that was a lie. It was one of Jason's friends who owed him a favour.

Leanne Livesey told the police about what happened at the house in Inkerman Street. Said how Jason had given her something to smoke, drink. He was high himself when he suffocated his own mother. Leanne described how Craig managed to knock Jason out and help her escape, how he'd called the police to tell them where she was. She repeated verbatim the words Jason used when he confessed to murdering Lucy and Jenna. Told the police how he laughed at Craig for being too pathetic, too stupid to notice that he'd set him up.

What kind of reporter did that make Luke? He'd missed all the signs. Rebecca Savage wanting to give him an interview? He thought she was a trapped woman, but she was doing what Jason had wanted her to do: casting doubt on Craig's alibi. Jason had manipulated everyone.

Luke discovered, when he looked into the history of the place on Inkerman Street, that another woman had been murdered there over thirty years ago. Her husband had accused her of having an affair and stabbed her twenty-three times while their children slept. Houses can seem haunted with painful memories sealed into the walls. Perhaps that's what Erica Wright's house was like. She'd spent all those years living like a ghost – a shadow of herself, neither alive nor dead. All that will change now. Finally, she can be free.

Luke bows his head as the pallbearers carry Denise Bamber's coffin out of the church. He waits until Craig, Jim and Caroline pass before joining the rest of the procession. After the vicar speaks his words, Luke is offered dirt to toss on to the casket. He throws the daffodil instead. It doesn't make a sound as it lands.

He doesn't linger afterwards – it doesn't feel right to join the family at the wake. He promised Erica he'd visit her and tell her how it went. It must be difficult for her to have missed her best friend's funeral. All the lies that both women were told. It could have been so different. They could have gone on being friends if they hadn't been so intent on protecting their sons.

But, Luke supposes, that's what parents do for their children. It's all about sacrifice.

Epilogue
One year later

It's four in the afternoon, and it's pretty cloudy, but I'm sitting outside anyway. The Cumbrian views are every bit as beautiful as I imagined they'd be. My place is tiny, but I don't need much.

I reach over for my cup of tea, cradling it in my hands. I tried white wine again, but I don't have the taste for it. They can have a glass though, with the dinner I'm going to make them. I'm cooking tagliatelle with roasted asparagus (they didn't have artichoke in the shop up the road), with butter and grated parmesan. I have chicken, too, in case the pasta's too plain for them.

I've spent most of the day getting the spare room ready for Craig and his girlfriend. They've only been seeing each other for ten months, but already they've a baby on the way.

'Didn't want to waste any more time,' he said.

I wasn't one to judge, was I? I'd been seeing Craig's father for a lot less time than that.

Craig didn't tell me about his father until after Denise's funeral.

'My father found me,' he said.

'Your ... father?'

'He saw everything on the news. I wish you'd told me his name, Mum. I know you were trying to protect me, but I should've been able to see him myself – make up my own mind about him.'

'I tried to contact him, but I had no address, nothing.'

'I know. He said you'd written to him. He still has the letter.'

After everything that's happened, I no longer feel angry that Alan got in touch.

I close my eyes and relish the silence.

It's so quiet here. It's times like these I think about Denise. She lost her life, but at least she lived it not knowing her son was a murderer ... well, not until her final moments.

I miss her terribly. Sometimes I have imaginary conversations with her – and she doesn't half make me laugh. That sounds ridiculous, doesn't it? Perhaps I'm losing my mind. But what better place to lose it?

There's a breeze on my face and I hear a car pull up outside the front of the house.

I jump out of my seat and rush through to the hall-way. I open the door and they're walking up the path. I step outside, and the sun appears from behind the clouds.

'Son!' I say, opening my arms. 'It's so good to see you.'

Acknowledgements

A massive thank you to the brilliant Harriet Bourton for giving me the opportunity to tell Erica's story. Thank you to my wonderful editor, Bethan Jones. Writing a book is such a collaborative process, and Harriet and Bethan's ideas and insight have been invaluable.

A huge thank you to my amazing agent, Caroline Hardman, and the brilliant team at Hardman & Swainson.

Thank you to the lovely Sam Carrington, Lydia Devadason, Caroline England, Carolyn Gillis, Claire Allen, Claire Reynolds, Louise Fiorentino, and Al Stokes for the friendship and support.

A big thank you to Steve Annand, Tom Earnshaw, Kath Sey, and Neil White for your advice. Any inaccuracies are my own.

Thank you to the fabulous journalists Aasma Day and Nicola Adam.

A big shout out to the bloggers for the time and energy you spend reading, reviewing and blogging.

To Janet Dyer and the lovely art class ladies: Kath, Amanda, Kate, Hazel, Glenys, Collette, Sheila – a big thank you (especially for the times I have brought my laptop instead of using a paint brush!).

Thank you to my readers – receiving your lovely messages really makes my day.

Finally, a massive thank you to my family – your support has been amazing (and you all deserve a medal!).